UPPER LONDON

'I absolutely loved it! Danger, excitement and kissing – it's got the lot. I can't wait to see what happens next' **Lucy Porter**

'Captivating, accessible and, of course, hilarious, Hutchinson Crouch has created a world of mythological and paranormal lore that's completely unique. Magical, funny and addictive with characters you'll fall in love with'

Sara Gibbs, author and comedy writer

'A spectacular romp through Elizabethan London, with all the wit you'd expect from a writer with comedy talons as sharp as Hutchinson Crouch's. A hugely imaginative read!'

Rose Biggin, author of *The Belladonna Invitation*

'A pacey urban fantasy that manages to be both sharp and warm – a satirical blast of supernatural romance with a host of loveable weirdos you want to hug'

Margaret Cabourn-Smith, comedy actress

'Hutchinson Crouch's London is dark, dangerous and very funny. A chuckle on every page guaranteed'

Mark Stay, author of *The Witches of Woodville* series

'A dazzling supernatural romance in the vein of Terry Pratchett and Neil Gaiman. The world Gabby has created is so rich, captivating and full of heart. You'll want to immerse yourself until the very last page'

Emma Nagouse, writer of *You're Dead to Me* podcast

'I loved *Cursed Under London*. Funny, joyous, subversive'

Joanne Harris, author of *Broken Light*

'A funny, emotional rollercoaster'

David Quantick, author and script writer of *The Thick of It*

'Very funny and completely gripping'

Gareth Gwynn, script writer of *Tourist Trap*

'A gleeful swashbuckle around a twisted Tudor London underground, with the heart of *Nimona* and the jokes of *Ghosts*'

Joel Morris, comedy writer and author of *Be Funny or Die*

CURSED UNDER LONDON

Cursed, Book One

GABBY HUTCHINSON CROUCH

This edition published in 2024 by Farrago,
an imprint of Duckworth Books Ltd
1 Golden Court, Richmond, TW9 1EU, United Kingdom
www.farragobooks.com

For bulk and special sales please contact info@duckworthbooks.com

A catalogue record for this book is available from the British Library

Book design by Danny Lyle

Printed and bound in Great Britain by CPI Ltd, Croydon, CR0 4YY

Hardback ISBN: 9781788425032
eISBN: 9781788425049

For my family

CHAPTER ONE
The Unundead

It begins where it should have ended, in an alleyway at the rough end of Upper Blackfriars. It was night, not that there was much distinction between night and day beneath the tight-packed buildings that loomed over the cobbles in this part of Upper London. Be it sunshine or moonlight, whatever natural light dared to peek through the glorious English clouds or the smoke of the city tended not to venture all the way down to an alley like this. Tiny candle flames in windows overlooking the alley faintly illuminated the scene below in timid orange flickers, as if they were afraid of what they might see down there.

And, well they might be afraid. There in the gloom lay something that was very nearly, but not quite, a corpse. For now, it was still technically a man, but it was a mess of a man. The cobbles around him were slick with dark red. The man slumped in the blood and the filth, waiting for the inevitable.

After a while, there came a soft, heavy sound. Padded paws on stone, the faint click of claws, the dragging of a long, thick tail of scales along the muddy alleyway. It stopped close to the man. The creature sat next to him and waited.

'Don't mind me,' said the creature in a husky, friendly voice after a while. 'I'm not going to start until… you know. I would never. Just, I smelled the blood, and wanted to get here first and call Baggsie.'

The man managed to turn his head a little and opened an eye, to squint at the creature. She was small, for a dragon. Either a lone juvenile or a runt who had somehow managed to scrap it out and survive to early adulthood. Whichever it was, this dragon clearly needed a decent meal, and as soon as he was dead, his fresh carcass would provide one. His death would help her survive. That was something, he supposed. And, he did appreciate her not starting to eat him until he was dead. He knew that the law expressly prohibited killing, or eating living humans on the Upperside, but he also knew that times were hard, criminality was rife and that a crafty dragon could drag him down below to Deep London where it was legal to kill him. One could even argue that the laws agreed with the Tudor throne to protect the people of Upper England shouldn't apply to him, because he was foreign.

'Besides,' continued the dragon, 'thought it might be nice for you to have a bit of company at this difficult time.'

The man huffed a painful sigh. He really had been hoping to die alone. It was what he deserved. Oh well. Maybe there were some other upsides. He spat out a glob of blood and gritted out a question.

'Did you see a cat?'

'A cat?' asked the dragon.

'With an injured tail,' added the man.

'Um,' replied the dragon, 'hang on…' she sniffed the air, then snuffled over to a barred basement window a few yards along the alleyway. 'There's one in this basement,' she announced. 'Don't know how she's injured, but I smell cat blood.'

'She going to be OK?'

The dragon gave another sniff. 'She isn't losing enough blood for it to kill her, and she's safe and warm down there.' The dragon came ambling back to the almost-corpse. 'Unlike someone I could mention. Why'd you ask about her?'

The man didn't answer.

'Don't tell me that's how you ended up getting all beaten and stabbed?' asked the dragon. 'Stepping in to help a little street cat?'

Still, the man didn't answer.

'That's adorable,' added the dragon, 'I mean, as far as fatal beatings can be adorable.'

The man groaned a groan that he hoped conveyed an emphatic 'just let me die in peace'.

The dragon sat down again, and they both waited – the dragon exhibiting rather more anxiety than the dying man. The dragon kept looking around, nervously. Clearly, the rules of Baggsie didn't count for much in a city full of crime and hungry dragons, vampires, zombies and so on. The man had no doubt that this dragon was starving and that she stood no chance of winning a fight if any bigger creatures came to steal her meal before he was dead.

He tried dying faster, for her. It didn't work.

'Is there anything else I can do for you?' asked the dragon. 'Any last words you want me to pass on to a loved one?'

The man snorted, derisively. The dragon shifted anxiously again.

'Would you mind if maybe I took you down to the Deepside?' she asked after a while. 'The tube's not far at all, and once we're in Deep London, I can make it instant and painless for you… oh, hang on, actually…'

The darkness was closing in, now. Not the darkness of the alley; a different darkness. A more final darkness. A darkness that silenced sound, and made pain dwindle to nothing. He couldn't even smell the stench of the alleyway anymore. Here it came. No more running, no more guilt, just the peace of death. And, perhaps, at the other end of the peace, someone would be waiting for him. He was coming! He embraced the absolute darkness.

And then, in the darkness, a spark. A spark! Oh no! It hurt. His heart… his lungs… they were working again. Heaving, pumping, painfully. Stop it, you horrible organs, just let me die, he wanted to cry. The darkness fell away from him, insubstantial as a shadow. The alley was still there. The dragon was still there, her mouth open, glistening fangs inches from his face, her expression frozen with guilty embarrassment. She pulled her head back.

'I am so sorry, I could have sworn you were… you know.'

The pain was searing. He could hear the blood in his ears, and it all hurt so much. 'What happened?'

'I don't know! I swear, your heart stopped, all of you stopped. And then you just… restarted.' She anxiously looked around herself again. 'I should go.'

'No… wait.'

'No. I shouldn't be here. You're not dying, you're not dying at all! You used to smell of death, but now you smell all weird. This is wrong, this is bad.'

The dragon started hurrying away, waddling along the narrow alley as fast as her little reptile legs could take her. The man tried to get up, tried to follow her. Everything hurt so horribly. He just about managed to push himself painfully onto all fours before the dragon disappeared into the gloom, in the direction of Blackfriars tube.

Great. Now he was alive and in horrible pain and stuck in an alley. He didn't feel like he was dying, anymore. It was nothing as peaceful as that. This felt worse. And, not dying meant that he now had to deal with the problem of how he was supposed to get all the way to Upper Southwark. South of the river, in this state, at this time of night. He managed to get some purchase on the wall of one of the nearby buildings, pushed himself onto his wobbly legs and began to make slow, aching progress along the alleyway, dragging himself along from beam to beam like a nervous first-time ice skater. This was going to take forever.

He persisted, step by shuffling, painful step. Left foot. Right foot.

But then, he thought to himself as he made his slow south-bound trek, hadn't his whole life been a slow, painful journey, step by terrible step? He'd really thought the journey had come to an end, tonight. He should have died. It didn't make sense. This was yet another problem for him, right when he'd hoped his problems may have finally been over.

Typical, thought Fang.

Left foot, right foot, left foot, right foot.

Fang was already five thousand miles away from the only place he'd ever called home – give or take a few hundred miles or so, honestly he'd stopped counting somewhere in the Ottoman Empire. What was another mile or two, on bloodied, bruised and shaking legs?

Left foot. Right foot. Left foot. Right foot. Left.

*

'Well, then.' Lady Alice Feignshaugh paused, cleared her throat and started again. 'Monsieur Quitbeef. Yes. Well, then.'

Lazare de Quitte-Beuf smiled winningly at his employer and tried to pretend that he couldn't read from her tone that she wasn't going to be his employer for very much longer, at all.

Lady Alice clapped her hands together with a pretence of pleased satisfaction. 'I must commend you, Monsieur, on your tutelage. After a mere nine months, I must say that Cuthbert's command of the French language has come on in leaps and indeed bounds. He speaks it as if a native of your land, I have no doubt!'

Cuthbert Feignshaugh could not speak French as well as any Frenchman, and it didn't take a Parisian to know that. Cuthbert could speak French as well as a bored child with a thick English accent, and even then was only able to tell you whether the boulangerie was on the left or the right, and that on Tuesdays he enjoyed riding horses with his cousins.

'And Cecily plays the flute like an absolute cherub following your months of instruction,' continued Lady Alice, with a cheer as thin and as hard as varnish.

Lazare had never seen cherubim, nor heard whether they were known to be proficient flautists. There was, he supposed, a chance that cherubim were only capable of squeaking out a tune that occasionally veered into something like Greensleeves, the way Cecily Feignshaugh was after nine difficult, patience-straining, if reasonably paid months.

'So, I do believe your mission has been a complete success,' concluded Alice. 'Bravo, Monsieur.'

She smiled at him, expectantly. Lazare smiled back, mentally unpicking what she'd said to locate the meaning she'd buried deep amongst layers of flattering lies.

'Are you,' he hazarded, his smile never dropping, 'firing me, Madame?'

Lady Alice beamed at him. 'Goodness, no! We're setting you free! To pursue other avenues! You have your acting career to concentrate on after all, you don't want to waste any more of your time after achieving what you temporarily joined our household to do.'

Lazare continued to smile politely. 'Is this because I'm French?'

'Monsieur, you're so delightfully amusing, why, we *hired* you because you're French!'

He nodded, aware that his smile was losing its lustre. 'Is it because of the wings?'

And there was the glint in her eye. 'Noooo,' she cooed, 'goodness, no. We Upper English do not discriminate against our friends from the other side. Why, you saw for yourself, Mr Peaks was taken good care of, even though he was a zombie.'

Lazare didn't reply. Mr Peaks had been kept as a footman in Lady Alice's employment for a mere six weeks after being turned into a zombie. Lazare had had his little misfortune only a month ago.

'I'm sure that, as with Mr Peaks when he felt it was time for him to move on, you'll find London to be simply packed with fresh opportunities for a talented young vampire such as yourself.'

'I'm not a vampire, Madame,' Lazare replied, ensuring she could see his normal human teeth through his renewed smile.

'Or whatever it is that you actually are,' continued Lady Alice, smoothly, and Lazare had no answer to that. He knew that the one thing he very definitely was, was fired.

Lazare wasn't a vampire. That much, he knew. To become a vampire, one must be turned by another vampire. It hadn't been a vampire attack that had started Lazare's recent troubles, but humdrum, run of the mill human muggers, with boring old cudgels and knives. Vampire attacks were actually very rare in Upper London, in spite of all the lurid rumours and whispers about their kind, and it was even rarer for a vampire to revive a dying human by turning them without their consent. No, none of this was a vampire's doing. In fact, the only vampires that ever bothered Lazare even now were…

'Sir? Good sir? Excuse me?'

Lazare sighed inwardly, and painted his smile on for the approaching vampire.

'I couldn't help but notice that you appear to be afflicted, sir.'

The vampire seemed to be a boy of around ten or eleven, although his eyes, like the eyes of any vampire, were old and tired. Like Lazare, the boy had a large pair of leathery wings, the same shade as the skin of his face. There was something familiar about him that at first Lazare couldn't quite place.

'Wulfric, sir,' continued the child, holding out a hand for Lazare to shake.

Lazare accepted, politely. 'Lazare de Quitte-Beuf, at your service. Um… have we met?'

'Possibly?' Wulfric shadowed Lazare's own expression as they tried to place one another. 'Do you frequent the Moon and Werewolf? Upper Deptford?'

'Guilty as charged.' He clicked his fingers. 'You're a pot boy there.'

Wulfric looked offended. 'I'm the owner.'

'Of course you are, Monsieur,' replied Lazare, hurriedly. 'Forgive a poor mummer's foolishness.'

'You're that French fellow who drinks with the actors,' said Wulfric. It was the vampire's turn to look apologetic. 'Your affliction must be very new, in that case. I truly hope your vampirism isn't down to any of my clientele, I've been *very* firm with undead customers that they are not to—'

'They did not,' said Lazare, cutting the boy off, 'as I am not "afflicted" as you think.' He flashed another wide, deliberately toothsome grin.

Wulfric noticed the teeth, and Lazare watched the by-now familiar expressions of surprise, confusion and disappointment flit over the vampire's face.

'Oh,' said Wulfric.

'*Oui*,' replied Lazare, smoothly.

'So, you're... you're not actually...'

'I am not. Same old human teeth, same old human appetites, I was able to go outside that one afternoon last week when it was sunny.'

Wulfric sighed. 'That's a pity, Monsieur.'

'I know.'

'I was hoping to invite you to join our support network.'

Lazare nodded. He'd had this conversation before and yes, he agreed, it truly was a pity. One vampire had managed to get a good five minutes into trying to sell the support network to him before noticing that he wasn't actually a vampire. It sounded marvellous.

'We have lawyers and everything,' continued Wulfric, 'we could have helped you get a base in Deep London, keep your connections Upperside, or help with any discrimination cases, in terms of employment, or lodgings...'

Wulfric gave a meaningful little glance to Lazare's bags of belongings.

'I am indeed between jobs and lodgings right now,' Lazare admitted, 'at least nobody chases one with flaming torches in these enlightened days.'

Instead, thought Lazare, in the forward-thinking and ever-so-civilised Upper London of 1599, they waited a few weeks so that it didn't look like they were sacking you because of the wings, and then turned you out of a live-in tutoring position so that you were immediately without income or board and under threat of being arrested for vagrancy. In many ways, that was worse than a lit torch – it was insincere and cowardly. You weren't allowed to fight back. You just had to say 'thank you, Madame' for the insipid letter of reference and politely be on your way.

Wulfric's smooth little face creased with a bewildered frown, and the vampire's top lip curled up slightly as he gave Lazare a good sniff. 'So… what *are* you? Where do you belong? Are you undead, at least?'

'I don't know,' replied Lazare, truthfully. He didn't *feel* undead, but how else could he possibly describe the sudden change that had happened to him a month ago? He had almost died… no, that wasn't quite it. For the briefest moment, it had felt as if he *had* died. And then, there had been a sort of spark in the darkness, and a searing pain, and then he simply hadn't been dead anymore. He wasn't dead, but he wasn't entirely alive, either. He definitely wasn't human anymore – the massive wings he'd woken up with made that pretty clear – but in the past month he'd discovered he wasn't a vampire, a ghoul, a zombie or any of the known magical demographics of Deep London either. As for the question of where he belonged, he definitely didn't know the answer to that either, but certainly hoped it wasn't 'in the gutter'.

'Before you ask,' added Lazare, anticipating what usually came next whenever a vampire respectfully approached him, 'I don't want you to take me Deepside and finish me off or fully turn me, either. I just feel like that would make things more complicated.'

'No.' Wulfric stopped sniffing and stood back again, with a troubled expression. 'I don't think I could, even if you did want that. You smell... off.'

As an enthusiastic consumer of the finest perfumes available on a tutor's wage, Lazare couldn't help but feel a little affronted at that. '"Off"?'

'Off,' repeated Wulfric, still frowning. 'I'm so sorry, Monsieur. I don't think I can help you, at all.'

Lazare tried another smile, even though his heart really wasn't in it. 'That's all right.'

'And I certainly can't try turning you or drinking you, because you really do smell...'

'Off,' replied Lazare with forced cheer. 'Yes. I get it.'

'I should get back to it,' continued the vampire, turning back the way he'd come, 'there was a dead fox in the gutter over there that should make a decent meal for a couple of... oh, for pity's sake!'

Lazare gazed over the little vampire's head to see what had annoyed him so much. There was indeed some of a dead fox lying in the gutter, although the back half of it was a cleanly picked skeleton by now. A stumpy, brick-brown runt of a dragon was making fast work of scavenging the carcass.

'I was going to have that,' cried Wulfric. 'I called Baggsie!'

The dragon looked cowed. 'You were chatting, I didn't think you'd mind. D'you want me to save you a leg?'

'No! I wanted...' Wulfric sighed. 'Fine, I'll have a leg. And the heart, unless you've snaffled that, too.'

The dragon backed away from the fox corpse, before sniffing the air and staring at Lazare.

'*Bonjour*,' said Lazare, politely.

'We don't have to share with him,' Wulfric told the dragon, reaching into the cadaver's chest cavity. 'He's not one of us.' The little vampire pulled the heart out easily and tucked into it as if it were an apple.

The dragon approached Lazare with a combination of trepidation and wonder, still sniffing. 'I recognise that stink.'

'I don't stink…' Lazare complained. He was wearing his second best pomander, for crying out loud.

'I can smell it even under all that lavender you're wearing.' The dragon sat down in front of him, the fox corpse seemingly forgotten. 'God's Scales,' she exclaimed, 'it happened again. I found another one!'

'Lavender is very in fashion right now,' argued Lazare, before breaking off suddenly. 'Wait… what do you mean, "another one"?'

'Another one,' repeated the little dragon, brightly, like that was enough of an explanation.

'Another… not-quite-a-vampire?' asked Lazare.

The dragon turned tail and started waddling off. 'I'll show you him. C'mon.'

CHAPTER TWO
THE OTHER ONE

Lazare wasn't even entirely sure what he was doing, or where he was, besides the obvious: he was lugging all of his worldly possessions around a dark, dangerous alley somewhere in Upper Blackfriars, following a small dragon he had bribed with the promise of as grand a meal of butcher's scraps as he could afford – a dragon who appeared to be completely lost. As for why he was doing this… well. It wasn't as if he had anything else to do or anywhere else to go, right now. The dragon's insistence that she had stumbled upon another man with the same mysterious affliction as Lazare intrigued him – gave him hope. Maybe this other fellow knew what was going on, knew how to turn Lazare back to normal.

Of course, the little dragon would have to actually find the fellow first, which was proving much harder than he'd initially been assured.

'He was right here.' The dragon sniffed a patch of cobblestone. Lazare could just about make out some smears of red amongst the mud and muck, but patches of dried blood were common sights in the back alleys of Upper London, and this blood was days old.

'How long ago did you see this poor man?' Lazare asked, politely.

'Two… no, three nights past?' replied the dragon, still sniffing about.

Lazare deflated. 'Three nights? He could be anywhere by now!'

'He was injured,' the dragon told him. 'And you Upper Londoners never go very far, even when you're fit and well.'

'I am not an Upper Londoner, Mademoiselle dragon,' Lazare told her, mustering what pride he still had left. 'I am from Paris.'

'How long you been living here, then?'

'Ten years.'

'Then you're an Upper Londoner.'

Lazare gave her his best, Frenchest huff of derision.

'Deny it all you like. I bet you still know all the main thoroughfares by heart and have a favourite little foreign restaurant down a side street that you think nobody else knows about.'

'Majlad's Grill on Knott Row,' muttered Lazare, on instinct, 'never go to The Merrie Moor on Watergate, it's a total tourist trap.'

'Such an Upper Londoner. Amber, by the way.'

'Hmm?'

'My name.'

'That's pretty,' said Lazare, even though he knew enough about Deep London culture to be aware that it was a thoroughly common name for an urban dragon.

'Oh!' Amber perked up a little, sniffing around a filthy wall. 'I think I found his trail. He was leaning against the walls. Come on!'

Lazare pulled a face. It was never a good idea to lean against an alley wall in this city, for the same reason that it was never a good idea to walk under houses' eaves early in the morning, or ever lift up your head with your mouth open if you heard an upstairs window open. True, Paris was no better, but he couldn't help but feel the city could use a better sewage system than 'chuck it out of the window and hope you don't get cholera'. He could see the wet, brown lines of the residents' morning movements staining the walls of the alley. *Merde.* This fellow must have been *really* injured to drag himself along *that.*

Amber started waddling at speed down the alley, sniffing at the wall and ground. 'He was heading south.'

Lazare followed her, glad to be getting out of the alley. Unfortunately, the alley opened up into a second alley, and after that, an even narrower, darker alley than the previous two.

'Um,' said Lazare, pulling his bags of belongings closer to himself.

'I think he was heading to the bridge, you know,' said Amber, still cheerfully following the trail.

'The bridge?' murmured Lazare. 'He went south of the river? In the middle of the night?'

'*Such* an Upper Londoner,' muttered Amber, smugly.

Well, thought Lazare, at least the South Bank was pleasant enough in the day. And, once they got to the bridge, they'd be back in civilisation again. Yes, the shops and bars that crowded Blackfriars Bridge were touristy as anything, but it had to be an improvement on the alleyways where his person – and, more importantly, all of his stuff – were in peril. He could see the opening of the narrow alleyway ahead, and hurried to reach it, to embrace the relative safety of the bridge's many 'I Love Upper London' tankard stalls and Ye Emporium of New Worlde Sweetes, but just as the end was in reach, two shadows appeared at the opening.

'Well, well, well,' said one of the shadows.

'Well, well, well, *well*,' added the second shadow, like a menacing, mocking echo.

The shadows of the alley shifted, and suddenly their way was blocked by two figures.

'What are you two doing on the Upperside?' asked the first voice.

'We're allowed,' said Amber, quietly.

'This is *our* London, Sunshine,' added the second voice, eyeing up Lazare's wings. 'Oop, sorry. Are you offended by the word "Sunshine", Sunshine?'

'I'm not a vampire, actually,' Lazare said, as levelly as he could. 'Upper London's my home, just as it's yours.'

'Your accent suggests otherwise, *Señor*,' said the second voice.

Lazare bristled a little at that. Yes, he was accustomed to comments about his French accent and the tone of his skin, yes he supposed he should now get used to people assuming vampirism, but, even under threat from these would-be muggers, he still took exception to any insinuation that he might be Spanish.

'As do,' added the first voice, 'your wings. And your little dragon.'

'And your wings,' chimed in the second voice.

'I just said wings, Herbert,' hissed the first voice.

Lazare decided to use the moment of self-inflicted distraction between the shadowy figures to take a couple of steps backwards.

'No you don't, Señor Vampiro,' snapped the first voice, stopping Lazare in his tracks.

The shadows finally approached Lazare enough for him to make them out. One of the men had the arrogant swagger and moderately expensive clothes of someone who was doing fairly well for himself in the thriving industry of organised crime. The other, younger man, apparently named Herbert, was more shabbily dressed and was sporting a freshly broken nose. Some lad dragged from poverty, no doubt, having to do the dirty, dangerous work as he attempted to move up the ranks before his inevitable early grave. Lazare might have felt pity for Herbert, were he not very clearly about to beat Lazare up and steal all his things.

'What you got in those bags, Señor?' asked the well-dressed gangster.

'Vampire gold?' asked Herbert.

Again, the older gangster sighed. 'They don't have gold.'

'Well, they're not allowed silver, are they, Randall?' added Herbert. 'Health and safety hazard, in Deep London.'

Lazare took another step back. And another. Behind him, he could hear Amber turn tail and start scurrying away. He tried taking another couple of backwards steps, in the hope that if he didn't turn just yet, they might not notice.

'He's making a run for it!' shouted Herbert.

'Cheeky sod,' Randall exclaimed.

They both lunged at Lazare, who turned and ran. Ahead of him in the alley, he saw Amber, running as fast as her little stumpy legs could carry her – which wasn't very fast, not that Lazare was anyone to judge. He wasn't one of nature's great athletes. Generally, if an activity was worth Lazare messing up his hairdo or rumpling his doublet for, it had to be something he really enjoyed. As far as he was concerned, those activities were confined to acting, dancing and/or making love, so while he considered himself *extremely* skilled in those three things, he was not at all practised in the art of running away – let alone while encumbered by all of his worldly possessions.

Lazare just hoped that Amber knew of some hidden tunnel or corner where they could duck and hide, because there was no way either of them were outrunning their pursuers. A little runt of a dragon such as Amber had to have some neat little way of avoiding peril, right? Otherwise how could she have survived either Deep or Upper London so far? At that moment, unfortunately for Lazare, he saw what Amber's means were of avoiding danger in Upper London's alleys. The little dragon opened up her stubby wings as she ran at full pelt and lifted herself into the air with all the confidence and grace of a fledgeling goose, until she was just a little too high up for the pursuing humans to grab, and flew away.

Merde!

Someone grabbed one of Lazare's bags from behind. He turned, again. Herbert had his satchel of spare shoes and accessories held tight, and was doing his best to yank it off Lazare's shoulder. Not his shoes and jewellery. Not today, Herbert. Lazare's years of theatre training had left him extremely well versed in stage fighting. He could wield a grand array of different stage weaponry with swift finesse. So too could he pull off the intricate foot and fistwork of a complexly choreographed bare knuckle stage fight. He had recently discovered as he had bled out in a gutter, that none of these skills did him the first bit of good in an actual fight with actual weapons.

'Randall?' called Herbert. 'He's not letting go.'

Randall pulled a wooden stake from his well-tailored padded hose. 'Well, we know what to do with his sort, don't we?'

Oh, no. Oh, no no no. The thing about staking someone in the heart was, it didn't matter if you were a vampire or not, it was still going to kill you. Maybe this was how Lazare was going to get killed for real, this time. Or, if he still couldn't die properly, it was going to really, really hurt. Dying sucked. He'd already done it once this month and he didn't want to do it again so soon. It was agony, and who knew what new weird additions to his body he'd wake up with if he went through it all again. Horns? Chicken feet? He didn't want chicken feet, none of his shoes would fit. He should probably let go of his precious bag of things. But he couldn't! This was his stuff – he couldn't afford to lose anymore stuff! This was so unfair. He didn't want any of this, he wanted to play Mephistopheles and recline on cushions recounting scintillating anecdotes and drinking wine and generally being exotic. He wanted to write sonnets over some gorgeous soulful Lord, Lady or Other with eyes as dark as night – and not just because he had a lot of good rhymes in the bank for 'dark as night'. He wanted to fall in love, he'd never fallen in love, and now he was about to get stabbed in an alley over a mugging gone wrong, *again*, and... and...

'Unhand that poor vampire.'

Wait, what?

Both gangsters paused, although neither of them unhanded Lazare as instructed by this mysterious new voice. Herbert looked as confused as Lazare felt. He frowned across at Randall, who blinked at his accomplice, still holding the stake aloft.

'I recognise that voice,' muttered Randall.

'Tis the Turk,' Herbert exclaimed.

Both of them turned to a new man standing in the alleyway. Lazare followed their gaze to look at him.

The man, from his complexion, was not in the slightest bit Turkish, but most likely had a lineage hailing from the Ming Empire, or some other land in the eastern reaches of Asia. He wore simple, scuffed and dirtied travellers' attire that didn't fit him properly, and looked too threadbare for the cold and damp of Upper London. The man beneath the clothes looked just as muddied, battered, torn and worn as his attire. He looked as if he'd spent the past week sleeping in a ditch, and the ditch regretted it. He looked as if he'd just been expelled from a haunted swamp for bringing down the vibe of the swamp. He looked, thought Lazare, how a hangover felt. He was *not* well groomed. Nor, from his expression, was he happy about a single element of the situation. Likely, being mistaken for Turkish was only a small part of that.

'Didn't we already kill you?' asked Randall.

The stranger's scowl deepened in reply. From the cuts and bruises he was sporting, this was a display of displeasure that likely caused the stranger some pain.

Wait. Was this… could this be the Other Guy?

'You broke my nose, you Ottoman bugger,' added Herbert.

The gangsters' attentions were on this furious stranger, now. Lazare could probably use the distraction to prise his bag from Herbert's grip and make a dash for relative safety.

Lazare did no such thing, much to his own consternation. He told himself to do it. Told his hands to wrench the bag from Herbert, even as they balled into fists. Told his legs to run away, even as they planted themselves firm.

'Maybe he's a zombie,' noted Randall, 'or some filthy foreign ghoul we haven't heard of from all Constantinople and that. Maybe we just need to kill him again, like this dirty Spanish vampire, here.'

The stranger took another step towards them. 'Leave that fop alone – vampire or no, he's unarmed and clearly incapable of fighting back. Attacking the defenceless, just like the last time. Well, why don't you pick on someone your own size?'

Lazare couldn't help but notice that the stranger was the shortest of all four of them in the alleyway. He was also as unarmed as Lazare was. Lazare wasn't a fighter – he was a lover, an entertainer, a caperer and cavorter – but he couldn't in good conscience run away and leave this bruised husk of a stranger to fend off two armed ruffians alone, after he'd stepped in to help him.

Randall turned, his stake raised, away from Lazare and towards the stranger. 'I enjoyed crushing you foreign muck into the filth last time. Cheers for coming back for an encore.'

The stranger tilted his head a little at Randall. 'Filth, is it?'

Something off to Lazare's side caught his eye. The wall of the narrow alley was wet with sewage, as if gong buckets were tipping out from every window above, all at the same time. He glanced at the other wall – it was doing the same. The filth was coming down thick and fast, a great unending torrent of it, slick, and dripping lumps. Lazare tried to pull his bags closer to himself and folded his wings even tighter than usual over his shoulders, to avoid touching the disgusting walls. The muggers noticed it too.

'What the...'

'Sloppy buckets time, Randall,' noted Herbert.

'But that's at dawn,' Randall muttered. 'What's going on?' He turned to the stranger again. 'Be this magic?'

'No, this be poo-poo,' Herbert explained. 'Happens all the time.'

'Herbert, look up. There's no windows!'

Lazare looked up, along with Herbert. There were indeed no windows along either of the narrow alley walls. Filth was just streaming down it from nowhere.

'What is this?' Randall demanded, turning the stake from the stranger to Lazare and back to the stranger again. 'Is it a spell or something? Who casts a spell to make walls of magic gong? It's weird. Stop it. Whoever's doing this, just...' He looked upwards again, and his eyes widened. 'God's Bones.'

High above, in the narrow strip of sky visible between the sewage-spewing walls, the murky grey clouds darkened with a great and terrible shadow. Mighty wings flapped ahead. There was a downwards whoosh of air and the great, razor-clawed talons of an immense dragon gripped the rooftops. The huge dragon, the size and colour of a townhouse, bent her neck down towards them. Her head loomed over them in the alley – almost as wide as the alleyway itself, brick-brown, with fiery eyes and great, wet fangs, shining with spit.

'There you are,' growled the dragon. 'I've been looking for you.'

'Argh,' screamed Randall and Herbert.

'Argh,' screamed Lazare, not to be outdone.

'That's not right,' cried Randall, 'it's not right! Big dragon out here, in broad daylight, and the walls, and... This is some real Deepside stuff, I don't care what the law says, whoppers like that shouldn't be allowed up here! We're being terrorised! In our own city!'

The spooked ruffian grabbed his younger accomplice by the sleeve and started trying to pull him away, back towards the bridge end of the alley where they'd come from.

Herbert couldn't take his horrified eyes off the dragon. 'We'll tell a guard on you,' he threatened.

'Herbert,' said Randall, 'have you biscuits for brains?'

'Not a guard,' continued Herbert as Randall continued to drag him away, 'cause they'd arrest us too. We'll get the gang! We run with Avis Hapenny. You heard, you're in big trouble now. We'll be back with the Hapenny boys. And more weapons! Then you'll be sorry We'll stake the lot of you!' Herbert turned to Randall as both ruffians skuttled away. 'Do all Turkish ghouls and that still die from a staking?'

Randall continued to drag Herbert away. '*Everyone* dies from a staking, you egg.'

'I'm not Turkish,' sighed the stranger.

'Foreign's foreign, to their sort,' growled the dragon – who wasn't the size of a house at all, come to think of it, but in fact barely bigger than a badger. As she flapped to the ground on unsteady wings, Lazare realised the 'mighty dragon' he'd been so scared of was actually just Amber.

'They thought Lazare here was Spanish even though he's extremely French. Um. Was it one of you two just then, making it look like the walls were all dripping droppings?'

Lazare looked around at the walls. They were… not 'clean' by any stretch of the imagination, but they certainly weren't pouring with effluent, and they looked as if they never had. 'You went all big,' Lazare told Amber, confused.

'Did I?' Amber sounded happy about this. 'Ooh, how big? Big as a horse? Can one of you gentlemen make little dragons look big as a horse?'

'I think that was me,' muttered the man. 'It's… I still don't really understand it yet, but it got you out of getting mugged, Monsieur, so you're welcome, and if you don't mind, I have important business to attend to, so…'

He tried to push past Lazare and Amber.

'Hey! Woah there, friend!' Amber tried to get in his path but he just stepped over her. 'We were looking for you.' She looked up at Lazare, excitedly. 'Told you I'd find him!'

Lazare let the fact slide that the stranger had in fact found Lazare, after Amber had immediately reacted to a dangerous situation by flying off and leaving him. 'You're the other one?' Lazare asked.

This stopped the stranger. '"Other"?' He narrowed his eyes at Lazare. 'You have human teeth. You're *not* a vampire?'

Lazare shook his head.

'But you have wings.'

Lazare nodded.

'Did you... die, recently? Or, that is, did you fail to die and just end up alive and awake and... changed?'

Lazare nodded again.

'He's like you, mister,' added Amber. 'Like when you didn't die the other night. Remember? Remember how I nearly ate you?'

The stranger sighed. 'Yeah.' He looked Lazare up and down. Lazare wasn't sure that he liked the tone of face he was being appraised in. 'So, I'm not the only one. Confucius's Toenails, it's worse than I thought.' He gave Lazare a look of distaste. 'What did you do?'

'"Do"...?'

'Did you not do something terrible, to bring this on yourself?'

'I don't think so,' Lazare told him, hoping that the enjoyable vices of pride, sloth and lust didn't count as 'something terrible'. 'Why?' he asked the man. 'Did *you* do something terrible?'

The man ignored his question. 'You – dragon.'

'Amber,' Amber told him.

'Whatever,' replied the stranger. 'Take Monsieur Lazare to the safety of the bridge, he can buy some souvenirs to take back to la belle France.'

'I do actually live in Upper London, you know,' Lazare told him, affronted. 'You can tell from my doublet. This is a London doublet.'

'Go to the bridge where it's safe, Monsieur London Doublet,' the stranger told him. 'I have urgent business to attend to and then I'll come find you, we can compare notes on this curse we appear to both share, and find out how to undo it so that we can both get on with being dead.' The stranger patted him on the elbow and began walking down the alleyway.

'Being... dead?' asked Lazare, weakly.

'You know your urgent business,' said Amber, 'does it have anything to do with all the roast chicken in your pockets?'

The stranger stopped dead in his tracks, and turned to face the little dragon, looking faintly embarrassed. '...No.'

'But you do have roast chicken in your pockets,' replied Amber, sniffing.

'...Yes.'

'Why?'

'None of your business.'

'Can I have some?'

'No.'

'You're going to feed that little cat, aren't you?' asked Amber. 'The cat in the basement, the one you were asking after.' She turned to Lazare. 'He got beaten to a nearly-dead bloody pulp rescuing a little kitty cat, isn't that adorable?'

Lazare cocked his head at the stranger, who flushed a little. 'Yes, fine,' blurted the stranger, 'therefore what's the point in my going through all that and waking up with a curse on me if she then dies of starvation while she's healing up? It's just common sense I feed her once a day til she's better, OK, Monsieur Lazare?'

Lazare liked that little bit of bothered pinkness around the stranger's nose. 'Can we help you feed your kitty cat?' he asked with a smile. 'Be easier than splitting up and you having to find us. That bridge is simply packed, this time of day...'

The stranger turned, and started marching down the alleyway again. 'Do whatever you want, just don't slow me down or try to eat my pocket-chicken.'

Lazare and Amber took that as a 'yes', and followed him.

'By the way, it's not "Monsieur Lazare",' Lazare told him, 'Lazare is my first name. Lazare de Quitte-Beuf. Not "Quitbeef" as the Upper English keep saying. But just "Lazare" is fine.'

'Fang,' replied the stranger.

'Is that family name Fang or personal name Fang?'

'Just Fang,' said Fang, who didn't speak again until they reached the spot where he'd been killed.

CHAPTER THREE
Why Won't You Die?

Finding out that what had happened to him wasn't a one-off after all was the last thing Fang needed. He knew he shouldn't still be alive. Nell couldn't find any information in her books that might explain what exactly had happened to him, or what his newly acquired magical power was – besides 'disgusting, stop it, Fang'. She had just advised that, while they looked for answers, he shouldn't let himself die again, on the grounds that he could make it all get worse. His only succour had been that as far as their research had been able to show them, it was only he who was affected. But now, there was this grinning fop of a Frenchman. He was cursed with it too, and Fang had absolutely no idea why.

As Lazare chatted about himself, Fang couldn't think of a thing that connected them, besides their being of a similar age, and both residents of Upper London from foreign lands, although there was no link between Lazare's upbringing in France and Fang's own. Fang had assumed, when he'd thought he was the only one, that the curse was to do with The Incident back home, but now Lazare had turned up, that hypothesis was blasted to smithereens. The Frenchman seemed to have committed no deed dreadful enough to warrant a magical punishment as powerful as this.

And then there was the new, disturbing bit of information Lazare had blithely brought up as he'd chattered – Lazare had been struck by the curse almost a month ago – weeks before Fang. Fang wasn't the first to be cursed. And the curse had given Lazare *wings*. He kept them self-consciously folded over his shoulders like a soft brown leather cape, but Fang could see that they had to be huge – at least as big as a full-grown vampire's wings. How come Lazare got those incredible wings and he got a weird little gross spell that only half worked? No. Focus, Fang. That wasn't the issue. The issue was that he now had another cursed person to add to the research, and every bit of new data from him torched all the hypotheses he and Nell had pursued so far. Also, this French guy was far too cheery for comfort. Grinning and twittering away. You have a curse on you, Monsieur, act like it! At least when he'd thought it was only him, there had been no issue with trying to find a way to break the curse and die properly. Fang hated life. This new fellow seemed to love it – one of these real *joie de vivre* fools. The idea that he may soon have to find a way to ensure this other man died properly as well made Fang feel bad.

Yet another problem about Lazare was that he and the dragon Amber were intent on following him while he fed the cat, which, while not exactly the most pressing issue, was still pretty annoying. He reached the spot where he'd failed to die, and found the barred window to the basement where the cat had fled after he'd stopped the Hapenny boys hurting her. He fished out the chicken, crouched by the window and lowered his voice.

'Mi mi mi mi mi?' he called, in what he hoped was a level loud enough for the cat to hear but quiet enough to avoid Lazare thinking he was being 'cute'. 'Mi mi mi meow meow mi mi mi? Here, mimimi?'

'Mimi?' cooed Lazare. 'Cute!'

'It's just how people from my country say "pspsps".'

Lazare crouched next to Fang. He smelled overwhelmingly of lavender. '*Minou minou*,' called Lazare, much louder. '*Ici, minou, minou*!'

There came a rustle from the basement below, and the little cat came nosing out of her nest of sackcloth. Her tail was healing up nicely, and her limp was less pronounced. The leaky windows allowed enough rainwater into the basement to create a small puddle she could drink from, and she'd eaten up all the chicken he'd thrown down for her yesterday. Hopefully in the next couple of days she'd be able to go back out on the hunt and start fending for herself again. She actually managed to stretch up on her hind legs a little towards the chicken as he ripped the meat into manageable shreds for her.

'You're looking better, Mimi,' he told the cat. He held a finger up towards Lazare. 'Don't,' he warned Lazare, before he had chance to say anything.

'What?' replied Lazare. 'You're funny.' The Frenchman paused. 'Those jokes earlier, about finding a way for us to die…'

'I rarely joke, Monsieur, and that was no exception.' Fang kept his tone gentle as he continued to feed the cat. 'We shouldn't be alive. If this gets a chance to snowball, it could endanger the whole world.'

'But people wake up from death all the time, these days.'

'Yeah. Vampires. Ghouls. Lycanthropes. Zombies. All well-known, well-established subsets of the undead magical population. We know what they are and how they're turned, society has structures in place to accommodate them. We know where they came from. Us folk from the Great Ming know *all* too well where they came from, and the stupid, selfish hubris that caused them to be…'

'Ohhh,' sighed Lazare, 'you're taking all of this so seriously because of that old Emperor. God's Balls, man, that was millennia ago.'

'No,' Fang told him through gritted teeth, 'I am taking this seriously because it's serious. We don't fit any of the undead demographics, we don't know how we were turned or why, we both have new magical embellishments that are completely different to one another. We don't know how it spreads or how it can be stopped. Do you have any idea how dangerous a new type of undead could be, in powerful hands? Because my people do. My people lived it, for generations. Old Emperor Qin Shi Huang just had to devote himself to finding the elixir of life, and look what happened when he found it – eight thousand of his soldiers turned into the first undead.'

'Yeah. Two thousand years ago, though.'

'Eighteen hundred years ago, *actually*,' retorted Fang, 'and we all still feel its shockwaves even today, all over the world. And, who gets the blame for it? My countrymen. With good cause, I suppose. Until you came along, Nell and I were working under the assumption that, like the others, even this new curse had its source in the Empire...'

'Who's Nell?' asked Lazare.

Fang threw down the last scrap of chicken and sighed, wiping his hands on his breeches. Well, he was going to have to let Lazare and Nell meet, if she was to research this curse properly, wasn't he? This was going to be awful, Nell was always so *Nell*, especially when Fang turned up with someone new, and *especially* especially when that person was kind of good looking. He may as well prepare Lazare at least. He got a flyer from his satchel and passed it to Lazare as they watched the cat finish eating and pad back to her bed. 'You may as well have one of these. I said I'd hand some out, as a favour. Drum up business and whatnot.'

Lazare stood up and read aloud from Nell's flyer. 'Be your bedchamber a wretched den of misery? Suffering from the flops? The drops? Nightly terrors? Sleeping habdabs? Gentleman's whoopsadaisy? The monthly curdles? Fear ye not, but come to Mistress Nell's Emporium of Tinctures, Exotic Spices, Etcetera! All the latest potions and herbal expertise from far flung and forbidden lands e.g. Ming Empire, Mughal Empire, Ottoman

Empire, Ethiopian Empire, Aztec Empire and The Lost City of Llanelli! Yes, we also have Tea, Coffee and NEW IN Chocolate! Private consultations for marital complaints, wink wink, that's NELL'S APOTHECARY, Griffin Alley, Southwark (above the fish shop, knock really loudly).'

'You already have a witch on the case,' noted Amber, impressed.

'She's not a witch, she's just Welsh. An apothecary,' Fang replied. 'And a very good one… don't tell her I said that.'

'Why wouldn't you want me to tell her you said something nice?' asked Amber.

'She *actually* wrote "wink wink" on a business flyer,' muttered Lazare, pocketing the flyer. 'Also, is it true she has coffee? And, if so, why aren't we in Southwark right now, drinking coffee?'

This was a good point. The cat was fed, it was cold, Fang really didn't like hanging around in the spot where he was beaten to not-death and he too was gasping for a coffee. He nodded, and led the others back down through the alleys, in the direction of the bridge. Honestly, the sooner they were out of these shadowy, hemmed-in, dangerous Upper Blackfriars alleyways the better…

'Well well well well *well.*'

Oh, thought Fang, for crying out loud. The Hapenny boys stepped out again from the very same spot in the alleyway where he'd accosted them not twenty minutes previously. And, as threatened, Randall and Herbert had brought back-ups along. Half a dozen of the Hapenny gang now blocked their paths. All, Fang noticed, were wielding stakes.

'Avis Hapenny sends her regards,' sneered Randall. 'She had to agree with us that a vampire and a Turkish ghoul…'

'He ain't Turkish,' interrupted the one woman amongst the gang. 'My granny's from the Ottoman Empire, he looks nothing like her.'

'Well, he's not an old lady, is he, Thomasina?'

'No, I mean he's like Cathayan or something. Vile place, the Ming Empire. Granny says it's where zombies come from. And they play at put-pin with Ghost Foxes and all.'

'Eurgh,' cried Herbert, with a delighted expression.

Fang balled his fists. It was OK – whether it was against two, or six, or twenty, he'd just use his magic again and frighten them all away. There'd be no need to fight.

'Will you let me finish?' Randall snapped. 'Avis thinks it's not right, you doing all gong related magics with a big dragon…' the confidence in Randall's tone wavered considerably as he looked down at tiny little Amber. '…and… and so instead of waste the guards' time, she sent us to clean up the streets directly. Right, lads? And Thomasina?'

'Yeah,' chorused the Hapenny boys plus the one Hapenny Thomasina.

They strode towards Fang's group, stakes raised. Fang concentrated. Vile, was it? Well, since his kind was so 'vile', he should see just how vile he could make things.

'Er. Randall?' called one of the Hapenny boys, gazing at the alley walls. 'The walls are bleeding and the blood's got faces in it and the faces have all got fingers coming out of their mouths.'

Randall kept his gaze squarely on Fang. Damn it, thought Fang.

'Remember what Avis told us, lads, it's just a Turkish trick.'

'He's not Turkish,' snapped Thomasina.

'Fine! Or a Cathay trick or something! What I mean is, it's magic, and we know how to fight magic, don't we, gang?'

Herbert lunged at Amber, who yelped and fluttered out of the way, causing Herbert to lose his balance and tumble to the ground.

'Get the dragon first,' wheezed Herbert, 'before she goes big again!'

'She didn't really get bigger, you codpiece, it was more foreign magic!' Randall swung a stake at Lazare. Fang caught Randall's fist and twisted his arm backwards.

'Still,' replied Herbert, scrabbling back onto his feet, 'She's got all claws and teeth.'

Fang continued to grapple with Randall, and tripped up Thomasina before she too could get to Lazare. Fang locked eyes with the stupefied Frenchman. 'Get out of here! Fetch a guard or something.'

'OK,' shouted Amber, far too keenly, and swiftly flapped away to safety. Fang tried to give Lazare a glare that said 'you too, Monsieur, you literally have wings', but Lazare wasn't moving. Fang concentrated harder. Maybe he could disgust Lazare into fleeing.

'Randall! There are worms all over you,' cried Herbert.

'There's worms on *you*,' added Thomasina. 'Eurgh, they're coming out of your nose!'

Herbert put his hand to his nose, on instinct. 'No there's not.'

'It's an illusion,' shouted Randall, still trying to get out of Fang's armlock. 'Ignore it!'

'But it's gross,' shouted another of the Hapenny boys, stepping away. 'Herbert's all maggoty, I'm sorry, I can't do 'em, they make me sick. And if I'm sick, Thomasina'll be sick, she's got that automatic response thingie.'

'Don't tell him that,' shouted Thomasina, recovering from being tripped, and wielding a stake of her own. 'He'll... too late.'

Fang had already made the walls start dripping vomit. Thomasina took one look at it and gagged, helplessly. Fang took the opportunity to let go of Randall and give Lazare a shove. 'Go!'

Lazare bunched his fists, with his thumbs tucked in like an absolute egg. 'No.'

One of the Hapenny boys ducked down low and charged Lazare, grabbing his hips and pulling him to the ground.

'That's it, lads,' shouted Randall. Fang's magic or illusions – or whatever it was that could make things look disgusting – had only neutralised two of the gang so far, the maggot-phobic one was backing off with a disgusted expression, and Thomasina was retching away. Fang and Lazare were still hopelessly outnumbered, especially considering Lazare clearly couldn't fight a jot and was just some big preening popinjay that Fang now had to protect.

Fang ducked out of the way of another Hapenny boy and threw himself onto the one on top of Lazare, trying to pull him off the Frenchman. He noticed that both Lazare and the Hapenny boy had their eyes shut. He conceded he might have overdone it on the maggots coming out of people's faces.

Strong hands grabbed Fang's hair and yanked him up to his feet. He was spun around to face the biggest of the Hapenny boys – apparently undeterred by the illusionary grubs falling out of his various face holes. Fang recognised this fellow from when he'd stopped the gang from tormenting that cat. He noted the scoundrel's sling and recalled dislocating the bigger man's arm during that previous fight. The Hapenny boy's snarl suggested that he had taken the injury very personally. Good, frankly. What sort of coward hurts a poor little kitty for fun? The ruffian swung his own weapon at Fang – not a stake, this time, but a length of lead pipe which he wielded one-handed. Yikes, this guy was strong. Fang ducked away, almost in time. The pipe skimmed the side of his head. It didn't concuss him, but it still really hurt. The ruffian swung again and again with it, each time just missing Fang as he ducked and dodged. The Hapenny boy punctuated each swing with a frustrated grunt.

'Why… won't… you… die?'

With the last swing, Fang pressed himself against a wall, and pushed himself off it again with force, lunging at the Hapenny boy in a counterattack from the side.

'I don't know!' Fang grunted in reply, slamming an elbow into the ruffian's ribs. 'That's what…' he twisted around behind the man, 'we're trying…' he kicked the back of his knee, toppling him, 'to find…' as he continued to twist around the man, he grabbed the slinged arm and tugged it, dislocating it again, 'out!'

He punctuated the 'out' with a swift kick to the downed man's head, knocking him out cold – which would at least keep him from feeling the initial pain of his arm being re-dislocated.

Lazare was still struggling to make any progress with the rest of the Hapenny boys. Two of them were on top of him now, both trying to keep him from wriggling for long enough to stake him. Fang leapt at them, and decided he needed to shift his magical strategy away from manifesting maggots.

'Randall?' Herbert called. 'Guards!'

That stopped the rest of the gang in their tracks. At the southern end of the alley stood two Royal Guards – fierce and huge, with glossy feathers and vicious beaks. Both were impeccably dressed, as were all Royal Guards, in red livery with gold brocade and stiff ruffs. Beady eyes on the gang, they strutted towards the fray.

'Hang on, nobody go anywhere,' muttered Randall, watching the guards, but the rest of the attackers didn't want to hang on. They scattered and ran for it, two of them pausing only to scoop up their unconscious and dislocated comrade and carry him off with them.

'It's another trick,' shouted Randall.

The image of the two guard ravens was a bit much for Fang to keep up for long. As soon as the rest of the gang fled, the two mighty creatures dissipated into a thin fog. Fang went to try to help Lazare up, but was stopped by Randall, grabbing Fang by the throat and shoving him against a wall.

'You think you're so clever, don't you, ghoul? Well, Avis is smarter than the likes of you. She knows what to do about your lot.' With his spare hand, Randall pulled something from his jerkin that made the breath catch in Fang's throat. Randall grinned. 'Oh, what's that? You've seen something that scares you? Not very nice, is it?'

Fang eyed it. An impossibly slim and delicate knife – the blade so thin that it was translucent, and glowing with the magical luminescence of...

'That's a fae weapon,' gasped Fang. 'What are you doing wielding something like that up here?'

'I told you. Avis Hapenny is not a lady to trifle with.' Randall grinned, clearly enjoying the boot of fear being on the other foot. 'She has contacts. And if you Deepside scum insist on bringing your dirty magic Upperside, well, we can fight that with even deeper magic.' He brought the fae knife right up to Fang's face. '*This* is but a trinket, compared to some of the artefacts she's acquired lately.'

'You idiot,' breathed Fang. 'Stealing artefacts from the fae. You *idiots*! Do you have *any* idea what you've done?'

'All I've done is scare the breeches off of you, foreign ghoul,' leered Randall. 'That's almost good enough for me. Almost. See, you hurt my lads, so why don't you pay that pain back for us now?'

Given Lazare's fighting prowess so far, Fang really wasn't expecting the great fop to rescue him, which made it all the more surprising when Lazare loomed up behind Randall at that moment and grabbed his knife-wielding hand with an angry string of French curse words. While Randall may not have factored Lazare into the fight, so Fang hadn't factored in that Thomasina had still been too busy retching to run away from the illusion of the guard ravens at the time, and still lingered in the alley. But now Fang could see over Lazare's shoulder that she had stopped throwing up. Worse yet, she had a stake.

The stake was raised, positioned well in both hands, and she was already running with it, aiming squarely at Lazare's back. Fang didn't even think. His hands were already on Randall's shoulder, his foot already on the ruffian's thigh, he pushed himself up and vaulted over both Randall and Lazare's shoulders, one leg curling back as he dropped down the other side of the two men to kick the stake out of Thomasina's hands before landing.

He lashed out a foot. It hit nothing but thin air. He'd mistimed the kick.

Thomasina was still lunging, her eyes widened in alarm at the man who had just dropped down between her and her intended target.

Fang tried to make a last-ditch grab for the stake.

But it was too late.

There was a terrible, meaty sound of sharp wood entering flesh, and Thomasina's face was right next to his, etched with shock.

'Sorry,' she mumbled. 'That wasn't meant for you.'

Everything was going dark, again.

Maybe, maybe this time he would die. Maybe someone was waiting for him. Underneath that peach tree, that big peach tree back home.

'Fang?'

Both ruffians looked down solemnly at Fang as he crumpled to the ground, his hands, slick with blood, clutched over the wooden stake in his guts.

'We warned him, Thomasina,' Randall told her gently, as if *she* were the one whose distress deserved to be allayed. 'A dangerous ghoul, swept from our streets where he can haunt no more…'

'What did you do?' Lazare's voice was quiet with horror, and with… with something else. What was that feeling?

'We removed a meddling Deepsider from our streets,' said Randall, 'and if you know what's good for you, vampire, you'll…'

'What did YOU DO???' Lazare screamed. Now he understood what that feeling was. It was rage. The sort of rage that snaps around the nerves, tensing the muscles and bypassing the rational parts of the mind. He was aware of something behind him, something huge. A great shadow, a flap of leathery wings, as before when Fang had created the illusion that Amber was a giant and dangerous beast. Perhaps Amber had come back. He didn't care. At that moment, he only cared about what was in front of him.

Randall and Thomasina were staring at the whatever-it-was behind him.

'That's not a trick,' breathed Thomasina, 'is it?'

'Get *out* of here,' Lazare screamed. 'Leave us alone! He needs a physick, or…' He bent down to scoop the limp Fang up off the ground. 'Or…' Fang was pale, unresponsive. He was losing so much blood.

The apothecary. The apothecary in Southwark. She would have medicines, right? Medicines or potions? Perhaps some surgical knowledge? It was the only option his panicking, furious, whirring mind could think of. The two villains continued to stare in terror at the whatever-it-was behind him, and without warning, they were hit by a great gust of air that knocked both off their feet. A second gust sent them sliding from him on their knees. On the third gust, they seemed to become smaller, lower to the ground. They both scrabbled to their feet and ran.

It was only when Blackfriars Bridge came into view beyond the rooftops that Lazare realised what was happening. He glanced to his side and saw what they'd been looking at – his wings, unfurled, had to be six foot in span apiece, edged with four sharp claws, just like a vampire's. They looked to be great, ferocious things. Ever since waking from death, Lazare had been too anxious of scaring anyone to open them properly, even to take a real look at them for himself. He had certainly never tried to fly. He'd had no idea if he could. Until now.

CHAPTER FOUR
THE APOTHECARY

Fang was so tired, everything was so dark. He wanted to sleep beneath the big peach tree, with the one he loved, like they used to all that time ago, but the wind was whipping up. It buffeted him and it was freezing.

With the wind came something else. That spark, again. That terrible agony to his heart and lungs and head. He gasped, and choked, and coughed up blood. The dark receded, but that horrible cold wind did not. If anything, it was worse than before. It was everywhere. There were hands beneath him, lifting him by his back and thighs, and nothing else but the lashing wind. He found the strength to open his eyes. A man glanced down at him – around Fang's age, attractive – the Frenchman. Lazare. Yes, Lazare was here, his visage a picture of concern, his carefully coiffed curls and immaculately trimmed beard ruffled by the mysterious wind. His wings, his mighty, tawny wings open and flapping hard with a great, deep *swoof* every few seconds.

...Wait. What?

Fang drooped his head, and squinted down. The rooftops of London sped past, several yards beneath them. Confucius's Eyebrows, they were *flying*.

*

Lazare's heart leapt when Fang stirred and opened his eyes a smidge, but the man was still horribly wounded, seeping blood, barely conscious and confused. They weren't out of the woods yet. He had to get Fang to the apothecary in Southwark as fast as he could. As Fang slipped into another swoon, Lazare became aware of a second set of wings, flapping up behind him. Amber, the little dragon, struggled to fly into his line of sight, her stubby wings straining to keep up with Lazare's pace.

'Couldn't find anyone to help, sorry,' puffed Amber, 'but it looks like you have the situation in hand – why didn't you just fly to safety from the start?'

Lazare chose not to answer that, on the grounds that 'I'd been too scared to try flying before and didn't know if I even could' didn't sound very cool. He decided to change the subject, instead.

'Fang's hurt.'

'Oof, I can see that. They staked him good.'

'They didn't just have stakes, either.' Lazare glanced at Amber. 'You live Deepside, right? Have you heard anything about stolen fae materials, lately?'

'Fae? They'd be *really* hard to steal from, they're deep, deep dwellers. Sounds fake, *mon ami*.'

'Oh, it wasn't fake. I know fake weapons when I see them, I am an actor.'

'Wait, a bunch of Upperside street ruffians had fae weapons? That's… no. That's impossible.'

'I saw one,' insisted Lazare. 'A knife. It was glowing with fae magic.'

Amber considered Lazare's statement for a moment. 'This is bad.'

'That's an understatement.'

'Where are we going, by the way?'

'An apothecary in Southwark. Griffin Alley.'

'I'll escort you,' announced the dragon, nobly.

'It's just down there, I can see it.'

'Nevertheless,' said Amber, and carried on flying by Lazare's side. Lazare wondered why she was being so helpful until he remembered apothecaries usually stocked plenty of dried newts.

*

Not all of London's women would hurry to see what was causing frantic knocking at the window of their second storey apartment. Of those who would, most would likely be shocked and horrified to discover that the cause of the commotion was a small urban dragon and a distraught looking vampire, flapping his great leather wings to stay airborne enough to remain at her window and carrying a man who was bleeding profusely from the guts.

Nell ver'Evan was not shocked. She was a bit horrified, but it was a weary horror. Ugh. It had happened again.

'Again?' she groaned.

She opened up the door.

'You could have just come in, you know,' she told them, 'these are my business hours. Even out of hours, I'd be no Welshwoman if my door weren't open to dragonkind.'

'*Prynhawn da, dynol*,' Amber muttered respectfully.

Nell gave the dragon the usual little bow of the head with her hand over her heart that she'd been raised to greet all dragonkind with, before turning her attention to the very good-looking vampire still carrying her injured friend. 'And I'm *always* receptive to an impromptu visit from a handsome young man.' She gave the vampire a little smile as he touched down on the balcony entrance to her shop. She afforded the barely conscious Fang a little smile too, even though she didn't mean it. 'Even if he is carrying an idiot.'

She ushered the dragon and the vampire through – and on closer inspection, realised that actually, he wasn't a vampire at all. Human teeth, human eyes, just he had those great big wings. She told herself to look up just what the stranger might actually be – once her best friend had stopped bleeding all over her nice clean floor.

'You can give me the juicy gossip on how exactly he mangled himself this time once he's patched up.' She got out the same cloth she'd used the last time and laid it over the same table as before. 'I'm interested in where he found a nice fellow like yourself to sweep him off his feet, all macho like that.'

The stranger grinned at the compliment, as if automatically. The grin didn't reach his eyes, which were still etched with concern. The stranger placed the horribly bloodied and visibly unrepentant man onto the table.

'Thanks,' replied the stranger in a strong French accent, 'but I just wanted him to get help as soon as possible. He showed me your flyer.'

He watched as she cut Fang's bloodied tunic off him. Farewell, horrible ragged old brown-grey woollen shirt. Fang would just have to find an equally disgusting and ill-fitting replacement for it out of a dead beggar's leftover effects, which is where Nell assumed he got all his clothes. She noticed the stranger's expression. Alarm, at the state of Fang's wound, and a concerted effort not to look at the rest of the injured man's bared torso.

The Frenchman swallowed audibly, before speaking again. 'Do you have potions or poultices to stop the bleeding?'

'Not if it's this bad.' Nell glanced from the wound, up at the Frenchman. 'No need to fret, Monsieur, I've done this sort of thing plenty of times.' Too many times, she thought to herself, and now the great idiot knew he couldn't die, this was going to get worse, wasn't it? She'd only just patched him up a couple of nights ago, and here he was again. And now as well as getting Nell involved in his self-sabotaging nonsense he'd roped in some poor gullible little dragon and a… a whatever it was this Frenchman actually *was*.

She carefully pulled out the stake, and Fang bit down a howl of pain. At least he didn't squirm. At this point, he was as used to this as Nell was. She inspected the damage. 'Well, who's a lucky numbskull? That stake managed to miss every major organ, although I don't think your gallbladder will ever be what it was.'

'Does he need that?' asked the dragon.

'Nah, it stores bile, and Fang here always just lets that flow anyway.' She nudged the Frenchman, handing him a clean rag. 'Put pressure on the wound for a tick?'

'Won't that hurt him?'

'Oh, yes,' Nell told him, cheerfully. She listened to Fang grit down another squeal as she got together her needle, thread and a couple of potion vials before washing her hands. 'Take it you want something for the pain, Fang?'

'No,' replied Fang in a tone that Nell supposed was meant to be one of stalwart stoicism, but was rather undermined when it came out as a painful whimper.

'Sure?' She waved the vials at him. 'If cost is the issue, don't worry. I'm already charging you for my time and expertise patching you back up again, the small surcharge for pain relief will be a drop in the ocean, comparatively.'

'Nnysshh,' managed Fang, which Nell took as acquiescence. She dropped a little bit of liquid from one vial between Fang's unprotesting lips, and rubbed the contents of the other vial on the skin around the wound, before getting stitching.

'Mistress dragon, Monsieur, you could do me a great favour and put the kettle on for me,' she muttered as she worked.

'Amber,' said the dragon as she waddled over to Nell's stove. 'The French fellow is Lazare.' The little dragon lit the stove with a single puff.

'I'd appreciate a bowl of boiled water, Lazare,' Nell told him, not looking up from her work. 'Also, a cup of tea.'

'Of course,' Lazare told her from the sink, anxiously washing Fang's blood from his hands. 'Er… how does one make tea?'

'Just steep the leaves in hot water, jar's behind the sales desk. Help yourself to a drink too – I've got all the fancy new imports in stock. It's one of the main reasons I put up with Fang's nonsense – he put me in touch with my Coffee Guy.'

'Ah. My mother's family were merchants – I do understand the importance of having a good Coffee Guy.' The kettle on the stove began to boil. Lazare gave Nell's coffee jar a sniff. 'God's Beard, that smells fresh.'

'Yeah, my contact's an azhdaha, he can fly from Qom to London in two days. Help yourself, Lazare. Payment for the trouble you took getting this prize plum pudding back to me in approximately one piece.'

'I'll take my coffee strong and unsweetened…' grunted Fang.

'No you will not,' snapped Nell. 'Idiots don't get coffee. Amber, there's dried newts in a bottom basket for you.'

'Ooh, ta,' replied Amber, snuffling in the baskets.

Nell finished off her stitching, as Lazare brought over her water and inexpertly brewed tea. She readied bandages as she waited for her sterilised water to cool. 'You'll have yet another rugged scar to add to your rapidly growing collection there, Fang,' she told him, 'it could be much worse, if not for Monsieur Lazare's quick action.' She noticed Lazare was still resolutely refusing to look at Fang's chest.

'Oh, come *on*,' replied Fang, 'we all know it's not as if I could have died.'

Lazare and Nell blinked at one another. 'You know about his curse?'

'Of course he knows, Nell. Look at him. He's cursed too.'

Ah. So that explained the wings.

'Look on the bright side,' said Nell, cleaning the stitches. 'We can find out more – do you know how you were cursed, Monsieur? Or why the wings?'

Lazare shrugged, sadly. 'Sorry. I do know the wings work now, at least. That's something, right?'

'No!' Fang tried to sit up, huffed with pain and flopped back down again. 'You stuck out like a sore thumb, back there. Why did you insist on flying me here? What if we'd been followed? What if it alerted guards?'

'But...' the poor Frenchman floundered. 'You were bleeding out. I wanted to get you safe as soon as possible...'

'You didn't need to!'

'You were suffering.'

'So? What's new about that?'

'Fang! Behave!' Nell began bandaging the wound and continued to regard Lazare in sneaked glances. Oh dear, not this again. For all that Fang's habit of showing up at her door alone, bedraggled and injured frustrated Nell, more upsetting still were the occasional times he showed up injured and barely conscious in some worried stranger's arms. Said strangers were usually well-intentioned, kind-hearted and blissfully optimistic regarding their romantic prospects. Fang would reward them for their trouble by being as rude to them as he possibly could, sending them away quickly with desperately hurt feelings and the sense that, sometimes, a good deed could go roundly punished if the recipient of that good deed were ungrateful and unpleasant enough. The least Nell could do for these unfortunate saviours and would-be suitors was to offer them a nice tea or coffee for the road. If this good soul had taken the trouble to scoop Fang up in his arms and fly him over London on newly grown wings, even though he knew Fang couldn't die... oh, Lazare, you poor sweet streak of sunshine.

'We didn't just come here because of your injury though, Fang,' said Amber, munching through her newt.

'Didn't you?' asked Nell.

'Well, no, you're an apothecary, aren't you? And a Welsh one at that. Very magicky.' The dragon indicated with her snout at some of the particularly magical potions, amulets and artefacts dotted around her shop. 'Practically witchcraft, some of the stuff you've got here.'

'I practise and purvey a fusion of magic and human medical science,' Nell told the dragon proudly. 'It's a unique, state-of-the-art study.'

'She means, everybody else thinks it's dangerous and heretical,' added Fang.

'I don't see you complaining, or did you want me to unstitch that hole in your belly again?'

'Well then, would someone with your sort of expertise in magical items know anything about fae weaponry?' asked the dragon.

Nell frowned. 'Fae? Not really. They keep to themselves in the Deepside, don't they? Their weapons are defensive, to make sure nobody bothers them, there's no way I'd be able to get hold of anything like that, nor should I. It would probably cause a major incident if any fae stuff found its way Upperside.'

'Exactly,' growled Fang.

'Sorry – are you all speaking in code?' Nell asked.

Lazare gave Fang a little 'sure you can trust her?' glance, to which Fang nodded.

'What?' asked Nell again, exasperated.

'Just, if fae weaponry making its way Upperside would create a "major incident", we're going to have to be really careful who we speak to about this,' Lazare explained. 'It's already happened. They're already here.'

CHAPTER FIVE
FEATHERS

The Tower gleamed as much as was possible in the drab grey daylight of Upper London. It was its usual noisy nest of activity. Queen's Guards strutted, flapped and waddled about the Investigations Hall, arguing about cases, half of them mumbling due to having to carry witness reports and scraps of evidence in their beaks. There was no reverent hush as the grand doors opened and their captain strode in, her great webbed feet slapping on the stone, her snow white feathers flexing around her ruff as she bent her long neck in greeting to her team. Captain Honkensby wasn't the sort of boss who demanded her subordinates stand to attention when she was around – quite the opposite. Keeping the Queen's peace in a city like Upper London was a constant frantic pedalling against the rushing stream of crime, and Honkensby didn't want her constables to take their energies away from that for even a second, not even to acknowledge her seniority.

The Royal Bird Constabulary of Upper London had only been established a little over a century ago, by the first Tudor king. At the time it had been seen as a sop, just a means of buying the loyalty of magical birds to the Upper English Crown, because, there *definitely* wouldn't be another war between Upper England and the magicals of Britain, not with the peace treaty keeping so well, not after the terrible losses on both sides following 1277's attempted invasion of Wales, no no. Just, if there *were* another war, well then Upper England would rather need some sort of air force, would it not? This cynicism had proven hollow and ignorant. The peace had kept, and Honkensby's kind had taken considerable pride and earned great status in Upper English society by keeping said peace as warders of the splendid Tower, as guards and even courtiers to the Upper Throne. Truly, besides of course the precious centuries of peace, was there any greater tribute to the Upper English Crown's diplomacy and generosity than the Royal Guard? Magical swans and ravens not only granted full citizenship to Upper London on hatching, but entrusted with the moral hygiene of the land? Perhaps, if one were to catch her in one of her rare lighter frames of mood, one might be able to have Honkensby concede that her great personal pride in the Royal Guard possibly coloured her judgement a tad, and she would be able to reel off a great many other testaments to Queen Elizabeth's wisdom and grace.

The tube system would be one of the Tudor Crown's accomplishments, of course – allowing residents of Deep London to visit the majesties of the Upper city at will. Technically, Honkensby supposed, the tubes also meant that Upper London residents could visit the Deepside streets that existed beneath the ground of her beloved city, although why any human might want to do that unless they had a death wish was beyond her. Sometimes, civilians would assume that the Royal Guard hated the tube system and the extra work it created, but honestly, Honkensby didn't mind them, as long as Deepsiders behaved and remembered just how inevitable and terrible the punishment would be if they were to break Upper London's laws. Honkensby took personal satisfaction in being one of the main reasons the vast majority of Deepsiders made sure to obey the law while visiting the Upper city. And those few who didn't... well. Honkensby always ensured that what happened to those individuals was a learning moment for the rest of the population.

Elizabeth's cordial and diplomatic relationship with King Llewellyn of Wales and Redthroat, the dragon Queen of Britain's magicals was also a testament to her Queen. At least, Honkensby assumed the whole diplomatic relationship was cordial; she was always invited to embassy balls with the rest of the swans, but she was always far too busy keeping the city in order for any of that frilly stuff. Obviously it was a good relationship between Elizabeth and Redthroat – it had to be. Otherwise, the complex system of dividing England wouldn't work, and it *did* work, very well, thank you. Not many monarchs could maintain peace by gifting the earth beneath their very feet to an independent magical state that based its own seat of power in a neighbouring rival kingdom, but for three hundred years, the Kings and Queens of Upper England had pulled it off with aplomb.

People always asked Honkensby what Queen Elizabeth was really like. Honkensby had a feeling that she didn't particularly know the answer to that, despite being in her court since a cygnet. She just hoped that Elizabeth loved the yoke of responsibility as much as Honkensby did.

Honkensby had always considered herself a 'wings on' kind of a boss, a real 'my nest is always open if you need anything' type, and as she strode through the Investigations Hall, several constables hurried over to her for advice on cases. Spates of muggings, as usual, gang warfare in the streets – the Hapenny gang were getting particularly belligerent, she'd noticed. Avis Hapenny remained as slippery as a marsh worm though. Honkensby imagined she'd never have enough firm evidence on the gangland matriarch to actually put her away. One of the incidents stood out to Honkensby as odd. She stopped, and turned to the nervous young raven constable who had shown her the case.

'A vampire attack in the middle of the day? Are you sure?'

The constable nodded. 'Several eyewitnesses reported it, Captain. Flying southbound over the river, near Blackfriars Bridge. Carrying a human… said they couldn't tell if the victim was a woman or a man with long hair, but the human looked injured. Um. And we don't yet know if it's connected, but minutes before that, witnesses near the bridge saw an urban dragon in flight, calling for help.'

'Deepsiders playing silly buggers,' sighed Honkensby. 'That's all we need.'

The constable bowed her head, unhappily. 'I know. I've pinned down a set of alleyways where the attack may have taken place, I was wondering if we could get a unit together to investigate.'

Oh, no. If Deepsiders were flouting her law, she wasn't about to throw some poor fledgeling constable out of the nest to deal with those dangerous intricacies. As much as she hated to take a case off a hatchling...

'You will pass over all the paperwork on this case to me, Constable.'

'But...'

'I will personally oversee this one. You can assist Constable Pebbles in the Whitehall stabbings case.'

'But...'

'Are we a chicken, Constable?'

'No, Captain.'

'Then I want to hear no more "butbutbut" from you. Understood?'

'Aye, Captain.'

The constable shuffled away to get the paperwork. Great. This vampire had attacked a human, in broad daylight, in *her* city, *and* it had made her shout at a subordinate. That rotten bloodsucker was going to lament ruining the day of Captain Dame Isobel Honkensby, of the Queen's Royal Swan Guard.

*

'That's bad,' said Nell.

'Yep,' said Fang.

'No, I mean that's really, *really* bad.'

'Yes, I know.'

Nell, having nervously paced to one end of her shop, turned and paced back to Lazare again.

'And you're sure it was definitely a fae dagger?'

'Its blade was glowing,' Fang told her. 'Where's my shirt?'

'Yeah, that sounds fae-made.' Nell sighed, shakily. 'God's Duckies. And you both got cursed after being attacked by Hapenny boys?'

'You think it's linked?' Lazare asked, sipping one of the best cups of coffee he'd ever tasted.

'Could be,' Nell replied. 'I mean, fae magic would explain Fang's new power, too.'

'Where's my shirt?' repeated Fang.

'I euthanised it,' Nell told him.

'Oh, *what*? That was my only shirt!'

'Yes, it smelled like it.'

Lazare was still trying to ignore the fact that the other man was topless. There was being a lusty red-blooded dandy about town, and then there was 'ogling a man's chest in the context of him having received emergency surgery', which Lazare felt was beyond the pale.

He kept his gaze fixed on Nell. 'I was going to ask about his spells – he kept making things look all disgusting, like the walls were dripping with gong and gore – is that a fae trick?'

'Kind of.'

'I need a shirt,' interjected Fang.

'I have spare shirts,' Lazare told Fang, still not looking at the man, but rummaging in his bag of clothes.

'You've heard of fae glamour?' Nell asked. 'A common illusion they use to make things look much prettier, fresher and more inviting than they truly are.'

'They use it for luring prey,' added Amber. 'Or misdirecting enemies. Wish I had something like that. I can just breathe fire a bit.'

'When Fang woke up from death, he found he could do the opposite of that,' said Nell, 'didn't you, Fang?'

'I can create a disgusting illusion,' replied Fang. 'Or make situations look more dangerous than they are. That's all. I tried making other illusions, but they didn't work, they just ended up looking horrible. Dirt, rot, sewage, nightmare images, impending doom… that's it. It's useful as a short-term distraction against attackers I suppose, but it's very limited.'

'It's like… a reverse glamour,' Nell said. 'Like someone took fae magic and gave it to him all backwards. I don't understand what happened to give you wings, though.'

Lazare finally found a shirt he felt he could part with. It was old, from his skinnier years so it was on the small side, and it had gone rather grey.

'Fang,' said Nell, 'tell me you're not going to borrow another man's shirt without washing all the blood off you first.'

Fang and Nell glared at one another, both of them going through the facial journeys of a silent argument.

'Wash basin's just over there. And, I didn't get good soap in for it not to be put to good use.'

Fang sighed and shuffled over to fill the basin with warm water from the kettle.

Something about the way Nell and Fang interacted was bothering Lazare. He decided to take that particular bull by the horns as soon as possible. He hoped that the answer would give him another reason not to look at Fang's chest.

He lowered his voice. 'Are you and he… amorous?'

Nell laughed a disconcertingly loud laugh. 'What gave you *that* idea?'

'You're always quarrelling.'

'I quarrel with him because he's quarrelous, Monsieur.'

Fang sighed a loud, passive aggressive sigh from the wash basin.

'See?' Nell continued. 'No, while I personally am a *very* amorous individual, Fang and I are not a love match. We're friends.'

'We're associates,' grumbled Fang.

'We're best friends,' Nell said, emphatically.

'I put her in touch with traders I met on my travels, she stitches me up and gives me coffee,' Fang told them, finishing up with his wash.

'I told you,' replied Nell with a mocking smile, 'idiots don't get coffee.'

Fang turned and, whoops, Lazare's eye just *happened* to slide over towards him, to see the other man hit by a rare shaft of sunlight peeking through one of Nell's windows, the blood and filth at last washed off his bandaged, naked upper half.

Cock-a-doodle-doo, he was attractive. Lazare had guessed from the way Fang had fought that he'd have to have considerable lean strength, but it was quite a different matter being faced with those forearms, those shoulders, that chest and that midriff, still half wet. The man's skin was far from the sort of perfect porcelain purity that would be romanticised in sonnets. Black hair grew thin as lichen on his chest and thickened as it disappeared in a merrily widening path down the front his breeches. The body hair had bald, discoloured lines of scar tissue cut into it in one, two, three, four… five places on his torso, and several on his arms. Fang had pushed his long hair back to wash his face, and *bonjour* neck, jawline and cheekbones. The bonnest of jours to all of that.

It had only been a second – but what a second! Lazare would be thinking about that second for some time to come. He looked away again, holding out the spare shirt. He reckoned he'd probably managed to get away with that moment of weakness – or, at least he did until he spotted the expression Nell shot at him.

'Thanks,' said Fang, taking the shirt, and mercifully putting that torso away. Unfortunately, he still looked really good in the shirt. It hung far too nicely over his clavicles and biceps.

'Sadly,' said Nell, still giving Lazare that strange look, 'one major limitation to Fang's reverse glamour is that he can't make it work on himself.'

'Goodness knows I've tried,' sighed Fang. 'I can't magically alter my own appearance one bit.' He put a rough, ill-fitting old grey jerkin over the shirt. *Zut*. He still looked hot.

'We should tell the Queen's Guards,' suggested Lazare, trying to pull his thoughts away from the general handsomeness of Fang and back to the problem in hand. 'About the fae dagger.'

'Oh, no no,' replied Nell, horrified. 'We are *not* getting the law involved with this.'

Lazare hadn't had a chance to properly investigate Nell's shop, but from some of the items sitting around, and a few of the locked drawers he'd discovered while making tea and coffee, he could guess why Nell didn't really want guards pecking around the place. Lazare was, of course, too gentlemanly to draw attention to this.

Fang wasn't, though. 'Half her stuff's contraband,' he said with a vicious smile, 'or not properly taxed. Or so new it hasn't been given Royal assent yet.'

'I sell my customers the very latest in medical and magical produce, plus exotic tonics from all over the globe,' Nell argued, '*and* I prefer to pass the savings onto the customer, rather than the Upper English Crown.'

'*Now* who's the idiot?' Fang grinned. He sauntered over to the kettle. 'I'll have that coffee.'

'It's going on your tab,' warned Nell.

'Yeah, yeah, and the rest.'

'I've got to say,' said Amber, 'I agree with the illegal apothecary.'

'I'm not illegal!'

'Deepside and Upperside politics are strained enough as it is,' said Amber. 'Fae selling weapons to humans, or humans stealing from the fae, it's bad either way. Humans and magicals have gone to war over issues far pettier than this in other countries.'

Over by the kettle, Lazare noticed Fang scowl.

'Once it gets to the authorities, up here or Deepside, it'll be out of our claws,' continued Amber. 'Could spiral out of control.'

'It may already be spiralling out of control,' Lazare reminded them. 'If the fae magic cursed me and Fang, who's to say how many others are cursed that we just don't know about yet? And surely, the longer it's out there, the more people it could affect. We *must* do something.'

'We will,' Fang assured him, pouring out a cup of coffee.

'Fortunately for us, we already have a Deep London resident on our side,' said Lazare, offering a little smile down to the dragon sitting by his feet.

'Wait, who?' asked Amber. 'Oh, yeah! Me!'

'Might you ask around Deepside about talk of black market fae weapons?' Lazare continued. 'Or a spate of thefts from magicals?'

'Er,' replied Amber, nervously, 'I don't want to get in any trouble, down there.'

'You'll be fine,' Fang told her, 'just say you heard a rumour from a proper size dragon. Nobody'll pay much heed to a little thing like you.'

'Oh,' said Amber, sounding rather hurt, 'thanks.'

'Perhaps we can sweeten the deal by paying you in pig hearts?'

The dragon salivated a little. 'I'll see what I can do, but I can't promise anything.'

'That's fine,' Lazare told the group, standing up grandly with a flourish that almost spilled his coffee, 'because I have Deepside contacts of my own!'

'What, *you* know people in Deep London?' Amber asked, incredulously. 'Really?'

'Well… not *in* Deep London,' Lazare admitted. 'Upper Deptford. There's a pub I know, serves the undead. The owner offered to help me, recently. He alone has a world of Deepside contacts.'

'That's your plan?' Fang asked. 'Go to the pub?'

'Yes,' crowed Nell, delighted. 'Pub!'

CHAPTER SIX
Elysium to a New-Come Soul

Deptford – urgh. Fang had a considerable list of which of the many scars that criss-crossed his body had been given to him in Upper Deptford. For an area of Upper London, it was considered rather a fashionable stomping ground for the undead, so at least Lazare didn't stand out here. This was probably the only upside. Upper Deptford was also a hot spot for a vast array of violent criminals and worse, actors.

Lazare was in his element. Nell looked cheerful as anything, although that was the norm when she was getting a night out at the pub. Fang trailed behind, keeping an eye out for trouble.

The Frenchman led them to an inn close to the New Cross tube called 'The Moon and Werewolf'. It seemed a perfectly reasonable pub, if rather Deptfordy in its enthusiastic embrace of undead and thespian cultures. There were two signs by the door which delighted Nell so much that she read both aloud before they entered. The first was an official looking plaque reading: 'Please respect our neighbours as you leave! Any clientele found turning members of the public will be barred for 2000 years, by order of the management.' Another, hastily hand-scrawled sign read 'We do not accept soliloquies as payment (yes that means you, Kit)'. The owner had really overused skulls in the decor, but it was done in a way that felt less intimidating and more like a pretentious nod to its clientele. Indeed, even though it was only early evening, the pub was already filling up with groups of the undead and theatre types.

'All right then,' said Fang to the other two, 'let's plan a way to question as many Deepsiders as possible without anyone finding out what we're...'

Neither Lazare nor Nell were paying him a jot of attention. Nell split away from the others immediately and headed straight for the bar. Lazare was looking around the pub for something – or someone.

'Are you listening to...' Fang attempted, but at that moment, Lazare spotted whoever it was he'd been searching for. His eyes lit up with recognition and he waved manically at a pair of men sitting at a corner table.

The men at the table were around a decade older than Fang. One had muted, practical clothes, a receding hairline and a hang-dog expression. The other man was much more flamboyantly dressed, his beard neat, his thick mane of golden-brown hair expertly tousled, wearing a self-assured grin and an eyepatch that detracted nothing from his good looks, rather it added to his general air of rakishness. He waved back at Lazare and cheerfully beckoned him over. Lazare grabbed Fang's wrist excitedly and dragged him over to the table. It was only when they were close enough to pull up chairs and sit with them that Fang noticed the man with the eyepatch was in fact a zombie.

'Laz, you big shagger,' crowed the eyepatch man. 'Vampos got you, did they?' He slapped Lazare on the wings. 'Onwards and upwards, Lazzo, being zombified was the best thing that ever happened to me, don't I always say, Billikins?'

The man with the receding hair rolled his eyes and grunted an affirmation.

'Ah,' attempted Lazare, 'actually...'

'And you've pulled already, I see,' continued the one-eyed man, blithely. 'That's vampirism for you – sexes one up. Good job I didn't take that option, I'd be dehydrated within the first month.' The zombie gave Fang an appreciative glance up and down that Fang wasn't unused to, but never found any more tolerable. 'God's Cock, are they flocking to you all the way from Asia Major, you smug French bastard? This one's an absolute peach, look at those cheekbones, introduce me immediately.'

Lazare laughed affably at the one-eyed man even as Fang glared a 'why are we wasting time talking to this absolute arse' glare at him as hard as he could. Lazare's smile was… wrong, Fang noticed. He was wearing it like make-up. Had his smile always been so lacquer-thin?

'Fang,' he smiled, ignoring the glare, 'Kit and Bill are friends from my acting career.'

Bill raised a couple of ink-stained fingers in a half-wave of greeting. Before Fang could say anything to either of them, Kit reached across the table and grabbed Fang's hand.

'Bill writes and acts a bit for The Lord Chamberlain's Men.' Lazare continued. 'He's the Romeo and Juliet guy, did you see Romeo and Juliet?'

Why was Lazare asking Fang if he went to the theatre as if that was something he'd have the time, energy and patience to bother with? He shook his head.

'Ah! You should! It's really sexy stuff.'

'It's a tragedy,' interjected Bill in a plaintive voice.

'A really sexy tragedy,' continued Lazare, enthusiastically, 'with a funny nursemaid. Now, Kit you *must* have heard of. He's—'

'A genius,' interjected Kit, before planting a firm kiss on the back of Fang's hand.

'I was going to say,' added Lazare, 'Faust. Tamburlaine. You know? Or you may have read some of his poems? Maybe his translations of Ovid?'

Kit flicked his remaining deep brown eye up to catch Fang's gaze. 'They're deeply erotic,' he told Fang before finally letting go of his hand. '*Much* sexier than bloody Romeo.'

'It's not meant to be sexy, it's meant to be sad,' protested Bill, as Fang wiped Kit's kiss-slobber off his hand.

Kit completely ignored Bill's dismay and Fang's disgust. 'Lazare, you might have told me you were a vampire now.'

'About that,' said Lazare, scooching his stool over to sit between Kit and Fang, 'I'm actually not.' He showed the writers his teeth. 'It's a long story. I'll make it as brief as I can.'

Lazare's retelling of what had happened to the two of them really wasn't that brief at all, to Fang's continuing dismay. They managed to get through two rounds of drinks in the time he took to tell his tale, full of florid language and ludicrous embellishments. Lazare particularly romanticised flying over London's rooftops with Fang in his arms, Fang noticed. He also, despite them agreeing they should be subtle about the fae weapon element, just came right out and told the playwrights.

'Fae weapons, eh?' Kit concluded in far too loud a voice, once Lazare had finally finished. 'That's ill news, Lazzers. You don't mess with fae affairs, right Bill?'

'They'll turn you into a donkey,' agreed Bill, quietly. 'Least, that's what I heard.'

'And,' added Kit, 'it's ill news even further that you're not a vampire, Laz, but instead something all half-way and strange. I need to cast a new Mephistopheles, if you were in fact a vampire, I feel you'd be perfect.'

Lazare's eyes widened. His fingers clawed at the edge of the table. 'Mephistopheles? New? Cast? I was born to play Mephistopheles!'

'Yes, I remember your speech that time you begged to understudy.'

'And I have these wings now. I'd be perfect!'

'Aye, but it's a Deepside production, Laz. You can't go Deepside if you're still too human, they'd have you for breakfast down there. Literally.' Kit took a sip of his wine. 'You could always see whether being properly turned by an undead might fix your problem? Mr Fang, I would be honoured to make a zombie of you, at the very least.' Kit picked up his stool and pushed in to sit between Lazare and Fang, treading on Fang's foot in the process. 'Did I mention being turned was the best thing that ever happened to me?'

'Yes, Christopher,' whispered Bill, bitterly. 'Many times.'

'I was in a spot of bother with the Queen's Guards, Mr Fang, few years back,' Kit explained, his voice full of pride. 'The warrant was given for my arrest, in fact. Treason, espionage, sedition, generally being too sexy – all sorts – and then, lo and behold, the very night I was to be arrested I got into this silly drunken brawl with my old pal Ingram over a bar tab, he whops a dagger in my eye, stabs me in the brain, down goes poor old Christopher. Everyone's crying, all the busty wenches and lusty lads screaming and throwing up at the loss of the best shag in Deptford. Ingram's immediately wracked with guilt at robbing Upper England of her greatest literary talent, runs into the street in tears and grabs the nearest undead. Next thing I know, I'm up and about, and discovering that zombies are bound by the laws of Deep England, not the Upperside, and so any charges brought against me by the court of Elizabeth no longer apply. I can continue to work, with both Deep and Upper London open to me now, as long as I keep my nose reasonably clean from now on in. Couldn't have gone better for me if I'd planned it myself.'

'Mm,' muttered Bill, 'which is likely why rumour has it you *did* plan all that yourself, to get out of jail.'

'It is the sort of scheme a terribly clever fellow might come up with,' beamed Kit, 'but I couldn't possibly comment.' He rested a hand on Fang's knee, beneath the table. 'So. How's about it?'

Fang firmly removed the hand, and explained their concerns about complicating the curse, and making it any worse than it already was.

This at least made good sense to Bill. 'Cause otherwise they could turn you into donkeys,' he muttered, nodding.

'What is it with you and donkeys?' asked Kit.

'It's a thing!' Bill protested. 'I heard it growing up.'

'Ignore him,' proclaimed Kit, 'he's from out in the sticks.'

'Warwickshire isn't "the sticks"!'

'So,' said Lazare to Kit, 'if you're expanding your company, might that leave space at least for me to understudy Mephistopheles on the Upperside with Lord Strange's Men?'

'Lazare, that's not why we're here,' hissed Fang. 'You said this place would be good for Deepside information.'

'Hmm,' said Bill, 'who here'd be good to ask? Let me think.'

'And, what might good information be worth to you, Mr Fang?' Kit asked, leaning in close again. 'You know I *was* once suspected of espionage – wrongfully of course, but there never is smoke without a fire is there? Perhaps I could be persuaded to see what I might discover... for a price, of course.' Kit reached out a hand and ran one of the ties lacing up the top of Fang's borrowed shirt between his fingers.

Fang tried to shoot yet another exasperated glare at Lazare for introducing him to this lascivious pest, but noticed that Lazare was sporting a very strange expression indeed. Even the thinly painted smile had gone. The Frenchman was watching Kit with considerable unease – a touch of anger even. Well, he had just been turned down again for his dream role, Fang supposed.

'Most of the undead who come here are recently turned, like Kit,' said Bill. 'Fresh undead will be no good for information on the Deepside – for the first few decades, they generally stick to their old lives up here, only using Deep London as an official residence, to visit occasionally, show their face for appearance's sake, maybe get some rest and relaxation, somewhere to keep their stuff, etcetera.'

'Like your funny little house for your funny little wife and kids up in the sticks, Bill,' interjected Kit, resting an elbow on Fang's shoulder with a grin.

'I… hey! I worked hard for that house. I *love* Anne and the kids.'

'That's not what you said to fair young Henry, was it?' Kit kept his gaze firmly on Fang, and winked saucily at him – quite a feat, with only one eye.

'Christopher Marlowe, would you get your paws off that poor Cathayan,' replied Bill hotly, through gritted teeth, 'he does not like it!'

'Oop,' grinned Kit, sitting back and moving away from Fang. 'Touched a nerve. Apologies.'

Kit clearly didn't mean his apology in the slightest, but Fang was glad to have his personal space back, and not to be quite so assaulted by the smell of Kit's floral pomander, and the faintly meaty zombie smell it was trying to mask. He noticed Lazare relaxed a little too, as Kit sat back. Bill took a deep breath and tried again.

'I spotted an alchemist at the bar tonight. He might know something?'

Fang shook his head. 'No, where I come from, you don't listen to alchemists.'

'Because of that old Emperor?' asked Kit.

Fang nodded. 'That "old Emperor" paid an alchemist to discover the "elixir of eternal life". Sort of created a curse on the world that my people will always be blamed for and left the whole Empire under the yoke of dragon rule for hundreds of years last time someone listened to an alchemist round my way.'

Kit shrugged. 'Yeah, fair enough.'

'Also, alchemists are ten a penny in London,' Lazare added, 'what good are they really except for changing one metal into a different kind of metal? They're not even allowed to do gold anymore – it messes up the economy.'

'That just leaves Wulfric, then,' said Bill.

'The owner,' Lazare told Fang. 'He tried to get me to join his vampire union.'

'Classic Wulfric,' grinned Kit. He got up. 'Come on, he must have finished the stocktake by now.'

*

Wulfric looked pleased to see Lazare with Kit and Bill, although what a vampire tending a bar while inhabiting the body of a ten-year-old child had to look pleased about was beyond Fang. He had to use a little stool just to see over the bar.

The four men slotted themselves in at the bar, next to the alchemist, who managed to look conspicuous even in a pub full of actors and the undead, due to a decision to wear a particularly flashy alchemist's cape, all silver swirls and sparkles. It only really served to highlight how pathetic the alchemist seemed, hunched alone over his drink, very slowly turning wine into urine, the old-fashioned way. Lazare had to talk loudly over Kit, who decided to take this moment to flirt with the drunken alchemist, asking if he knew him, if he was rich, or at least if he'd been rich once in the past. Utterly ridiculous – no alchemist ever got rich. Wulfric was no better informed on any rumours about fae weaponry going missing than any of the others were.

'Nobody would really bother informing a lowly undead bar-keep on big political stuff like that,' he explained, getting a stepladder in position so that he could reach a bottle of sack from a high shelf. 'But I do know someone who could help.' He fetched the bottle, climbed down and poured out a round for the four men. 'You want to talk to someone of Deep London's political class, you're going to need a dragon, and luckily I befriended one recently. You met her too, Lazare, she's very easy to bribe with butcher's offcuts…' he trailed off, gazing at Lazare and Fang's disappointed expressions. 'What?'

'Do you mean Amber?' Lazare asked.

'That's the one! What, you already asked her?'

‘This is a dead end,’ Fang sighed. ‘Let’s just get Nell and go.’ He looked around. Nell was nowhere to be seen. ‘And, of course she’s wandered off.’

‘Maybe she’s found a lead?’ said Lazare, hopefully.

‘Maybe she’s found a docker,’ replied Fang with the grimly realistic air of someone who’d known the apothecary for a year now.

‘Wulfric,’ said Kit, ‘do you ever act, my lad?’

‘What?’ whined Lazare.

‘What you said about Mephistopheles really struck a chord,’ Kit explained. ‘A vampire would be the perfect casting for my Deepside production.’

‘Oh, but,’ Lazare protested, ‘but…’

‘You do know Kit’s not the only man with a theatre company in London?’ Bill asked. ‘He’s not even the only man with a theatre company at this bar, I mean I know we don’t get the same attention as his lot do, I know he plundered Burbage and Kemp off us…’

Kit snickered at the memory.

‘But why aren’t actors begging to join *my* company?’ Bill complained. ‘We’re successful! People enjoy our stuff, King John notwithstanding, but not *every* play can be a banger, and, I write magical roles too, and…’

‘Can I play Oberon, then?’ Lazare asked.

‘No, I have an Oberon.’

Lazare threw his hands in the air in frustration.

‘Can *you* act, Mr Fang?’ Kit asked, leaning close again.

‘Oh for crying out loud,’ Lazare exclaimed.

‘What?’ smiled Kit with feigned innocence. ‘You have a beard, Lazare, you can’t play a maiden. But I’m always open to pretty boys.’

‘Boy?’ asked Fang. ‘I’m twenty-five.’

Kit shrugged. ‘Beardless bar a bit of bumfluff we can cover with paint, lovely long hair, and those *features*. You would be a gorgeous Zenocrate, were you to pass the, ah, casting process.’

Lazare had that odd expression again. His knuckles were tight around his cup. 'Christopher?' he asked quietly.

Kit stayed pressed close to Fang, but turned his head to acknowledge Lazare. '*Oui oui, mon ami*?'

Lazare retained his strange, tense expression as he swiftly, seemingly impulsively, lashed out an arm and threw his cup of sack in Kit's face.

'W?' managed Kit, before Lazare grabbed the alchemist's drink off the bar, and threw that at Kit as well.

The hubbub at the bar stopped. Everyone watched in silence as the playwright blinked in surprise, dark liquor dripping off his perfectly manicured beard. Lazare retained that same strange expression of wordless anger, his fists bunched, his wings slightly raised off his shoulders as if trying to make himself look bigger. Next to him, Bill and the bar-prop of an alchemist gazed at the scene. Bill's expression had a faint twitch of amusement to it. The alchemist just looked bereft at the loss of his drink.

Kit wiped his face, agog, then threw back his head and laughed. 'That's the spirit, Laz! There's that gallic passion – want to go out back for a quick shuffle?'

'No thanks,' Lazare replied. 'Wulfric? Another round for myself and the alchemist, please, Kit's paying.'

'You're cleaning that up,' Wulfric grumbled.

'Fine. Another round, and a mop.'

*

Lazare mopped up the puddle of wine, and tried not to think too hard about why he'd thrown it. Kit had just been annoying, he told himself. But then, asked another part of his brain, was not Kit Marlowe always deeply annoying? That was just kind of Kit's thing, and Lazare had always just laughed along with it before. Throwing the drink had at least broken an unspoken tension that had been brewing. It had, at least for now, stopped Kit pestering

Fang for sex, and that was a good thing, of course not because it bothered Lazare, but because Fang had clearly hated Kit pestering him for sex.

Finally freed from Kit's attentions, Fang waited for Nell to show up, so that they could leave. And, while the man was no longer covered in London's greatest playwright, Fang was still deeply attractive – just objectively speaking, Lazare reminded himself. Several different patrons of the Moon and Werewolf backed up Lazare's findings re Fang's attractiveness by buying the man drinks.

Fang didn't seem particularly surprised by the steady flow of free drinks sent hopefully in his direction, nor did he express any particular flattery or offence over them. He merely accepted them, with a nod of acknowledgement at each benefactor in turn. It was as if he was very used to people buying him drinks – so used to it that he may have even come to start expecting it. Lazare had only seen one other person react to being bought drinks with quite such a casually indifferent attitude – the toast of London that was Richard Burbage. And even Burbage had occasionally taken a moment to sign a playbill, or allow a fan to gush at him. Was Fang prettier than Burbage was famous? And… did he *know*? He *had* to know, right?

Lazare wasn't so preoccupied by this that he didn't notice the constant supply of free drinks meant that Fang got through three wines, three cups of sack and a brandy in the time it took for Nell to finally show up, dishevelled and arm in arm with a large, hirsute woman.

'All right, lads?' Nell crowed happily, leaning against the bar. 'How's it going?'

'Not good,' Fang told her, a considerable slur to his voice.

'Ohhh, *someone's* been drinking on top of painkillers in contradiction to the express advice of his surgeon,' said Nell, 'hasn't he?'

'Well, can you blame us? Lazare got in a fight, a poet keeps trying to have sex with us, and we've been waiting for you all night after every single lead hit a brick wall.' Fang pointed a wobbly finger at Nell. 'Where'd you go? What d'yer find? It'd better be something good.'

Nell grinned and pulled the strange woman close by the hip. 'This is Edith. She works down the docks.'

'I *knew* it would be a docker!' Fang exclaimed.

Lazare held out a polite hand for Edith to shake. 'A lycanthrope,' he noted.

'Aye, sir,' replied Edith, shaking his hand with the usual firm grip of her kind.

'Hence her dockyard job,' said Nell, with pride. 'They're popular hires for heavy lifting work, they've got that werewolf strength.'

'Fine,' said Fang, wearily. 'Miss Edith, what rumours have you heard Deepside, about fae affairs?'

'Oh, Nell already asked, sir,' replied Edith. 'I know barely anything about the workings of Deep London, I was only turned a few years ago – my whole life is still up here for now.'

'Then what,' slurred Fang with exasperation, 'was the point of you going off with her all night? And don't say what I think you're about to say.'

Nell leaned into both of them, and spoke quietly, and soberly. 'She doesn't have information from the Deepside, but what she *does* have is information from the docks.' She leaned back again. 'But yes, it was what you were thinking too, Fang. An apothecary has needs.' She wound her arm around Edith's waist once more. 'Speaking of, I'm off to Edith's for the rest of the night. I'll fill you in on the details in the morning.' Nell met Lazare and Fang's eyes, meaningfully. 'OK?'

'But we were waiting for you because you have the only key,' complained Fang.

'What, the key to *my* shop and apartment, you mean?' asked Nell. 'I take it both of you wastrels think you're lodging with me for the time being, then?'

'Is that all right?' asked Lazare.

Nell reached out and pinched Lazare's cheek. 'How could I say no to this ray of sunshine? Here.' She tossed Lazare her key. 'You're in charge while I'm away, Lazare. No more booze for my favourite fool.'

'Gladly,' replied Fang, pushing what was left of his drink away. He got up off his barstool and wobbled for a moment, looking surprised, before grabbing the bar for stability and putting on a poor act of false sobriety.

'I'll be back for breakfast,' Nell told them, leading Edith away. As she passed Lazare, she very briefly dipped her head to whisper something in his ear that only he could hear.

'Don't sleep with him,' she whispered seriously, before turning back to Edith, giggling and kissing the werewolf on the cheek. Before Lazare could even react to her odd message, she had melded into the crowd and was gone.

Fang saw this as his cue to leave too, which was fine with Lazare. Lazare was at the happy, fuzzy stage of drunkenness and didn't want to push it any further, especially since he was now in charge of Fang, who was at the stumbly, realising-too-late-that-he-should-have-stopped-about-three-drinks-ago stage. Fang was the kind of drunk where you don't really notice it until you try to stand and go outside, and suddenly your head doesn't know what to do about being up so high and surrounded by quite so much not-the-pub. Lazare linked arms with him as they commenced the lengthy walk back towards Nell's. He reasoned that if he did this, he could help Fang stay reasonably upright and walk in a straightish line, as well as putting off any would-be muggers or suitors. That was all.

Nell's murmured message continued to bother him. Why had that even crossed her mind? It certainly hadn't crossed Lazare's. He'd only just met Fang! He'd helped the man when he'd got hurt, he was going to work with him to undo whatever fae magic had cursed them both, that was it. Yes, Fang was good looking. London was full of good-looking men, women and assorted others who were not as unkempt or ill-tempered as Fang. Lazare should know – he had bedded many of them already. He was certainly not going to attempt to bed this prickly Cathayan, who had so far only showed an interest in throwing himself into danger, and drinking coffee – he had shown none such interest in sleeping with anyone, least of all Lazare.

Lazare certainly wouldn't describe himself as 'picky' when it came to matters of courtship, but he made a point never to pursue those who did not have the good taste to display any sexual desire for him. Life was too short to chase anyone who didn't want to get caught.

'Sorry about your part,' slurred Fang.

'Mm?'

'Mephistomp… Mephimpolep… the… Marlowe thingie.'

'Mephistopheles? It's not the first time I've been turned down for a role, no call for concern.'

'You were upset enough to throw your drink.'

Lazare made the mistake of glancing down at Fang. The other man was hanging off Lazare's arm, walking at a strange, drunken angle. The alcohol had burned a flush onto his cheeks, and his eyes were big and dark in a way that made Lazare want to think of rhymes for rare black jewels and midnight oceans.

Lazare gave him a grin and an easy breezy shrug. 'An actor's hot-headedness, is all.'

'I think Christopher Marlowe wants to sleep with me.'

'Yes, he does. Take it from me – the man's all talk, not worth your while.'

'You carried me over London.'

'And you were right, it was risky, so I'm not carrying you home tonight.'

'Why'd you carry me?'

'You were hurt.'

'I'm always hurt.'

'Well, before today I wasn't around to help out with that, was I?'

'I should thank you.'

Lazare blinked in surprise and smiled at him again. *'Mon dieu.* Drinking gives you manners.'

Fang hooked a hand over one of Lazare's folded wings and half pulled himself up, half pulled Lazare downwards.

Lazare laughed, lightly. 'I just said, I'm not carrying you.'

But Fang had an odd expression. He wasn't silently demanding a lift. Nor was he joking. He leaned into Lazare further, still pulling downwards on Lazare's shoulder. His lips were half parted in a welcoming manner. Lazare could smell the brandy on the other man's breath. Lazare waited for Fang to whisper some drunken nonsense that he could make fun of in the morning, but none came. Instead, Fang leaned in even closer, his lower lip just brushing the top of Lazare's beard, and God's Cheeks, was Fang going for a kiss?

Fang closed his eyes. Argh, Fang really was going for a kiss. What on earth? Lazare was confused and drunk, and more importantly, Fang was much, much drunker and likely much more confused. There was something else about Fang's expression that Lazare didn't like. There was a sadness to it. Lazare wasn't going to kiss someone who was sad about it, and he certainly wasn't going to kiss someone who was this drunk. Lazare was a fantastic kisser, and his kissees should be clear headed and glad of the kiss. Lazare pulled away, telling himself it was the right thing to do under these circumstances. Unfortunately, he also barked out a laugh of surprise at the situation, which definitely wasn't the best thing to do. Fang's expression flitted briefly to one of bewildered hurt, followed very swiftly by one of haughty, cold anger.

'Not that I'm not flattered…' attempted Lazare, trying to smooth things over.

'What?' snapped Fang, letting go of Lazare's arm and faking a sober march in the rough direction of Southwark. 'I don't know what you mean.'

'It's just, we've both been drinking, let's not do anything we regre—'

'Whatever you think you're talking about, I assure you it's not the case,' slurred Fang, 'you're drunk, sir.'

He'd started veering off diagonally. Lazare hurried over to join Fang again.

'Indeed I am, sir, so you'd better help me back to Southwark.'

Fang wasn't looking up at Lazare anymore. He glared straight ahead. That flush on his cheekbones was, if anything, more pronounced than ever.

'Fine,' huffed Fang, and that was the last thing he said for the rest of the journey back to the apothecary.

CHAPTER SEVEN
ABOVE

There was no silence in Nell's shop to break, but for a while, the only sounds were the background noises of Upper Southwark starting its day. Commerce and commutes thrummed up from the street below, until boots ran lightly up the stairs and the door suddenly crashed open to reveal a loud Frenchman carrying food.

'Everybody with a hangover, give me an "argh",' he called.

'Argh,' groaned Fang from his blanket cocoon beneath Nell's desk. Oh yes, they'd gone back to Nell's. Fang always slept under the desk at Nell's because she only had one bed. He must have given Lazare the bed and now the great lanky actor was thanking him for his kindness by being far too noisy, far too early.

'There's a bakery next door,' continued Lazare, cheerfully, 'and the fish shop downstairs, of course. Wasn't too expensive, so I don't have to start pawning my jewellery for food just yet.'

Fang groaned again. 'You bought fish?'

The smells of bread and fish wafted past Fang, in the direction of the stove.

'Oily protein,' Lazare told him as the stove was lit. 'Good for your hangover. Unless… do you not eat flesh? Is it against your religion?'

'That's mostly Buddhists.' Fang allowed his face to sneak out from under his blanket a little. The London morning light was dull and grey as usual, but he winced at it nonetheless. How much had he drunk, last night? He could remember something about a poet and an alchemist and a werewolf, but every memory after the pub was all smeared. That was far from ideal.

'Are you not Buddhist, then...?'

'I'm not anything, really,' Fang admitted, still trying to defuzz his memory of the walk home. 'Technically Confucian, but that was before...' he trailed off, hit by a horrible memory. Oh no. Ohhhh no, he'd tried to kiss Lazare.

'Well then there's nothing to stop you enjoying a kipper,' replied Lazare merrily, putting a pan and a kettle on the stove. 'I miss many things about Parisian dining, but the English really excel in breakfasts. I can brew us some coffee too, really treat ourselves.'

Fang groaned again and hid back in his blanket nest. Everything hurt. He tried to concentrate just on the pain from his stitched-up wound, but even that reminded him of how he'd got far too close to that ridiculous Frenchman, far too fast. And worse still, Lazare had turned him down and now he was going to go around acting all gallant, and... urgh.

There was a leathery flapping noise, followed by the sound of clawed feet landing on the ledge of an open window.

'Ooh, are you cooking fish?' asked Amber.

'I saved you the heads,' Lazare told her.

'Cor, thanks.' There was a thump, followed by a horrible wet crunching. Fang could tell what it was even from the depths of his desk-cave, and felt too nauseous to check. Amber spoke again, her mouth full. 'Is Fang hibernating or something?'

'Yes,' groaned Fang.

'Fang had a little too much sack last night,' said Lazare breezily, 'but here we have starch, grease, salt and hot coffee, what else could a worse-for-wear gentleman need?'

‘Silence?’ hazarded Fang from his nest. ‘Solitude? The eternal release of death?’

He heard the footsteps of Lazare walking over. They were accompanied by a smell that made his alcohol-ravaged stomach gurgle.

‘Well, you’ll have to just make do with kippers on toast,’ Lazare told him, nudging him with a foot.

Fang supposed that was his cue to finally crawl out from the relative safety of his under-desk hideaway and greet the terrible new day head on. He made it to a seated position without throwing up, which was a good start. Lazare passed him a plate and a steaming mug of fresh coffee with a winning smile. Lazare looked great – why did he look so great? How dare he look great? Before going out to buy food, Lazare had found time to change into fresh clothes, style his hair and trim his beard.

‘So, I poked around Deep London like you asked,’ said Amber, her mouth still full.

Fang glanced at the dragon, then had to look away, quickly. She was very happily making her way through the last of the raw fish heads, and while that usually wouldn’t bother Fang, it was a bit much for a hungover morning.

‘Couldn’t find any fae,’ Amber continued, ‘they don’t really leave their enclave. But, I heard a few rumours about a human raid.’ She swallowed down the last fish head, and licked the blood from her snout. ‘Honestly though, it only got mentioned in the context of everyone thinking it was a confection. Nobody Deepside believes a human gang would ever dare disturb the fae. And, if there *were* any Uppersiders stupid enough to try such a thing no one thinks they’d manage to take one step past the gates without being turned inside out and set on fire, let alone actually steal anything. Everyone reckoned it was just propaganda spread by the Deep London trade association to keep us wary of humans, stop Deepside folk always scampering up the tubes to spend our money in Upper London.’

'I'm not so sure about that,' replied Fang, picking at his breakfast.

'Yeah, I know, it doesn't work, loads of us like it on the Upperside too much. Not just the newly undead – the food's better up here, certainly for us smaller dragons.'

'No,' said Fang. 'I mean, I'm not so sure that the fae would necessarily have all this power to immediately eviscerate any human that even tries to cross them.'

Amber gave him an incredulous look. 'Er, have you ever *met* the fae?'

'No. Have you?'

'Yes.' Amber blinked and looked down. 'Well. Those were more goblins. So, no.'

'I haven't either,' added Lazare, helpfully.

'All we have is conjecture,' said Fang, 'stories, which could all end up just being another kind of fae glamour. Maybe they *are* vulnerable to raids, even by common human gangs. You'd be surprised how dangerous and brutal humans can be. Humans can be capable of just... just the most...'

A horrible memory bubbled up. Human faces, contorted with hate. Human hands, strong hands, on his shoulders, holding him back. Screams, stones. Blood. Fur.

After a moment, Fang realised that he'd trailed off into silence. The others were still watching him, waiting for him to continue with his sentence. Lazare still had that damned gallant concern in his eyes.

Fang bit into his fish on toast. 'I'm just saying,' he continued with his mouth full, 'if there's a Deepside rumour that humans raided the fae, we should take it seriously.'

The shop door opened and in swooshed Nell, looking happily dishevelled. 'Morning lads, morning Miss Amber, do I smell breakfast?'

'Did your sweetheart not even make you breakfast?' asked Fang with a smirk. 'For shame.'

'She offered,' Nell explained, helping herself, 'but werewolf food is quite... doggy. Lots of boiled chicken and bone marrow. No judgement, it's just not for me.'

'Sounds delicious,' murmured Amber.

Nell ate, casting a wary eye around her shop, which was still in exactly the same state of cluttered disarray that she'd left it in. She nodded at Fang. 'Were you under my desk all night again?'

'I'll tidy the blanket away in a bit,' muttered Fang, perturbed by the almost approving glance Nell gave to Lazare. 'We *were* consulting with Amber,' he continued, 'who's been gathering information while you were off gallivanting.'

'Much appreciated, Miss Amber,' said Nell with a small curtsey. 'We can add to it the information I gathered while the lads were getting hammered and trying not to sleep with Kit Marlowe.'

'Let's have it, then,' sighed Fang, 'I know you're itching to tell us how your docker relates to this case.'

Nell perched on her desk, next to where Fang was still slumped in his hangover nest. 'We're trying to find out about contraband, probably stolen magic weaponry,' she explained, 'for gang use in Upper London, or to sell overseas, or a combination. If you were an Upper London gang with those goods, you'd need somewhere to store them, securely, with easy access to the streets and to transport hubs.'

Fang sighed the sigh he always sighed when he realised Nell had a point. 'The dockyard warehouses.'

Nell reached down and ruffled his hair fondly. 'He always gets there eventually.'

'Your Edith has seen suspicious activities there?' Lazare asked, topping up Nell's coffee.

'First of all – she's not "my" Edith, she's her own Edith, neither of us were looking for more than a nice night. Secondly, there's *always* suspicious activities going on at the warehouses. Do you have any idea just how much smuggling goes on in this city?'

'That's fair,' Lazare conceded.

'But,' continued Nell, 'she told me that since last month, this one warehouse has been putting her and the other werewolves on edge. It's been completely lined with metallic paint. She thinks it contains silver filings.'

'So,' reasoned Fang, 'someone's trying to keep werewolves out.'

'What if it's not just about keeping werewolf dockers out?' asked Nell. 'What if there's some powerful magic they need to keep in?'

'If I had a stolen stash of fae weaponry,' said Lazare, 'and I wouldn't, because I like my skin to stay on the outside of my body where it belongs, but if I did, I'd surround it in a lot of silver.'

Fang got to his feet, decisively. The effect was rather undermined when it caused him to be hit with a fresh wave of pain, dizziness and nausea, and he had to hunch and grip the desk for stability.

'Stakeout,' he wheezed. 'I'll go.'

'Not in that state, you're not,' Nell told him. 'What are you going to do if there's trouble – vomit on them?'

*

The dockyard was quiet when they arrived; the fog was still thick and most ships would be waiting for it to clear before docking or setting sail. Still, a few workers busied themselves in the gloom. Fang might have been able to blend in with them, but there was no hope for Lazare, even with his wings tucked closely into his back. It had taken more painkillers, a lot of water and a long, annoying argument for the group to agree Fang was in a fit state to stake out the warehouse, on the provision he brought backup. Nell had had to stay behind at the shop, since by the time they'd finished arguing it was late morning and she had a flurry of customers. The little dragon, exhausted from her night-long Deepside fact finding mission, had curled up on Fang's discarded blanket next to the sales desk and fallen asleep, and

Nell had refused to let them wake her, on the grounds that she was 'adorable', which meant that that the only backup available to Fang on this undercover mission was a gaudily dressed, loud actor. Fang just hoped that they could both go on pretending that his moment of extremely drunken foolishness the night before hadn't happened – preferably, on an indefinite basis.

Fang knew that they'd have to stay out of sight – Lazare would draw far too much attention were they were just to walk along the dock, and probably the first rule of a stakeout was 'don't draw lots of attention to yourself by sauntering up to your quarry alongside a garish, six-foot actor with a silly accent and magnificent wings'. Fang quietly led the way, darting around the back of one of the first warehouses, and clambered as nimbly as his injury and hangover would allow, up beams and ledges, until he reached the roof. It was a slightly easier climb up the slanted thatch. He was able to keep his puffing to a minimum, aching body parts notwithstanding. He crouched near the ridge, just about able to see over to the row of warehouses on the opposite side of the thoroughfare, and he waited for Lazare to join him. There was a quiet whoosh of leather and air below, rushing upwards, followed by a gentle billowing, and Lazare landed silently, effortlessly next to Fang. Of course, he'd scaled the whole building in a single flap. Lazare gave Fang one of his little grins that didn't quite reach his eyes. Fang just frowned and indicated Lazare should follow him closely. They clambered and jumped along the row of close-packed rooftops until a building on the opposite side of the thoroughfare made Fang feel uneasy.

'That one's setting my wings on edge,' whispered Lazare, nodding down to the same warehouse. 'Like... *coude en colère...* a banged elbow. Is that a magic thing? Can wings feel magic, do you know?'

Well, how was Fang supposed to know that? What he did know was that the warehouse jangled the newly created magic part of him, too. Fang squinted through the fog. A line of dark grey paint, approximately six inches wide, ran along the bottom of the building, and around its doors and windows. There were silver filings mixed in with the paint. His magic could just tell. The weeds growing through the cobblestones around the building looked different to the dandelions, nettles and fireweed growing around the other warehouses in shocks of green, yellow and pink. Around this warehouse, all of the weeds were stunted and blue. Bluebells. Newly sprouted ones, from the small size of them. Everyone knew to be careful where bluebells grew. They were markers of fae magic.

Four large men were sitting outside the warehouse playing a game of cards who Fang recognised from previous beatings as belonging to Hapenny's gang. The men were guarding what was inside.

'That's the one,' he whispered back.

'So what do we do?' Lazare asked. 'Break in?'

'We'd have to get past those fellows,' muttered Fang. 'Four against two, and there's no way to know whether there's more of them inside. The Hapenny gang would be alerted to what we know, and we'd put the safety of the dockers at risk if we started a fight here. We should stay hidden for now, watch for any shift changes guarding the door, or a delivery or something – an opportunity to sneak in undetected.'

'So,' whispered Lazare, 'we just... perch here? Quietly? All day?'

'And all night, if necessary.'

There was a pause.

'Sounds really boring,' whispered Lazare.

'You're welcome to flap away if you're not sufficiently entertained,' Fang replied. 'I can handle this by myself.'

'Your various recent injuries suggest otherwise,' huffed Lazare.

There was another pause.

'Cold, isn't it?' whispered Lazare. 'Are you warm enough like that?'

'I'm fine.'

'Don't you have a cloak?' Lazare asked. 'One of those moody, dark, mud-spattered cloaks all travellers seem to have, for covering your face mysteriously while you loom in shadowy corners?'

'I had a cloak,' whispered Fang, 'I lost it in a fight in Gravesend.'

'Yikes,' replied Lazare. 'I should give you my cloak. Doesn't fit me anymore, because of these things.' He lifted one of his wings, slightly. 'They keep me pretty warm though, so I don't need one.'

'Honestly, it's fine.' Fang *was* pretty cold in just a thin shirt and jerkin, but he was only shivering a little bit. 'You already gave me your shirt.'

'That's underwear, though,' Lazare said. He stretched out the lifted wing a little more, until he was able to drape it over both of Fang's shoulders.

Oh. It really was warm. Flexible leather, alive with the Frenchman's body heat. It was like a hug that he could wear. Fang allowed it – but only because he didn't want his shivering to make him lose focus from the stakeout in hand.

They settled into silence as they waited and watched. The men outside the warehouse, along with the cold, damp fog, continued to linger interminably.

Lazare continued to not mention what had happened the previous night. The unspoken knowledge of Fang's attempted kiss hung thick in the air around them. With every passing second of Lazare's continued polite silence, every moment under the warmth of his wing, the unsaid grew a little louder. Fang glared down at the warehouse, trying his hardest to ignore the awkwardness, spurred on by a determination not to be the first one to mention it.

Lazare gave a quiet, troubled glance at Fang's scowl. 'Are you upset because I turned you down last night?' Lazare whispered.

'What? No! I didn't...' Fang shook his head, still staring down at the warehouse. 'You misjudged the situation.'

'Did I? Because it seemed like the situation was you got drunk and tried to kiss me.'

'There was no sentiment in what happened last night,' Fang replied, quickly.

'Riiight,' replied Lazare, in a deeply sarcastic tone that didn't suit him in the least. Fang risked a glance at the Frenchman. He had a single eyebrow fully cocked.

'I was just trying to save time,' continued Fang.

'On this case?'

'On us.'

'On... us.' Lazare managed to cock his eyebrow further. Surely it couldn't get anymore cocked than this.

Fang sighed. 'We're going to have sex. It's almost inevitable at this point.'

Lazare's second eyebrow joined the first, with a few blinks for good measure. 'Is it, now? That's news to me.'

'Oh, come *on*,' Fang whispered. 'You're flying me around London, making me breakfast, now we're "sharing body heat" – you're seriously telling me that's all just you being gallant?'

'I am extremely gallant. I don't leave a hungover man hungry, or a cold man shivering, and I'm certainly not going to leave someone to infiltrate a criminal gang's cache of stolen magical weapons single handedly.'

'So you don't find me attractive?' Honestly, Fang hadn't intended for that to come out sounding as hurt as it had done, nor so incredulous.

Lazare gave him another little smile – a proper one, this time, that lit up his eyes. 'What do you think?'

'I'm asking you what *you* think.'

Lazare's smile remained. The light in his warm brown eyes danced gleefully.

'I think,' said Lazare, 'you're one of the most overly dramatic people I've ever met. And I've met Burbage.'

'I am *not* being dramatic, I am being *realistic*.'

'Piffle!' The smile brightened even further. At that moment, that smile was the single most annoying thing in Fang's whole life. 'Nothing is inevitable, good Fang. Not even death anymore, it appears. You are, objectively, attractive – I think you know this. But, if you are concerned you are *so* attractive that I simply will not be able to keep my hands off you as we try to avoid a diplomatic incident with the fae, then you are sorely mistaken, Monsieur.' He leaned in a little closer to Fang. Fang could smell the coffee on his breath, mingled with the lavender of his pomander. A light sensation of skin against the side of his hand informed him that Lazare had brushed his little finger against Fang's. Lazare had such soft hands. A workshy actor's hands. 'I am, after all,' continued Lazare, inches from his face, '*extremely* gallant.'

Was Lazare's wing getting warmer, or was it just Fang?

A movement below caught their attention as one of the men outside the warehouse stood up. Both Fang and Lazare tensed, watching the scene below in a sudden, focused silence. The man stretched, and cracked his back, and sat back down again. Fang and Lazare both exhaled. There was a brief pause, and then Lazare continued speaking as if they hadn't been interrupted – as if they were at a cosy table in a tavern, rather than on a rooftop stakeout.

'However,' added Lazare, 'once you and I have solved this little magical hiccup, foiled an international weapons heist and generally saved the day, if you were free for dinner one night, I wouldn't say no.'

Lazare's hand slid upwards a little, and turned, so the pad of his thumb rested on the pulse point of Fang's wrist.

Once all of this was over? thought Fang. But, once all of this was over, the curse would be stopped, the world would be safe from whatever new form of undeath this was, and Fang and Lazare would both be dead. There was no 'once all of this is over' for them. And, even if there was… no. He wasn't doing that again. He couldn't. It wasn't the same. It couldn't possibly be the same. So, Lazare thought Fang was good looking. So what? Fang couldn't help that, it was just the face he happened to have. And, so what if in turn he found Lazare attractive. Fang would admit to that, but that was it. A passing fancy, nothing substantial. Fang was most certainly not enticed to lie in the dappled sun with this ridiculous man under the peach tree… or under any tree, or in some boudoir or anywhere. He tried not to think about the thumb tracing a light circle against his wrist in a way that shot a jangling sensation along his arm and down into his belly. His eyes felt strange, his vision slightly blurred.

'I prefer to eat alone,' Fang managed.

'You had breakfast with me and the others only this morning,' countered Lazare.

'I don't go on dates.'

'You just kiss men in the street when you're so drunk you can barely stand, instead? Sounds like self-sabotaging nonsense to me.'

'I do not self-sabotage,' snapped Fang as quietly as he could manage. '*You* self-sabotage!'

There was that damned smile again, the smile that danced so merrily across Lazare's face.

'How so?'

Fang pulled his wrist away. 'Because you're interested in dating me.'

Now, that killed the smile. Lazare replaced it with an expression of concern and pity that was, if anything, even more annoying.

'Don't…' began Fang, but Lazare's attention was pulled away to the street below once more.

'Look!'

Lazare pointed below. A group of half a dozen armed men were walking towards the warehouse. Their doublets were a little shabbier than those of the warehouse guards, and again unlike the guards, were in an array of different grubby shades of yellow – these weren't Hapenny boys. This was a rival gang. Fang ducked further behind the roof ridge, thinking. If a fight was going to kick off right here and now over ownership of the stolen fae weaponry, perhaps he and Lazare could utilise the distraction. Of course, there was also the considerable chance that they could accidentally get drawn into the fight, or hit with crossfire, or even that they could be spotted and then both gangs would stop fighting one another and temporarily unite to fight him and Lazare.

Beside him, Lazare gasped quietly. 'That's the fellow who killed me.' He pointed at one of the approaching men in yellow. 'Or, you know… un-killed me. He's the one who stabbed me, the night I came back with wings and realised I couldn't die.'

Fang frowned. If Lazare had been stabbed by a rival gang to the Hapennys, maybe Lazare hadn't been stabbed with a magical weapon after all. If that was the case, then the curse could have nothing to do with the stolen weapons whatsoever, and here he was, stuck on a roof with a ridiculously annoying popinjay, in peril of getting drawn into an imminent gangland street war, and no farther forward in trying to undo his own curse. He swore to himself, under his breath.

The warehouse door opened, and a couple more Hapenny boys came out to join the guards, who were already on their feet, standing their ground against the approaching men. Fang braced himself, waiting for the first strike of what could only turn into a bloodbath. None came. Instead, one of the rival gang pulled out a purse, and set it on the floor. One of the Hapenny boys stepped forward, picked it up and opened it to inspect the coins inside, while the rival gang waited at a respectful distance. He nodded, clearly satisfied, and signalled to one of his fellow guards to open the big double doors to the warehouse. Out was led a horse and cart, which was laden with crates. The cart was covered in the same silver paint drawn around the warehouse, as were the crates piled on it. There was something else about one of the crates near the bottom of the stack. Something that hit Fang with a cold horror. There were airholes in that crate.

'They're selling the weapons on to other gangs, then,' whispered Lazare. 'What say you – follow this cart at a safe distance, see where it goes? Perhaps there'll be chance to quietly commandeer it on a side road and then… hey. What are you doing?'

Fang had barely listened to Lazare, he was too filled with dread at what he'd seen. He sprang out from the warm safety of Lazare's wing and scrambled over the rooftop, straight at the horse and cart. Yes, it would be him against a dozen armed gang members, yes there were still innocent workers at the other end of the dockyard, yes it was an impetuous act, yes it was more rational to wait and tail the cart. Yes, he was breaking their cover and running straight into terrible danger, but he couldn't let them take that bottom crate away. He couldn't leave that bottom crate in the hands of violent thieves for one second longer.

It wasn't just weapons they'd taken from the fae. They had taken and trapped something alive. Let loose, a fae beast could do untold damage in Upper London, but that wasn't what created the cold pit of horror in Fang's stomach.

The poor thing. It had been snatched from its home, imprisoned and traded like an object. It would be terrified and hurting. Humans were capable of such terrible, terrible things. *Hands holding him back. Screams. Blood. Fur.* Fang shook the memory away. Well, not again. Never again. He vaulted over the ridge of the roof and began sliding down the thatch towards the startled gangs.

He had to help it.

CHAPTER EIGHT
THE BOX

'Wait wait wait…'

But Fang wasn't waiting. He'd already vaulted the ridge of the roof. God's Buttocks, the maniac was going to get himself minced at this rate, if he didn't first break his legs jumping off the roof.

'Wait!' Lazare continued to cry – aware of how fruitless that was, even if Fang wanted to stop by now, the gangs were aware of both of them, and gravity had added its own momentum to Fang's acceleration down the roof. He was close to the edge, seconds from danger – if not death, thanks to the spell then possibly a fate even worse than death. Several of the gang members had already readied their weapons – worryingly, those weapons included two muskets. Lazare knew that firearms meant that there was no advantage to trying to attack or escape the gangs by air. He knew that they could shoot him as he flew, shred his wings. Only a fool would take flight under such conditions.

He took flight. He flapped in one great whoosh towards Fang at the same time that Fang launched himself from the edge of the roof towards the gangs. Lazare caught Fang under the arms and spared him the indignity of landing on his face several yards from his intended target, as his trajectory would have caused him to do without intervention.

A musket was levelled at him. He managed to duck away just at the right moment to avoid being shot.

'I'm getting you out of here,' he announced. He only cringed slightly at the knowledge that scooping Fang up and flying him out of danger without his consent was becoming a bit of a habit. Fang could shout at him again once they were safe – they were getting shot at, for pity's sake. Getting shot at was one of Lazare's least favourite things to do.

'You will not,' demanded Fang. He reached up, and with difficulty, grabbed Lazare's beard, pulling his head down to look at the cart. 'Bottom crate. Airholes.'

Lazare realised why Fang had intervened right then and there – why they couldn't just fly to safety without that crate.

'*Merde*.'

'The cart,' Fang told him.

Lazare turned, dodging another two flying musketballs. One of the gang members had already climbed into the driver's seat and was frantically slapping the reins, trying to make a hasty getaway. Two more ruffians jumped onto the back of the cart to protect the goods. Both carried large knives.

This would be fine, right? They couldn't die, and he had his wings and Fang had his reverse glamour or whatever you wanted to call it. This would be OK, they'd be OK…? He tried to speed up to catch up with the departing cart, heard the crack of the musket from behind him and tried to dodge blindly. Something grazed his thigh. Ow! It was only a flesh wound, but God's Liver, that flesh wound hurt to kingdom come.

He managed to drop Fang into the driver's seat right next to the rather surprised looking driver, who tried to elbow Fang out of the way, but with his hands filled with the reins was at a disadvantage. Fang managed to kick the driver's bum out from under him, before kicking him again in the shoulder this time, sending him tumbling off the cart.

'Roll,' Lazare advised the screaming, falling man as Fang grabbed the reins, 'you'll be fine.' He was shot at again. Now, there was gratitude for you.

The gang members who were neither falling nor shooting were now running, trying to catch up with the cart as it sped up along the main dockyard thoroughfare, any rivalry between the two gangs seemingly set aside as they rushed together to stop Lazare and Fang. The two gangsters already on the cart clambered towards Fang, knives at the ready. Lazare managed to land on a crate near the driver's seat, between Fang and the approaching knife wielders. Standing on his injured leg hurt. He was bleeding quite badly already. He gritted a grin through the pain.

'Not today, Monsieur et Madame,' he told the two gang members, 'we just need to borrow this cart. We'll be kind to the horsey, I promise.'

'Wait, didn't I kill you last month?' asked the man.

Ah, yes. This was the fellow who had stabbed him.

'Some dirty Deepsider vampirise you after we were done with you or something?'

'It's not vampirism,' said the woman, 'it's something else. Something interesting.'

'How so, Mistress Avis?' asked the man.

Oh, no.

The woman was Avis Hapenny. They were trying to steal a cart with the boss of the Hapenny gang on it. All in all, this attempted hijack was going from 'bad' to 'probably the worst decision Lazare had ever made'.

'The fellow he's with,' said Avis, 'the pretty one. My boys beat him to death, *and* staked him in the gut, and he's *still* back. Foreign magic, I'd say. They're tricksy, Cathayans.'

'Thought he was Turkish,' muttered the man.

'No, Thomasina says there's a difference.'

'Would you please get those two off my cart?' shouted Fang.

'It's not your cart,' snarled Avis.

'Yeah,' added the man, 'us Custards bought it fair and square!'

So, thought Lazare, the other lot were Jim Custard's gang. Lazare didn't know enough about the ins and outs of Upper London's gangs to be aware of whether it was particularly unusual for them to be doing business with Avis Hapenny. He supposed it didn't really matter – he and Fang were up to their sexy necks in it with both gangs, now.

Both Avis and the Custard boy lunged forward at the same time. Lazare managed, with the help of his wings, to propel himself over them, grabbing the wrist of the Custard boy as he went. There was the crack of a musket in the distance again as soon as he was airborne. He had to dodge awkwardly, and fumbled the landing back onto the moving carriage. He fell to his knees and his grip on the Custard boy's wrist slipped, meaning the only damage he'd managed to inflict was a slight friction burn. And now there was nothing between the assailants and Fang, struggling with the reins. Blast it! Lazare scrambled towards the criminals as they approached Fang. The Custard boy slashed at Fang, but thankfully missed, due to Fang ducking. Fang managed to elbow the Custard boy in the throat as he did so, which bought them a couple of seconds at least.

'Little help?' shouted Fang.

'This is difficult,' called Lazare, struggling along the rocking cart.

'So's this,' Fang snapped back at him.

The cart was coming to the end of the thoroughfare. They were going to have to take a turn, and if they didn't want to sink themselves, mystery crate and all, in the Thames, they would have to turn towards the street. As it was, dockyard workers were pressed against walls, watching the clattering cart of danger in horror. If this thing got onto a main street, heaving with innocent civilians, it would be putting so many more people in peril. Lazare had to stop this, fast. He jumped at the Custard boy and managed to grab him, only to feel a new sharp pain, on the upper edge of his left wing.

'Lazare!' Fang was gazing over his shoulder at Lazare, horrified.

Avis Hapenny dug her knife a little deeper into the top of Lazare's wing, smirking at Fang. 'I thought it might be like that. A woman has a sense for sentimentality. Surrender, or I'll shred his handsome new wings to pieces.' She held out her hand. 'The reins. Don't bother about disembarking – I think you should both stay with us. Two foreign fellows who can't die – I know someone who would be very interested to meet you.'

Fang gritted his teeth with concentration, and out of the side of his eye, Lazare saw his own wings begin to crawl with maggots.

Avis just laughed. 'I was warned about that Cathayan trick of yours. It only makes you all the more interesting to my contact.'

Fang exhaled, and the maggots vanished. Silently, Fang set his face, and yanked the reins hard to turn.

'No,' warned Lazare.

'Yes,' grinned Avis. 'Good lad, take us back to my boys, so we can—'

Fang's turn was far too sharp and too fast for comfort. In fact, it was too sharp and fast for anybody or anything, including the cart itself, to stay fully upright. It teetered briefly on its right wheels, throwing several crates to the ground, as well as the Custard boy and Lazare.

'The crate,' screamed Fang. The crate with the airholes was still on the cart, but the two boxes that had been stacked on top of it had fallen off. 'Take it,' Fang continued. 'Fly for your life, get out of here!'

He righted the cart, now fully facing the other way, back down the thoroughfare towards the warehouse and the approaching gangs. Avis regained her balance, and turned her knife to Fang.

Lazare scrambled to his feet and ran, ignoring the hot, throbbing pain in his leg and his wing as he flapped to get airborne. 'I'm not leaving you.'

'I'll be fine, I can't die, get the crate, *now*!'

'He can't die, Monsieur, but he can be made to beg for death,' called Avis. 'We can cut an awful lot of bits off a man who can't fatally bleed out.'

There was no way Lazare was going to leave Fang after that. All in all, Avis was making it very difficult for him to respect her achievements in rising to the top of a male dominated field.

He landed on the back of the cart.

'What are you doing?' Fang cried. 'Take the crate, you stupid... *Ow*!!!'

Blood gushed from Fang's thigh. The cart whizzed past one of the musket-toting gang members on the thoroughfare, his gun still smoking at the barrel.

'That's your fault,' Fang told Lazare.

'It's her fault,' replied Lazare, pointing at Avis.

'It's both of your faults,' Avis told them. 'Hand me the reins and surrender properly.'

'I don't surrender,' shouted Fang.

'You've got no choice,' Avis told them. Indeed, they were quickly approaching the large gaggle of assorted gang members still standing by the warehouse. They blocked the thoroughfare only a few yards ahead of them, all heavily armed. Only a handful of them flinched away as raw sewage rose from nowhere and lapped at their ankles. Most of them held fast, concentrating on the cart. Thick black swarms of flies descended around their heads, and only the woman Lazare recognised as Thomasina broke concentration with a miserable 'ewwwww'. A moderately sized plume of fire spread down at them through the flies, and still the gangs didn't flinch, which several of them realised moments later was a huge mistake.

'The flame's real,' one man screamed from within the flies.

'My hat's on fire,' shouted another fly-obscured gangster.

The illusion of the flies dissipated to reveal a small, brick-brown urban dragon.

'Thought you might need help,' explained Amber, soaring over to meet them. 'Oh, hang on, yikes, they've got muskets.'

The dragon dodged clumsily away from a flying musketball, clipping herself on a dockside pulley as she did.

'Ow,' she complained. 'Well, I did my best to help. Bye.'

'That's it?' yelled Fang.

Amber sighed, turned and made another approach in the direction of the few remaining gang members. 'Thanks for coming to rescue us, Amber; you're welcome, humans.'

The cart went past the remaining gangsters before Amber was able to get to them. There were still a good half dozen assailants who had neither been unsettled by Fang's illusions nor lightly set on fire by Amber, and most were able to jump onto the cart as it passed.

'It's over,' Avis told them. 'Stop the cart.'

'No,' Fang told her, even though they were again running out of thoroughfare.

'Stop it or I'll slice the Frenchman.'

'Amber, force Lazare off this stupid cart. Lazare, get the crate!'

Lazare was right on top of the crate. He could so easily just grab it and fly, while Amber created a distraction. He wasn't going to, and Avis knew it. She reached forward and plunged her dagger into the musket wound in Fang's thigh. Fang screamed a succession of foreign exclamations, none of which Lazare understood, other than that they were all definitely very strong curse words. Lazare added a '*merde*' of his own, for good measure. Behind them, Amber was struggling to keep up. She breathed a new plume of fire that missed everyone and everything except the heel of Lazare's boot. Lazare swore again and struggled to put his boot out while fighting off multiple criminals swarming the cart. He had to get to Fang. Maybe if he got to Fang, he could rescue him *and* the crate. Somehow. He had no idea how.

They were almost at the end of the thoroughfare. Again, their choices were either to turn into a busy street where there would be more than just the odd startled docker to worry about, or the Thames. Or, thought Lazare, they could fully turn around again and go back along the thoroughfare for a third time, in what was turning out to be a deeply ridiculous and repetitive cart chase. Fang, still screaming, grabbed the knife in his thigh and wrestled control of it out of Avis's grip. Before anybody else could do or say anything, he yanked the reins, causing everyone to tumble to one side as the cart performed another sharp turn towards the river. Then, mid turn, he reached forward to begin cutting the straps attaching the horse to the cart.

Avis lunged forward and grabbed his hand before he could cut them loose completely.

'What are you doing?' she demanded.

'Don't want to drown the horse,' he snarled, fighting to get the knife back, his fingers slipping on his own blood.

There was nobody holding the reins anymore. They were heading straight for the river. Lazare had no idea how many hands were holding him down and pressing blades threateningly against his skin, but it was too many to free himself from. Suddenly, Fang let go of the knife, let go of everything, just clamped his hands over his nose and mouth. There was a figure in a window directly above, then the sound of smashing glass, right in front of them, and then the world went soft.

Bright light. Comfort. Joy. Complete joy. Was Lazare in a bed? On a soft couch? He was on a stage, being applauded and cheered. He was amongst friendly peers, toasting him, promising to write him exciting new roles. He was alone with Fang, who groaned and sighed his name, his cheeks all flushed, his eyes all dark. Lazare was filled with absolute delight, and absolute love, and he never wanted to move away from this perfect moment.

'Lazare,' whispered Fang, his lips wet and parted and utterly inviting. Fang put his strong, elegant hands on Lazare's shoulders.

'Lazare.' Fang pulled Lazare towards him. Lazare held his own hands out and touched that lovely, scar-etched chest. 'Lazare,' Fang repeated, his voice urgent now, growing in a delicious crescendo. 'Lazare!' Fang gripped his arms, hard. It hurt, but in a nice way. Fang shook him. 'Lazare! Wake up, you ridiculous fop!'

Lazare frowned, and blinked a few times. Oh. He wasn't on a couch or a stage or making love, he was on top of a crate, on a cart teetering at the edge of the Thames. The air smelled strange. Ohhhh, and it made him want to go back to that joyful place of soft comfort and...

Fang slapped him. Lazare noticed the other man had pulled his shirt up over his nose.

'Try not to breathe in. We need to get out of here before they all wake up.'

Lazare blinked around. All of the gang members and several of the nearby dockers were still and silent, the hands that had battled, hurt and menaced them now slack at their sides, gazing into the middle distance with giddy, dreamlike smiles, as if under some enchantment. Even the horse had suddenly stopped, and was standing against the edge of the dock, its pupils blown, dribbling and looking as happy as a tired dray horse could look.

'A fae spell?' asked Lazare anxiously, tying a kerchief over his nose and mouth.

'No, Nell drugged them,' Fang explained, nodding to the shattered remnants of a number of glass bottles on the cobbles surrounding them, 'but the results are almost the same.'

'Er, me and Amber put good time and effort into saving you eggs,' called Nell, stepping out from the warehouse. 'You would have got stabbed and kidnapped or drowned in the Thames if not for our selfless actions, at no inconsiderable risk to our own safety. A little thankfulness wouldn't go amiss, since we're clearly getting no other reward for our bravery.'

'You got to test your new euphoria potion,' argued Fang, 'and Amber's having a great time.'

He indicated to the little dragon as she waddled slowly along, her tail drooped, her eyes like saucers.

'Queeeeeeen of the dragons,' she mumbled, happily, 'of alllllll I survey. Tremble, puny humans.'

'Yes, yes,' Fang told her gently, scooping her up into his arms so she could do no damage to herself, 'you're a mighty ferocious beast.'

'I shall build a royal nest from your skullllllllls.'

'Yeah,' sighed Nell, 'I can't sell it at this concentration, can I? It's way too strong.'

'I'd buy it,' Lazare admitted.

'The crate,' Fang reminded them. 'Come on. Let's go.'

'After all that fuss about not letting the Royal Guards know about the theft, you're just going to let them get their beaks on all this nicked stuff, then?' asked Nell, gesturing around at all the other crates littering the streets, many shimmering with spilled fae weapons.

'Fae hardware is small fry compared to something that needs air holes,' Fang replied. 'Leave the knives to the birds – we're also leaving them multiple wanted criminals, so we're doing them a favour.'

'They'll follow up on us anyway,' Nell told him in a sing-song know-it-all voice.

'Then let's stay masked and be fast,' replied Fang, aping her tune.

Nell helped Lazare pick up the crate, although on lifting it, Lazare realised that it was nowhere near as heavy as he'd expected it to be. He met eyes with Nell, who also seemed surprised at how light it was. He came close to commenting that there was a chance they'd put themselves in danger for an empty box, but as he carried it, he could tell it wasn't empty. Something was in there, lying quite still, probably under the effects of Nell's potion. If it was fae in origin, that would explain the weight. They had to get it somewhere safe immediately, which would be difficult while carrying a large crate and a drugged dragon.

'I surrender,' announced a gruff, familiar voice. Lazare and Nell followed the sound, and Nell broke into a broad grin.

'Oh hi again,' she began, before Edith the docker cut her off.

'I'm just an honest dock worker, there's nothing I can do about you ruffians hijacking my cart if you're going to threaten me.'

She nodded at the small cart next to her, attached to a mercifully non-drugged horse.

'Yes, that's right, me old mucker,' replied Lazare, playing along in the best Upper London accent he could muster, 'we gangsters needs must get away, gor blimey. Or we'll… slit yer from hither to yon.'

'Yeah, luvvaduck,' added Nell in a much worse Upper London accent, 'an' you'd better not go snooping around the Albany Coach House and Stables, guvnah, just cause that might be a really useful place for 'ardened criminals like ourselves to ditch our getaway vehicle for any dockers to pick up again laters so they don't get in trouble with their foreman, by crikey, eh… John?'

She looked to Fang, who reacted with a 'why on earth did you drag me into this nonsense' glare.

'Indubitably, by Jove,' grumbled Fang in honestly the worst Upper English accent Lazare had ever heard.

'Just take the cart and don't hurt me,' said Edith, pointedly, 'you won't get far anyway, not now someone's gone to fetch the guards.'

Lazare and his group hurriedly put the crate on the back of the cart and hopped on, Nell pushing Fang aside to take the reins.

'Well exactly, me old Jimminy,' called Nell, 'let's get a wriggle on up the old oranges and lemons, by crackers.'

She slapped the reins and they drove away onto the main thoroughfare, kerchiefs still raised, disguising themselves quickly amongst the other carts in the dust kicked up by hooves.

'That was lucky,' murmured Lazare.

'That wasn't luck,' replied Nell, quietly. 'That's the old Nell ver'Evan afterglow working in our favour.' She waggled her eyebrows at the others.

Fang glared at Nell. '"John"?'

'I left my shop during the lunchtime rush to help you boys. Let me have my fun. And now the guards will be looking for Upper Londoner gang members, not a Welshwoman, a Frenchman and a Cathayan.'

'Will they, though?' wondered Lazare, aloud.

'Well, they might be suspicious about Fang,' Nell replied, 'but us two had the accents bang on, I reckon.'

'The scourge of alllll London town,' sang Amber happily, still drooling in Fang's arms, 'they don't know who they're messing with.'

*

Captain Honkensby landed at the docks, choosing to make a water landing on the Thames and then hop up swiftly onto land, on the grounds that, while more convoluted, it was slightly less awkward than a dry landing. Constables had already tied up the gang members who had alarmed innocent dock workers with a violent fracas that morning. According to preliminary reports, when the constables had found them, the criminals had been in a seeming state of stupefaction, all standing or sitting quite still, gazing happily at nothing. Worryingly, the two constables who were first on the scene also reported a strange smell, and themselves feeling a vague but unmistakable sense of unwarranted elation. This ruled out hypnotism being the cause of the gang members' odd behaviour. As far as Honkensby could tell, it could be down to mass drugging through a gas attack, or a powerful spell. Both troubled her greatly.

Sergeant Peanut, a capable young raven, brought her the most up to date report.

'We now believe it was a fight between three gangs, rather than two,' she told Honkensby, 'since we've captured members of both the Custard *and* the Hapenny gangs, but from the dock workers' statements, a third faction interrupted a deal, stole some of the goods, threatened a werewolf, hijacked a cart and rode off – around a half hour ago.'

Honkensby hissed, quietly. 'That means they could be anywhere by now.'

'Quite, Captain. Sorry, Captain. We do have *some* bits of good news though, Captain.'

'Go on then, Peanut. Cheer me up.'

'Firstly, a bit of information on the escaped gang. The werewolf Edith said they had strong Upper London accents, and one of them was called John.'

Honkensby tried not to roll her eyes. That didn't exactly narrow things down.

'They were masked, but we do have a physical description of John,' continued Peanut, quickly. 'Um… "Gorgeous, just really nice eyes and hair, fit arms, bum like two tennis balls squeezed into a sock". There was also a woman and, crucially, the other man in the group fit the description of the vampire you're investigating.'

Now, that surprised Honkensby. That was twice this vampire had been seen in Upper London, assaulting humans in broad – if foggy – daylight. And he was apparently with a gang?

'They left with a small urban dragon, again like the one witnessed calling for help in the first report,' Peanut added, 'but it's unclear from witness statements whether she was working with them or if they were taking her hostage.'

It was, at least, slightly more information than before. Honkensby would take any lead she could, at this point.

'There's more,' said Peanut proudly, leading Honkensby towards where the gangsters were tied up. 'Now, this is what me and the girls are *really* hoping will cheer you up, Captain.'

Honkensby saw what Peanut was referring to and stopped in her tracks, impressed.

'Avis Hapenny herself,' she murmured.

'On a platter,' said Peanut, happily. 'Thought you'd like that.'

Avis Hapenny, the scourge of Upper East London, the thorn in Honkensby's flipper for over a decade, the previously uncatchable spider at the centre of a tangled web of crime, now glared at Honkensby, tied up amongst her own gang and several of Custard's boys.

'Well, *that* explains it,' Avis announced, cryptically. 'That explains why he was waiting. He just wanted to give me the satisfaction of seeing your stupid beak as you realise you've been bested by Avis Hapenny yet again!'

There was a pause. Honkensby gazed at Avis some more. Avis seemed to be waiting for something.

'What's she on about?' Honkensby asked Peanut.

'She was quite strongly afflicted by whatever physick or magic mesmerised the gangs,' Peanut explained, 'we think she's still under its influence, she keeps telling us someone's about to spring her loose, that...'

'You don't know who you're dealing with,' cried Avis. 'The things he can do! And, he won't forget his powerful allies! You'll see!'

'I'm afraid that's where the good news ends,' added Peanut, 'because with the gangs, we found some of the goods they were trading.' She showed Honkensby over to one of the crates, guarded by several constables, and ringed with silver chains. 'We don't know how many of these are missing, but we do know that at least one was taken away by your vampire.'

Peanut nodded to the constables, who carefully lifted the lid to allow Honkensby to look inside. It was full of faintly glowing weapons. Fae weapons.

'Oh,' breathed Honkensby in horror, 'quack.'

*

Wulfric was surprised to see Lazare de Quitte-Beuf and friends ride up to his inn dusty, bloodied and exhausted. It was the quiet period between lunch and the evening rush, so if Lazare and his weirdly good-looking companions wanted a bit of early afternoon hair of the dog, their custom was very welcome. He even had room around the back for their newly acquired vehicle and told them as such, but the Welshwoman Nell instead asked politely if there was a spare bartender who could possibly take it to the Albany Coach House and pay for the horse to be stabled there for the night. His cook had little to do at that point and so, out of respect for the alliance between magicals and the Welsh Kingdom, Wulfric sent him to run the errand.

Wulfric was rather less happy about the strange, unsettling crate covered in airholes and silver paint that they wanted to bring inside. They mumbled apologetically that they'd been closer to his place than Nell's shop in Southwark, that minimal attention would be drawn to them bringing a box into an inn, and that due to the nature of what they believed was inside, they considered it vital to have another Deepsider on hand that they could trust. Lazare promised they'd allow no harm to come to his property, and well, Lazare had always been a good customer, he'd paid off the overdue tabs of both Marlowe and Burbage in the past, so Wulfric relented nervously and let them take the crate through to a quiet back room of the inn.

'Can I get you anything?' he asked. 'Brandy...?' he trailed off, gauging Fang's nauseous expression. Ah. Someone was still hungover, then. 'I could fetch bread and cold meats? Split a pig's heart with Amber?'

'Yes,' replied the dragon, desperately. 'I have got a killer headache.'

'Do you have a needle and thread?' Nell asked. 'Boiled water? Rags? These two have got themselves stabbed *again*. And shot! I only stitched them up yesterday.'

'We don't have time for that right now,' snapped Fang, grabbing one of Wulfric's nice clean napkins to bandage his bleeding leg. That was a mercy for Wulfric, at least. Fang's open wound smelled odd, but it still made the vampire dribble.

'We need to get that poor thing out of there,' Fang continued. 'Safely. We still don't know what it is, or how affected it is by Nell's potion. For all we know, drugging it just made it angry.'

Wulfric looked at the 'dangerous' crate. It was completely motionless, if still unsettling in nature, although Wulfric wondered if that might be because of the paint. The silver filings in it made his stomach churn against the blood-hunger, and his wings and teeth jangle unpleasantly.

'We need to secure the room,' continued Fang. 'Wulfric, what silver have you to hand?'

Wulfric blinked at Fang. 'You're asking me, a vampire, if I have any silver lying around Upper Deptford's most popular undead nightspot?'

'OK, good point.' Fang paused. 'So, even the candlesticks?'

'Even the candlesticks! Everything's pewter.'

Nell rolled her eyes. 'I did come prepared, you know.' She pulled a spool of thin silver chain from her satchel. Wulfric stepped back out of instinct. Nell unwound the chain and placed it in a large, unbroken circle around the crate. Then she took out small silver necklaces for herself, Lazare and Fang, who took the chains with their own shudders of discomfort. Wulfric remained pressed against the wall, upset by the silver, and worried by the box as Lazare, Nell and Fang stepped into the circle to carefully prise off the lid.

The three looked down into it, and Wulfric heard all three stop their breath, his vampire sense for blood felt their pulses suddenly race.

'Oh, no,' breathed Lazare.

'What is it?' asked Wulfric. Now that the lid was off, he could feel another heartbeat in the room. It was fast, too. Whatever was in that box was as terrified as the rest of them.

'Oh, *no*,' sighed Nell. She sounded close to tears.

'Guys?' Amber hurried over the silver circle to the others. 'I smell fae. And… and human, mixed in with it. What *is* that? It's all wrong. It's—'

'It's all right,' announced Fang. Wulfric could tell from Fang's hammering heart that it wasn't all right at all. Fang took off his silver necklace, passed it to Lazare and leaned down into the depths of the open crate.

'Fang, don't…' managed Lazare, but it was too late to stop him.

Fang scooped something from the crate.

It was a fae child. Or… not quite a fae. Her blood didn't feel right for a pure fae. The dragon had been right, there was human blood in this child, too.

The fae was small. Smaller than Wulfric – barely more than three foot – younger looking too. A scrap of a girl – four, maybe five years old. Large, dark eyes and darker hair, tied back in a dishevelled ponytail, showing the pointed tips of her little ears. She was dirty, skinny, traumatised, terrified.

And she was, Wulfric immediately knew, one of the most dangerous creatures he had seen in all his 831 years.

CHAPTER NINE
THE CHILD

'God's Purse, those maniacs stole a bloody kid,' breathed Nell, shakily. 'This is so much worse than I thought.'

Lazare, for once, couldn't find the words. He just stared at the little girl, his feelings a horrible mix of fear, pity, bewilderment and hot rage. A fae *child*. Kidnapped from her community, dragged to the Upper streets, put in a box and traded like a weapon, like a… a *thing*. She'd been trapped in there, frightened and alone, as he'd drunk and made merry, and flirted with Fang. Bashed around during the fight due to his refusal to just take the crate and fly off straight away. If he'd known, he'd have acted quicker to rescue the poor poppet. He hadn't known. But, that didn't make things any better for the girl, did it?

'I mean,' Nell continued, 'we're definitely in "Diplomatic Incident" territory here, right? Upper Londoners abducting an actual fae child?'

'Half-fae,' Wulfric told them, quietly. 'You don't get them much nowadays in England since the peace treaty and the separation. The fae settled far into the Deepside, in part to stop interbreeding; it had become as taboo with them as it was with humans. To Uppersiders, even half-fae are dangerous and strange. To the fae, they generally saw half-human offspring as… lesser. Tainted. Back in the day, they'd dump them with the human parent, or leave them to the elements. Clearly, they changed their tune on that, haven't heard of a half-fae left on the Upperside in centuries, and clearly, somehow, some still get conceived – case in point.'

'If you could all stop talking about this little girl as if she isn't here,' interjected Fang in an uncommonly soft tone, 'that would be great.' He addressed the girl in the same gentle tone, still cradling her close as she shivered. 'Do you speak English?'

The girl nodded, not quite making eye contact with him.

'My name is Fang, I'm human… mostly. I'm going to make sure nobody hurts you again, and help you get home, all right?'

The girl still couldn't look at him, still trembled.

'Would you rather a lady look after you?' Fang continued, 'or another Deepsider? A dragon? A vampire?'

The girl shrugged, miserably.

'Would you like me to stop asking silly questions?' Fang asked, still in that same tone.

Lazare wasn't sure whether what he caught on the girl's expression was an attempted smile or the suppression of tears. She nodded.

'Very well.' Fang leaned over a little to try to deposit the girl on a nearby chair, but she grasped at his arms urgently. He stood back up, still cradling her, and now, she clung back.

'Tem,' she whispered.

Lazare wasn't sure what she meant by that at first. Fang, instantly, did.

'Your name?' he asked.

She nodded again, taking in the others, then spoke again in that frightened whisper. 'Thirsty.'

'I'll get water,' offered Wulfric.

'Don't they drink milk and honey?' Lazare asked.

'That's a treat food,' chorused the others, but Lazare noticed Tem's eyes had lit up at the words 'milk and honey'.

'I think if anyone deserves a treat right now, it's Tem,' concluded Fang, also noting her expression.

'Don't forget my pig's heart,' whined Amber, but Wulfric had already disappeared towards the kitchen.

Tem still didn't let Fang put her down as she drank several saucerfuls of honeyed milk in a row.

'Should we tell the Queen's Guards about this?' Wulfric asked quietly, topping up the girl's saucer again. Lazare could tell from Wulfric's tone that he really hoped the answer was going to be 'no, we need to get this kid out of your inn and Deepside as quickly and quietly as possible.'

'No,' replied Nell. 'The fae haven't gone public about Tem's kidnap, they must have good reason. If we get officials involved, there could be a fight over whether she counts as fae or human. Avis Hapenny and Jim Custard clearly thought she was valuable enough to buy and sell her – what if the Upper Crown wants to seize her? Try to use her as leverage to claw even more concessions and power from the Deepside?'

'You really think Queen Elizabeth would do something like that?' Lazare asked.

'I'm Welsh,' Nell reminded him, 'you can't exactly blame me for being extremely wary of the Upper English Crown.'

Lazare nodded with an understanding that came from a similarly thorny history of Anglo–Gallic relations.

'This could spiral,' said Nell. 'This could get really nasty.'

'We don't want to go back to humans and magicals being at war,' sighed Wulfric. 'It was bad enough last time.'

'It still *is* that bad,' said Fang, quietly. 'Some of the places I've been… England is far from perfect, the terms of the peace treaty are deeply unfair, but at least there *is* peace, on the whole. That's more than can be said for many of the places I've travelled through.'

'Spain,' murmured Lazare, his mind full of horror stories of his youth from his homeland's southern neighbour.

'Scotland,' added Nell, with a frown.

'Even the Great Ming…' Fang trailed off, as if hit by a sudden, unwelcome memory. 'We need to preserve the peace, fragile and imperfect as it is. The alternative is carnage, and nobody deserves that. We must get Tem back to her people quickly. Alerting the authorities will only complicate and delay.'

Tem had finally drunk her fill of sweetened milk. She was still shivering.

'Cold,' she whispered.

Fang looked to Wulfric. 'Do you have any warm clothes she can have? Any cast offs you've grown out of...?'

Fang, again, stopped suddenly. From his expression, he'd just realised his faux-pas.

Wulfric cocked an eyebrow. 'I'm a vampire, mister, I haven't grown since Cynewulf was king.'

'Cynewulf?' asked Lazare. 'Who's he?'

'Exactly,' replied Wulfric. 'I'll fish out some winter clothes, we can make adjustments to fit. And I'll heat some water. From what I remember of them, the fae always smelled like they enjoyed a lot of baths. Always wafting about smelling of roses...'

'Lilacs,' interrupted Tem.

That stopped Wulfric in his tracks. Everybody looked at Tem. She'd just corrected him. She immediately cast her eyes down, anxiously.

'We like lilacs,' she squeaked, her tone like an apology, 'And soap that smells all lilacy.'

'Do you have soap that smells all lilacy?' Fang asked Wulfric.

'I can do,' Wulfric told her kindly, before sighing and grabbing his purse and his sunproof cloak. 'Well, now I've got to go and buy fancy soap. *And* more milk.'

*

As they waited for Wulfric to return, the rest of the group came to a silent mutual decision that the ring of silver chains surrounding Tem was unnecessary. The silver was put away quickly and quietly, as was the silver-painted box. At the removal of the silver, Tem seemed to relax a little. She even asked for something to eat, and in the absence of Wulfric or the inn's cook, Lazare headed into the kitchen to see what he could rustle up. Amber followed him, although that was mostly to find the promised half a pig's heart, which still hadn't been delivered.

As Lazare departed for the kitchen, Fang asked to borrow a comb. There was no question over whether Lazare would have a comb upon his person – of course he did. Nell suspected that he carried more than one, in fact. Lazare was just that sort of person. He handed it over to Fang without question before disappearing off, pursued by a small and hungry dragon.

Something had happened between those two, in spite of Nell's warning. Perhaps it wasn't as bad as it could have been, but still. She liked Lazare. She didn't want Fang to get this one all tangled up in his sadness.

Maybe this time it could be different. Maybe trying to end the curse and help this fae child would keep Fang so distracted that he wouldn't find the time or energy to completely alienate the nice Frenchman.

Yeah. And Hippogryphs might not fly.

Nell watched as Fang fetched a shallow bowl of water, then sat cross-legged on the floor with Tem and, with soft directions for the child to tell him if she wanted him to stop, he began slowly combing the tangles from her hair. The little girl didn't complain about it at all, but closed her eyes peacefully, like a kitten enjoying the grooming of its mother's rasping tongue.

'We should get out of here soon,' Nell said.

'Agreed,' Fang told her, scraping the comb onto a clean napkin and inspecting it. 'The Queen's Guards will have found two drugged-up gangs and crates of stolen fae weapons by now, they'll have heard that we escaped with a stolen cart and the box. Depending on who's on the case, they may yet trace us to the inn. We'll get Tem cleaned, warmed and fed, then we go straight to New Cross tube, and hope Amber can get us to the fae enclave before we get eaten.'

'Fine,' sighed Nell. 'I packed some potions when I headed out to rescue you earlier, and I can always brew more as I go. I can gather a rudimentary first aid kit from Wulfric's stuff, and as long as I'm back by overmorrow, I shouldn't lose *that* much custom keeping the shop closed...'

Fang glared at her. '*You're* not coming.'

'Yes I am!'

'Nell, this isn't your problem.'

'It became my problem when my best friend was brought bleeding to my door—'

'We're not friends!'

'This, again. We *are* friends, you're always hanging out at my shop.'

'That's just a mutually beneficial arrangement. I helped you, you helped me.'

'Yeah. I help you. I patched you up, I found you that warehouse and then I swooped in and saved you from the gang.'

'Meaning, you've done enough.' Fang kept his voice soft and low so as not to startle the child, but his tone was firm. 'You've certainly more than worked off any debt you might feel you owe me for helping you out with that hold-up when we met—'

'Meaning,' argued Nell, matching his quiet, placid tone with her own, 'that you need me. I'm not going to let my friend get hurt. I'm not going to let that nice Lazare fellow get hurt. I'm certainly not going to let a dragon get hurt. But it's not even really about you three anymore, is it? It's about her, now.' Nell nodded to the little girl. 'I am going, because you need my help to get that kid back safe and fast. And I can't not help a fae in need.'

'Because you're a sentimental fool,' muttered Fang.

'Because I'm Welsh,' she told him, emphatically. 'Were it not for the magicals' help all those years ago, the English invasion would have succeeded. Magicals live Deepside in England partly because of concessions given by the Dragon Queen to ensure peace and stability for Wales. My people owe magicals an eternal debt, for over three centuries of freedom and sovereignty.'

'I thought the Welsh King paid Queen Redthroat back for that,' said Fang. 'Gifting her huge chunks of Wales, the whole city of Llanelli as her seat of power...'

'In return for our peace and liberty? A few square miles of land here and there only scratch the surface of what we owe the magicals. So I *will* go with you, Fang. It's a matter of national duty.'

Fang stared at her for a moment, then averted his gaze, inspecting the comb scrapings on the napkin again. 'Good grief. Well, if you want to play the patriotic Welshwoman in spite of living in London these past six years then I suppose I can't stop you. Even though your life will be at risk. Even though you'll lose trade with your shop shuttered. *Now* who's the "serial self-saboteur"?'

'Still you,' argued Nell. She paused for a moment, before lowering her voice even further. 'He's nice, you know. He could be good for you, if you weren't so... *you* about it.'

'Shut up,' whispered Fang. 'What did you say to him?'

'Just gave him fair warning for what you might try to pull. I know your method. Getting rid of a lovely admirer by going way too fast to "get it over with".'

Fang snorted. 'They only ever want one thing.'

'Then why are you always the one who pushes for that "one thing" as quickly as possible, only to show them the door? You just bring it on yourself so that nobody else has the chance to do it to you. But it means they don't have the chance for anything else, either. It's selfish. And cowardly.'

'Shut *up*.'

'What are you talking about?' asked Tem, her eyes still closed.

Fang shot Nell another glare, and she offered a little cringe of apology. She hadn't counted on the kid listening to every word they were saying.

'Nothing,' Fang told her quickly. 'Just a silly argument.'

'A friendly argument,' added Nell, just as hurriedly. 'It's normal for friends to talk like this, we're best friends.'

'What's a friend?' asked the girl.

Nell looked at Fang again. Fang met her gaze, his expression full of sorrow.

The door to the back room burst open, making everyone jump. '*Et voila*,' crowed Lazare, holding a plate. 'Fae food! Hot buttered fruit toast, with roast acorns and mallow cheese, picked fresh from the yard out back! And before you start, Fang, it's what fae like to eat, I'm not just feeding her weeds...' He noticed what Fang was doing with his comb. 'Oh. You're using my best beard comb to... eurgh.'

'To check for parasites, yes,' replied Fang. 'I'm not sending her back to her people itching and infested.'

'What's a parrot site?' asked Tem.

'Creepy crawlies, but the good news is, you don't have any.' Fang finished untangling the girl's hair and tried to toss the comb back to Lazare.

'Keep it,' Lazare told him, handing the plate to Tem. 'You could do with a comb of your own, with all that hair. It looks really nice when you brush it back a bit.'

Fang fidgeted with his own hair, scowling and pushing it forward to cover more of his face.

'I got soap,' called Wulfric from the hallway beyond, 'and... hey! Who ate all the pig's heart?'

'Sorry,' called Amber, sounding as if her mouth was full, and not actually sorry at all.

*

Fae weapons, out there on Honkensby's streets. There was no need to panic, absolutely no need to panic. She was just going to have to right this wrong as quickly as she possibly could. The dock was cordoned off, her birds were already questioning the dock workers and transporting the Hapennys and the Custards to the Tower for a rather more intensive questioning – the type of questioning that involved thumbs accidentally falling into screws, and fingernails going missing. Her first priority was to get all of the missing magical weaponry out of criminal hands before they could be used to endanger the public. Her second priority was to get the weapons into the hands of the correct authorities before the matter spiralled into some sort of diplomatic incident.

She would have to report this back to Elizabeth's court soon, of course, and when she did, it would be ideal if she could already have the missing crate and its contents secured to hand straight over. She would definitely need a more solid lead than 'we think it's got something to do with a vampire and a hot guy called John'. She wondered how long she could hold off on reporting it. Maybe until evening. That gave her a few hours. She could solve this in a few hours, she was Captain Dame Isobel Honkensby.

'Dame Isobel!'

Oh. Her official court name. This was never a good sign. Lady Gertrude Flipperings wheeled overhead. Honkensby sighed to herself. Obviously Lady Gertrude was not going to perform the indignity of a dry landing in public. Honkensby took off to join her in the sky.

'I bring word from Her Majesty,' called Lady Gertrude, unnecessarily. Lady Gertrude was hardly going to leave the comfort of the court and fly down to the docks for anything less important than an urgent missive from the Queen, now was she?

'The court has been informed of your discovery,' Gertrude told her. 'The stolen artefacts.'

Oh, quack. She didn't have until the evening at all. This was what came of instilling her subordinates with the importance of filing reports swiftly and effectively, she supposed.

'How they were stolen on your watch is not the main priority of the court right now, Dame Isobel, so don't you fret,' Lady Gertrude told her. 'Their return to their rightful owners is, however. This is now a diplomatic matter. All retrieved artefacts are to be delivered to Whitehall Palace immediately. The crown and her court will take it from there.'

'Understood. Sergeant Peanut is currently in command of the artefacts, I'll relay the order to her straight away.'

'And the remaining missing crate?' asked Gertrude. 'The one which, according to the sergeant's report, was stolen by a vampire, along with two masked humans and a dragon?'

'Captain?' Speak of the raven, Sergeant Peanut flapped over to join the mid-air discussion.

'Whatever it is, I'm sure it can wait until we swans have finished speaking,' huffed Gertrude.

'What news, Sergeant?' Honkensby asked Peanut, pointedly.

Peanut only dithered for a moment under Gertrude's disapproving glare. 'A breakthrough we believe, Captain,' she said quickly, as Honkensby gave approving nods for her to carry on. 'A cart matching the description was stabled at the Albany in Deptford but two hours ago. I was about to organise a party to fly up there right now, since you're so busy with swan matters, and...'

'I'll take the lead on this one, thank you Sergeant,' Honkensby told her. 'Lady Gertrude and I have finished our business, I can head there right now.'

Lady Gertrude opened her beak indignantly, then shut it again.

'I do hope you don't mind, Lady Gertrude,' Honkensby continued. 'Urgent Royal Guard business. Got to keep Upper London safe. You can tell the other courtiers that at this speed, my birds and I will likely have finished the case by nightfall.'

'When you do, ensure that all loot is sent for processing,' Gertrude told her.

'Of course.'

'*Whatever* loot it may be,' Gertrude emphasised. 'By order of the Queen.'

'Yes,' replied Honkensby, holding her beak so as not to add a sarcastic 'I heard you the first time'.

Without any sort of farewell pleasantry, Lady Gertrude turned on the wing and flapped away.

Honkensby rolled her eyes. The likes of Lady Gertrude were why she'd chosen law enforcement over a courtier role. Even though the pay wasn't as good and the hours were ridiculous. Well. That and the cephalophores. The Queen's court had far too many cephalophores for Honkensby's liking. One never knew where to look, when addressing someone who carried their head in their hands.

*

The lead at the Albany came good – it was indeed the stolen cart. The silver paint was a dead giveaway. It was a good turn up for the dockers, but finding it so quickly after it had been stabled was an even better turn up for Honkensby. It had been brought in anonymously, but a helpful passing alchemist in a deeply silly cape said he had recognised the man who had done so as a cook, who worked at a couple of inns nearby – the Pegasus, and the Moon and Werewolf. The Pegasus turned out to be a waste of time, the cook wouldn't be in for another two days. By the time Honkensby got to the Moon and Werewolf, it was late afternoon, and the inn was quiet. The proprietor welcomed them. It would have to be a vampire, wouldn't it? Honkensby didn't trust vampires one flap. It didn't help that this one had the wide, innocent eyed gaze of a small child, despite clearly being hundreds of years old. Honkensby asked him about his cook, knowing full well that she'd be told guilelessly that said cook was off and hadn't been seen all day.

'It's his day off,' said the vampire in guileless soprano tones. 'But I can rustle you something up if you're hungry, officer? Nice bit of bread and seeds?'

Honkensby sniffed. It smelled strange at the inn. Cutting through the usual pubby smell of stale alcohol and tobacco ash was a sweet note of lilac.

Wulfric noticed the swan's beak in the air and gave her a dimpled smile. 'Quiet day today. I actually had time for my monthly bath in the lull.'

There was something off about the place. Honkensby could feel it in her gut. For a moment, she couldn't put her flipper on it. She pushed into the back room while the vampire wasn't looking. There it was: silver. Just the slightest traces of silver paint, on the floor, but it had been enough to set the magic in her on edge ever since she'd got here. Now, why would an undead-friendly inn, owned by a vampire, have silver paint on the floor?

This was it. It had to be.

'Lock this place down, search it top to bottom. It's here!'

'What's here?' asked the vampire with that same infuriating false innocence.

Honkensby knew it wouldn't sound good if she admitted she wasn't entirely sure what she was looking for, besides 'something magic, something nicked', so she didn't tell him. She was aware that the optics of that weren't good. Nor were the optics of her officers detaining a popular local businessman who had the appearance of a sweet young boy and ransacking his inn on no more than a scrape of paint and a hunch, but she didn't do this job to be popular. Unfortunately, when vampires were involved, matters didn't just come down to optics and popularity.

There was an empty milk jug and recently used saucer in the pantry. This was completely normal for a pub pantry, but not a vampire's pantry after he'd sworn blind he'd barely had a customer all day. It smelled of honey. Honkensby didn't trust it. She was just about to call a constable to take it as evidence when the shadows descended in the pantry doorway. She looked up. A trio of vampires blocked her way.

'Kerridge, Yousefi and Grimm,' announced one of the three identically dressed vampires. He held out a card. 'Legal advisors, with the Mutual Aid Network of the Undead. We understand you are harassing our client on no charge? Tut tut, Captain.'

Honkensby ignored the card. 'Mr Wulfric is merely helping me with my enquiries, as I conduct a perfectly legal search for contraband materials, under the orders of Queen Elizabeth…'

'Ah, but you see,' said another of the vampire lawyers, 'while the Moon and Werewolf is indeed subject to Elizabeth's laws, Mr Wulfric himself remains under the legal and diplomatic protection of Queen Redthroat.'

'That doesn't mean he just gets to break my law!'

The three vampires gasped in unison. 'Are you baselessly accusing our client, a pillar of the community, of breaking the law?' The third vampire shook his head. 'What is your proof, Captain?'

She had none. A bit of paint, and a saucer – she was sure the saucer was a clue, she just didn't know how, yet. One by one, her team came back from searching the rooms of the pub, empty beaked. There was nothing. Even the stolen crate wasn't there. They eventually found its smashed shards in a nearby alley.

Honkensby swore to herself. The suspects weren't hiding after all. They must have already escaped. The New Cross tube, after all, was but a short walk away. She'd posted a couple of guards there when she'd started the search, but they could have already fled down there while she was wasting her time at the Pegasus. They must have snuck Deepside, where for all its many fraught dangers down there they might believe the long wing of Upper London's law couldn't reach them.

Honkensby took a deep, calming breath, and hung her Seal of the Upper Crown's Special Diplomatic Protection around her long neck.

Any thieves or villains who believed Captain Isobel Honkensby would shy away from pursuing a royally mandated case into the Deepside were, frankly, stupid. She just hoped they weren't stupid enough to get themselves killed first.

CHAPTER TEN
THE TUBE

'We're not leaving Wulfric in the gong, are we?' Nell asked with a frown.

They clustered around a food stall, all pretending to look particularly interested in the same sausage as three Royal Guards hurried past them on the other side of the street. It was the second set of guards to pass them in the direction of Wulfric's inn since they'd set out towards New Cross tube.

'Maybe,' admitted Amber, blithely. 'He'll bounce back, vampires always do.'

Lazare noted Tem's worried expression. 'He'll be fine. He has really good lawyers.'

With the guards out of view, the group turned away from the stall, to continue making their way as unobtrusively as possible through Upper Deptford's streets to New Cross Road.

'Are you not going to buy that sausage, then?' asked the stall-holder, irritably.

'Yeah,' added Amber, 'aren't we going to buy that sausage?'

Everyone looked at Nell, who sighed. 'Am I seriously the only one who has any money?'

'You did just insist on coming along to help us,' Fang reminded her.

Nell dug into her purse. 'I meant more rescuing you from danger and supplying cool potions than paying for everything, but fine.' She bought the sausage, and split it between herself, Lazare and a salivating Amber. Fang refused it, and Tem looked at it as if it were utterly alien.

Lazare had to remind himself that the Upperside must seem stranger to Tem than she seemed to them. For a being so 'dangerous' that criminal gangs had to keep her in a silver-lined crate, Tem appeared perfectly benign – sweet, even.

While he'd been warned since childhood never to trust what a fae made him see, he didn't believe that Tem was casting any sort of glamour over herself. Perhaps she was too young to be capable of doing so, or perhaps her fae magic was inhibited by being half-human. That was another thing about Tem – she looked *so* human. She could pass as human better than Lazare. She had no wings, no great horns, no luminescence, almost nothing that rumour had told him the fae possessed. The only things slightly non-human about her appearance were points to the tips of her ears, but those were easily covered with her freshly combed long, black hair. Her eyes were large and almost ink-black, but Fang's human eyes were no less dark. She had that same sad, tired, lost look to her as Fang did, too.

Tem really could pass as Fang's child, Lazare noted as he watched the little girl walking hand in hand with Fang. This was good, he told himself. It would help them avoid suspicion. At least, insofar as a small dragon and three foreigners – one with huge wings – could avoid suspicion while walking around with a little girl in clothes that absolutely did not fit her. Wulfric had tried his best, but even his smallest spare boots and breeches needed to be strapped up to keep them from falling down on the girl, his tunic and jerkin swamped her and every item of clothing was at least fifty years old.

Still, Fang was no less shabbily dressed. Perhaps people would assume they were a beggar and his child. All of this was moot in any case, since with every step they got closer to the New Cross tube, and once they'd taken the tube Deepside, they would no longer need to worry about passing as inconspicuous Upper Londoners, and would have to start passing as inconspicuous and inedible Deep Londoners, which would be much more difficult.

They turned a corner, and there it was. A sign read:

NEW CROSS TUBE
TO DEEP DEPTFORD AND DEEP GREENWICH
CAUTION: HERE BE DRAGONS

Lazare had been alarmed by the tubes when he'd first started living in London. He'd taken considerable diversions around them for the first year or so, unable to shake the sense of dread at walking past them, even seeing them. He'd grown more used to them during his decade of London living, but he still tended to hurry his pace when he passed one. You couldn't blame him. They were alarming looking things, to Uppersiders. Great holes dug into the sides of the road, fifteen feet in diameter, with sloping footpaths inside leading down, down, down into Deep London. The insides of the tubes flickered with lamplight day and night, giving off the impression of them leading down into fire. A second sign hung on the side of a building so as to be visible to any being coming up out of the tube, with arrows pointing the way to Upper Deptford, Upper Greenwich and Upper Southwark, along with reminders for Deepsiders:

UPPERSIDE LAW TO BE OBEYED AT ALL TIMES:
NO KILLING.
NO EATING ALIVE.
HUMAN/LIVESTOCK CORPSES TO BE EATEN
WITH EXPRESS PERMISSION ONLY.
BY ORDER OF THEIR MAJESTIES ELIZABETH
REGINA & REDTHROAT THE INVINCIBLE.

As Lazare watched, a grey dragon around the size of a dray horse emerged from the tube, glanced at the sign reminding him of the laws, rolled his eyes and flapped away, to do whatever it was horse-sized dragons enjoyed doing on a daytrip to Upper London.

'Well,' announced Amber needlessly, 'here we are. Any of you lot been down one of these before?'

The others all shook their heads.

'Probably for the best, it's totally legal to kill and eat you people down there. Good job you've got a dragon guide with you, eh?' She paused. 'Cards on the table though, I absolutely can't protect you guys from getting eaten down there. If you're attacked by anything bigger than I am, I'll be losing that fight, and I don't know if you've noticed, but I'm on the small side for a dragon. I just know my way around really well.'

'Brilliant,' Fang's voice dripped with sarcasm, 'thanks for your help.'

Nell slapped his arm. 'Attitude! Miss Amber isn't obliged to help us; she's being kind. And, instead of waiting til we got here and then complaining, *some* of us thought ahead to this problem and came up with a plan.'

'What's your plan?' Fang asked her.

'A smell,' she said, proudly.

'Of course.'

'Well – a smell for me and little Tem, since you and Lazare already smell "off" to Deepsiders – at least, that's what Amber and Wulfric told me.'

'They do smell off,' Amber told her, matter-of-factly. 'No offence, gents.'

Lazare sighed. He had already taken offence to Amber telling him he smelled 'off' once, he wasn't ready to rescind that offence yet.

'I don't want to smell bad,' fretted Tem.

'It's just a disguise, like your hat – you'll smell no worse than Fang,' Nell soothed her, 'that won't be so bad, will it?'

Tem just looked from Fang to Nell, her expression etched with anxiety and a desperation not to say something that could hurt Fang's feelings. This was fair – the man still smelled of old brandy, blood, and the sweat and grime of the dockyard fight.

'You'll smell no worse than Lazare, I mean,' added Nell, smoothly. Tem looked relieved.

'I don't smell *that* bad,' grumbled Fang.

'It's not a "bad" smell,' insisted Amber, 'it's just "off", I don't want to eat either of you.'

'It'll be due to their curse,' Nell said, taking out a vial. 'It's not the same as an undead scent, but it's close enough for Deepsiders to consider you off limits for eating. A few years back, I finally found a way to mix a pretty good approximation of the fresh zombie scent. Mostly for the human spouses of the recently turned.' She opened the stopper. Lazare recognised the smell – it was the scent Kit was always trying to hide. It wasn't a bad smell as such, just... a little off.

'And you just happened to pack that when you came to rescue us from the docks, did you?' asked Fang.

'Oh, I prepared for almost every eventuality, I didn't know what you boys were up against,' Nell told them, cheerfully. 'My bag is *so* heavy – you're welcome to take turns carrying it for me if you like.'

Tem took a cautious sniff of the vial. 'I have to lie that I'm a zombie or I'll get eaten?'

'Nobody would eat you,' Fang told her, gently, 'but we think it would be easier if we... played pretend, until we get you home to your family.'

'What's "play pretend"?'

Fang blinked and frowned. 'Um. Do the fae have actors, like Lazare? People who pretend to be someone else for a while? Just for fun?'

Lazare's acting career was *not* 'just for fun', thank you very much, but Lazare was hardly going to pick Fang up on that right now. He exchanged concerned glances with Fang over the girl's seeming bewilderment at any mention of fun, friendship or play.

'I don't know,' she told them quietly, sadly. 'Mummy says, "we have to mind our own".'

Fang nodded. 'And we'll get you back to your mummy as fast as we can.'

Nell put the zombie scent on herself and, after letting Tem check that it didn't smell too bad, put it on the child as well. Fang adjusted the too-big hat on the girl's head to make sure it definitely covered her fae ears. Lazare girded himself to venture Deepside for the first time… And froze. There was a new problem.

'Er, guys?' said Amber. 'New problem.'

As they'd been discussing zombie smells and actors, two Royal Guards had approached from above. They landed now, at the entrance to the tube. Nell hurriedly got a large map of the city out of her bag and they all crowded around it, pretending to read it, obscuring their faces and hoping to give off 'clueless tourist' vibes.

'Are they leaving?' asked Fang in a whisper.

Lazare snuck a glance. The two huge raven guards most definitely were not leaving. They were positioning themselves on either side of the gate to the tube entrance, to inspect everybody who passed through. He told the others as such, and learned new swear words in Cathayan and Welsh for his trouble.

'What do we do?' asked Amber.

'Where's the next nearest tube?' asked Fang.

'You're literally looking at a map,' Nell reminded him.

Fang squinted at the map until Lazare pointed out London Bridge tube on it for him.

'London Bridge,' Lazare told him, helpfully. 'Few miles.'

'Fine. Come on, then.'

Fang hauled Tem up in his arms and as a group they began walking west, as nonchalantly as they could muster. Unfortunately, it wasn't particularly possible to be very nonchalant when your group includes a dragon and a tall, striking man with leather wings. Lazare risked a side glance at the guards, and saw to his dismay that both were watching his group with suspicion.

'Oh, they're going to tail us,' noted Amber, quietly. 'Do we split up? Do we run?'

'That'll attract more attention,' Nell reasoned.

'They can't tail us all the way to London Bridge though, surely?' Fang sounded worried.

'Fang, they're birds. They probably have eyes in the sky already. If we don't get inside or underground quickly, they'll have one of their airborne intelligence divisions lock on to us and we'll never get shot of them.'

'Excuse me?' said a voice.

Should they stop? It was only as Lazare snuck another glance behind him that he noticed the voice hadn't been a guard trying to stop them, but some man trying to get the guards' attention.

'Excuse me, officer?'

Lazare elbowed Fang in the rib to alert him. The guards were still trying to keep an eye on the group, but the man was loudly distraught and doing a commendable accidental job of distracting both guards, as well as a considerable number of passers-by. Lazare noticed the man was wearing the particularly shiny cloak of an alchemist. Maybe they weren't quite so useless after all, even if this one's usefulness was by no means deliberate.

'It's my purse, it's been stolen,' wailed the man.

Lazare nudged Amber with his foot to turn her back towards New Cross tube. Nell was already walking quickly, quietly and purposefully, straight at the tube entrance.

'Can't you just make some more gold?' asked one of the guards.

'I'm not allowed, you *know* we're not allowed to make gold, do you mock me, Officer?'

'I do not mock you, Master Alchemist.'

'Alchemists accidentally crash *one* regional economy *one time* and we never hear the end of it!'

'Can't you make silver and then sell it for gold?'

'You *do* mock me!'

They reached the gate. Both guards were still dealing with the increasingly loud and agitated alchemist. All attention was on him. Quietly, Nell opened the gate for the others to pass, before slipping through herself and shutting it. Lazare would have loved to have made a dramatic speech or something – bid farewell to the sky and the Upper world, while embracing the enticing mysteries of the Deepside city that lay but a short stroll ahead of them. He didn't get to do any of that. He kept his head down, his mouth shut and his gait at a fast walk as he followed the others down the sloping tube. The murky, foggy natural light of day gave way quickly to the shadow of the tube's rough carved ceiling, and within a matter of half a minute, he was in a world of gloom and flickering orange lamplight. He passed a painted line on the tube's walls running horizontally, level with the surface. This, he knew, was the boundary – the line thirteen yards below the ground which marked where Upper London ended and the Deepside began. When the line was up to his shoulders, there was another sign.

DEEP DEPTFORD
DEEPSIDE LAWS APPLY
DRAGONS ARE OPERATING IN THIS AREA
THE EMBASSY OF REDTHROAT THE
INVINCIBLE BEARS NO RESPONSIBILITY
FOR ANY DAMAGE TO HUMANS ON THESE
PREMISES

Lazare was hit with a horrible feeling that he was never going to see the sky again. He really wished he'd been able to make a speech.

*

'Are they following us?'

'For the last time, no.'

Lazare couldn't quite breathe a sigh of relief. This tube was very quiet. Even though they weren't being followed by the guards, it was still eerie. The sign reminding them of Deepside law had bothered him, and they still weren't even in Deep London proper yet. There were shadowy shapes approaching them. Two human-ish figures, with tell-tale wings. Vampires. Deepside vampires, going by Deepside rules. Every ounce of Lazare's natural drive for self-preservation was screaming at him to turn around and go back up top where it was nice and illegal to exsanguinate people. He knew he couldn't do that. He knew that, once his group got down to the end of the tube, they'd be faced with beings far more dangerous than a couple of ambling vampires. He drew himself close to Fang and Nell, opened his own wings a little, and hoped that their various smells really were as off-putting as Amber and Nell said.

One of the vampires didn't even look at them, just kept her gaze blankly, awkwardly ahead. Her companion gave Fang, Nell and Tem a curious side-glance, and sniffed.

Lazare kept his eyes forward while watching the vampire anxiously with his peripheral vision. The vampire sniffed again, pulling his top lip up a little over his sharp front teeth, to taste the scent of them.

Fang stopped, fists bunched in anticipation for trouble. 'Can we help you?'

That vampire regarded them for another horrible few seconds, before coming to a silent decision. 'Not sunny up there, is it?' He asked Lazare, in falsely friendly tones.

Lazare shook his head. 'Plenty of fog cover.'

'Perfect, cheers.' He gave them another curious glance, and strode away to join his companion on their way to the Upperside.

Lazare gave a small exhale of relief. He felt as if they'd just passed a test, if only just.

They continued down the tube. The few Deepsiders who passed them paid them no heed, besides the occasional surreptitious sniff. After ten minutes or so of descent, the decline of the tube levelled off, and the tunnel ended with a large brick archway, beyond which lay something vast, and dark, and dancing with torchlight flames that dwindled into tiny spots of fluttering orange in the distance.

They passed through the archway, and Deep Deptford opened up ahead of them. Lazare couldn't help but stop and stare for a moment – he noticed Nell had done the same, and even Fang, for all of his travel-worn weariness at the world, took a moment to drink in the strange new sight of the subterranean city of London's undead, dragons and assorted magical beings.

CHAPTER ELEVEN
BELOW

By the acre, Deep London was actually a little larger than its Upperside counterpart. It needed to be big because, even though Deep London had a population of around half that of Upper London, many of its inhabitants were dragons, and even commonplace dragons could be up to twenty feet long. One waddled through into the tube, ignoring the group. A bottle-green, twelve feet long, fangs glistening in the torchlight of the city. Was it any wonder that Amber, with her tiny three-foot frame, was always scavenging desperately for murder victims and roadkill on the Upperside?

The city was younger than Upper London – like all of Deep England, Nell informed them with some pride, it had been created as part of the three-hundred-year-old peace treaty. The streets were wider in Deep London – to accommodate the larger residents, Lazare assumed, and the cobbles were in good condition. Far fewer of this city's residents relied on horse and cart to transport themselves and supplies. Lazare noticed that the buildings were largely made of stone and slate, not wood and thatch – sensible, given the fiery nature of dragon lungs, and the dependence on torchlight in general.

There were some shafts of natural light streaming down from holes in the high, cavernous rock ceiling, so that trees and crops could be grown in areas below. These holes were of no surprise to Lazare – all Upper Londoners knew of the holes dotted around in Upper parks and squares, fenced off to prevent anyone falling in. Lazare knew from undead acquaintances that the light patches were similarly fenced off on the Deepside, to prevent crop theft and, vitally, to prevent a vampire wandering in and getting caught in a beam of sunlight. It was as illegal for any of the Deepside's many winged residents to take a shortcut to the Upperside through the light holes as it was for an Upper Londoner to throw anything down them. Everyone in Upper London knew the story of a builder who had used a nearby light hole as a means of dumping some rotten planks of wood and caused a major diplomatic incident. It was a fatal mistake, although in that case it had thankfully only been lethal for the builder himself, on the grounds that it is impossible to survive when one's head is being used as a decorative and educational finial atop a post in the middle of Upper Cheapside. Everybody steered clear of the light holes now.

There was no sign of the Thames, since the ceilings of Deep London were dug beneath the river, but its many subterranean tributaries provided ample fresh water supply to the underground city. Indeed, to the west, Lazare could just about make out the narrow banks of the River Peck. He could see quite far from where they had emerged, since the tube's exit was on a high platform just above the rooftops of the buildings. He could even make out, far in the distance, the thick, well-lit pinnacle of rock jutting down from the carved ceiling that denoted another tube entrance – London Bridge, probably.

New Cross tube's platform had a landing area marked off for winged residents, and a steep set of stairs for tube users without wings to access the street level below. It was only when Lazare had struggled down almost all of the dizzying steps that he realised he could have just flown down carrying Tem and raised no suspicions at all – in fact, as Amber pointed out after waiting for them from her comfortable landing spot, now they were Deepside, it actually looked more glaring to have a winged man attempt the stairs than fly. *Bof.*

The streets of Deep Deptford seemed utterly mundane. Lazare had been expecting something stranger than this, but the real strangeness was in how normal it was, how like the London he was so used to. Ghouls, zombies, vampires, dragons and the like got on with their days, continuing to ignore the group. So far, so good.

'Right,' said Amber, 'so the bad news is, I've never actually been to the fae enclave, I'm not even sure precisely where it is.'

Fang sighed. 'Your one job is to be our guide.' He glanced at Nell. 'Can we get another dragon?'

'Stop being horrible,' Nell told him.

'Shan't.'

'Shall. You're setting a bad example.'

She nodded towards Tem. Fang tried and failed to hide a sheepish expression, which rather suited him.

'They're secretive folk,' continued Amber, defensively, 'but as I was about to say, the good news is, I know that it's roughly the other side of Redthroat's Embassy, and since there's a fae-folk ambassador, that's probably the safest place to take her. Even if I could take you directly to the gates of the fae enclave, they wouldn't just let us stroll in, not even with a dragon in the party. The embassy's a different story, dragons are in and out of there all the time. I went there last year to get my passport renewed.'

'Dragons have passports?' asked Lazare.

'Course we do. Upperside is literally a foreign country.' She thought about this for a moment. 'So, if anyone checks your papers, tell them you turned undead within the past six weeks so you're within the window to get your status changed from "human".'

Ugh, Lazare hadn't thought about needing to get all his paperwork changed. If he survived this but remained cursed, he'd have to get loads of forms from the French consulate. Maybe Fang had a point about them being better off dead.

'Well, take us to the embassy, then,' said Fang, 'since you think you're so high and mighty you can get us an audience with the ambassador…' he trailed off, noting Nell's expression, and then casting a guilty little glance at the child in his arms, taking in everything he said, '…please.'

'Yeah, so that's the bad news,' replied Amber.

'You already told us the bad news!'

'This is the bad news part two, then,' the dragon told them, smoothly. 'The embassy's a bit of a trudge – a little past Deep Westminster.'

'Westminster?' Fang sighed.

Amber gave them a little shrug. 'Deep London's big – what can I say? Since we have to go on foot it'll take a while, so we may as well get a wriggle on. Come on!'

Fang opened his mouth, grumpily, then closed it suddenly as he met eyes with Tem, and tried again. 'Thank you, Amber.'

They made their way through the streets of Deep Deptford in relative quiet. The buildings were wider, squatter and more spaced out in the deep, which led to a less claustrophobic atmosphere, but had the downside of making Lazare feel more exposed, and generally taking much longer to walk anywhere along the oversized streets. Walking in one big defensive clump looked too suspect, so they spread out a little, with Amber taking the lead, Fang in the middle carrying Tem and Lazare forming an unobtrusive rear guard with Nell, a few yards behind.

'So,' said Nell quietly, after a while.

Lazare could already tell what this was going to be about. 'I didn't sleep with him.'

'Oh, I noticed,' Nell replied. 'After all, you're still here.'

Lazare bristled at that. 'I don't like what you're insinuating. Do you suggest I don't care about the curse? About the child? That I just wish to seduce a man for one night and then be on my merry way? After everything I've been through so far? Getting marked with wings? Assaulted? Shot? Risking if not death then horrendous, eternal injury, and now braving getting eaten in Deep London? What would happen to someone who cannot die were he to be eaten? It doesn't bear thinking about, yet here I am.'

Nell sighed. 'Sorry. I came across as rude, didn't I?'

Lazare grunted an affirmation at that. 'I can see why you and he are friends.'

'It's not you who I'm worried will push a good man so far out of bed that he can never get him back,' Nell said, jerking her chin towards Fang, 'it's him.'

Lazare frowned at the back of Fang's head. 'He never struck me as a one-night stand cad. For starters, he's too obnoxious up front. I've met a lot of cads, and they're all more... well, you've met Kit Marlowe. All smiles and charm, until the second he pops it back in his codpiece and then you're out on your rear because he's got an important folio to finish. That's not Fang.'

'Well, in a way you're right about that,' Nell conceded. 'Fang doesn't smile about it. When he tried to sleep with me, he made it sound like it was some chore he was begrudgingly getting out of the way for me so I could get on with my life without him.'

'He tried to sleep with you, too?'

'I think he noticed we were becoming friends and panicked,' said Nell. 'Declining a night of passion doesn't come naturally to me, but by then I knew him well enough to be aware acceptance would be a terrible decision. Besides, he seemed so sad about it. It shouldn't be sad.'

'Right?' Lazare agreed. 'It was the same with me. He tried to kiss me and he just looked miserable. I would have said no to that self-pitying puckery even if you hadn't decided to be weird with me about it.'

'I wasn't being weird, I was warning you. Because, for all his many, many faults, so help me, I do love that ridiculous man, and I think you'd be good for him. And, I like you.'

He smiled at that and gave her a little bow. '*Merci.* I try.'

'Didn't want you immediately pushed away by his nonsense,' continued Nell, 'leaving you stuck alone with that curse, and me stuck alone with that mope.'

Lazare's gaze drifted towards Fang. He'd already managed to make Lazare's spare shirt absolutely filthy with mud and blood, and he was still as rumpled as ever. He was a haunted house of a man, every mucky smear and unkind sneer a warning sign upon the wall, a ghostly howl of 'beware'; every taciturn huff a locked door to a cellar of shadowy mysteries.

Yet, as Lazare watched, he saw Fang gently adjust Tem's hat to stop it falling down over her eyes. He spoke to her with soft words that Lazare couldn't make out. His expression was open and warm. The haunted house had melted away into a welcoming home in front of Tem. Lazare had been an actor since boyhood, he knew artifice when he saw it. He didn't believe he was seeing it now. Fang's demeanour didn't seem like it had been painted on out of kindness, to keep the child from being afraid. Tem said something to Fang, and Fang smiled at her. Lazare realised he hadn't seen Fang smile like that before. There was no falseness to the smile. It went all the way into his eyes, and it was soft, with crinkles at the edges like early morning pillow lines.

Fang glanced over his shoulder, noticed Lazare watching him, and the façade went back up. Lazare offered him a winning smile. Fang scowled and went back to concentrating on the dragon ahead of him.

Lazare turned his grin to Nell. 'He's not so bad, for an annoying mope. *You* let him into your life, after all.'

Nell returned his smile, with a little shrug. 'It's more exciting when he's around, and not just because he's always getting beaten up. I could be keeping shop right now, yet here I am on a quest in the Deep. What's life without a little danger?'

'Or, dare I suggest, a little self-sabotage?'

Nell gave Lazare a pointed look. 'Perhaps that makes three of us.'

Lazare laughed lightly, earning himself another over the shoulder glower from Fang.

'I do believe I like you too, Miss Nell,' Lazare told her.

'*Diolch*,' smiled Nell. 'Although I'm not going to sleep with *you*, either.'

'I didn't ask!'

'No harm in making it plain.'

They walked quietly for a while longer, until Tem shuffled uncomfortably and whispered something urgent into Fang's ear.

'Er,' he said, awkwardly, 'oh mighty dragon guide, is there anywhere a little girl might go to use the privy?'

'You're in luck,' Amber told them. 'Every Deep London Borough has public houses of easement for the human-shaped and beast-shaped alike. It was the cat-siths idea – you know how fastidious cats are with doings.'

'Wonderful potted history of your sewage system,' Fang said, dryly. 'Where is it? She's only young, so every request for the privy is immediately an emergency.'

'Just up to the left,' Amber told them, nodding to a building further along the thoroughfare.

Nell lifted Tem from Fang's arms. 'I'll take her. I have to go, myself.'

She marched towards the house of easement with the urgency that came naturally from being in the company of a small child who needs to go. Amber followed after them, announcing that if the other girls were going, she may as well. Lazare sauntered up to Fang as the two men took a more leisurely stroll over to wait by the door.

'Would you object horribly if I asked you a personal question?' enquired Lazare.

'I know for a fact you're about to ask it whether I object or not,' sighed Fang.

'Are you a dad?'

Fang just gave him an incredulous, horrified look.

'No mystery tragic family you've come all the way from Cathay to find, or save, or even get away from?' Lazare continued.

'No,' Fang told him. 'Not that I'm aware of, at least.'

'Really?'

'Really! It's the sort of thing a man would remember!'

'Then how do you explain how you're so ludicrously good with Tem?'

'I'm not. She's just a small, scared person who needs to get back home. I'm being kind. I *can* do "kind".'

'No little brothers or sisters you had to care for back home?'

'Well, of course there were, we were…' Fang cut himself off, suddenly. 'I have no family. I haven't, for some time now.'

This was obviously a touchy subject. Admittedly, it seemed most personal subjects were touchy as far as Fang was concerned, but Lazare had a feeling he really needed to drop this one for now.

'What was Nell talking to you about?' asked Fang, after a brief, awkward silence.

'Oh, just about how she's worried your addiction to self-sabotage might break my poor little innocent heart,' Lazare told him with a smile.

Fang scoffed.

'She thinks I would be, and I quote, "good for you",' Lazare added, surprised by his own pride in the statement.

'You two are still thinking in the long term,' said Fang. 'That's extremely misguided of you both. Once Tem is back with her mother, I'll ask the fae if this curse was cast by their stolen magic and if so, find out how to break it. And then, we die. You're welcome to have one of your undead friends on call to turn you in that instance, so that you can carry on as a full vampire or zombie or what have you. But I intend to just die. Life is pain, and another few hundred years of it is the last thing I need. Therefore – as I believe I told you before – you and I have no future together for me to ruin. I'm not trying to break any hearts, here. I'm trying to do you a kindness.'

Lazare watched Fang's expression, carefully. 'You've had your own heart broken. Haven't you?'

Fang didn't meet his gaze. 'Shut up.'

He may as well have thrown Lazare a parade full of dancing girls carrying banners with 'The Frenchman's Right' embroidered on them.

'Who was it? Who hurt you?' Lazare asked. 'I would relish the chance to give them a piece of my mind, assuming they don't already rue such a silly mistake.'

Fang did meet Lazare's gaze at that. His eyes were bright with angry tears.

'I said, shut *up*!'

Too fresh, Lazare. Too fresh and too far. 'Apologies,' he said. And, he meant it. *Merde.* So, the whole 'haunted' thing wasn't *all* an act.

One thing about haunted houses was, it was never the house's fault that it was haunted. It was just a vessel, into which the ghosts of years of sadness were poured and trapped. Lazare watched out of the corner of his eye as Fang concentrated on blinking away the tears without letting a single telltale drop fall. He wanted to say something. He wanted to dispel Fang's ghosts. He wanted to scoop the broken shards of Fang back up together, and stick them into an approximation of what they'd once been. But how does one go about removing ghosts from a house that wants to cling to being haunted? The problem was, Lazare told himself, that poetic as his thoughts of Fang were, they kept comparing him to an object, a possession, and he wasn't a house or a broken vase, he was a person. And people were more complicated than that.

'They've got *paper* in there,' came a loud, Welsh voice, breaking Lazare from his thoughts.

'In the privy?' asked Lazare, confused. 'You mean, pamphlets to read in case it takes a while?'

Nell shook her head, passing Tem back to Fang. 'For wiping!' She sounded scandalised, and indeed she might, as far as Lazare was concerned.

'There's nothing strange about that,' muttered Fang, defensively.

The others stared at him. People from Cathay used *paper*? It wasn't enough to put Lazare off him but still – eurgh. The reactions only made Fang all the more defensive. He passed Tem back to Nell.

'Well, if there's paper for a change on this uncivilised island, I may as well go myself.'

CHAPTER TWELVE
Bed (Singular)

'And nobody suspicious headed down the tube?' asked Honkensby. 'Nobody matching the description?'

The two guards at the tube entrance glanced at one another nervously.

'Iff'n you please, Captain,' said one, 'the description is merely "a vampire of reasonable height", and quite a lot of vampires use this tube.'

Honkensby sighed. 'And what of the victim-slash-accomplice? A human, or possibly a zombie, possibly Turkish, reportedly gorgeous and possibly called John?'

'A lot of zombies using it today too,' admitted the guard, 'several named John – it's a common name. Not sure I'd describe any as "gorgeous".'

'Not sure about Turks, either,' added the second guard. 'And, I wouldn't be able to gauge a human on its attractiveness because it's all subjective, Ma'am.'

Honkensby deflated a little more. 'No fae magic, no beasts? No silver paint?'

Both guards shook their heads.

'Nobody would bring silver down a tube, Captain,' said the first guard. 'That stuff gives magicals the heebie-jeebies.'

'We had an earful about silver from that quacking alchemist,' sighed the second guard. 'Pardon my language, Captain. Bleating on about getting robbed, wasting our time. You know how alchemists can be.'

Honkensby was beginning to regret not stationing guards at some of the other tubes as well. 'You truly saw nothing untowards being taken through the tube all afternoon?'

'No, Captain,' replied the first guard. 'But... well... permission to conjecture?'

Honkensby raised a wing slightly to indicate the guard could go ahead.

'If it's fae magic we were looking out for, well, they cast glamours. They could parade a whole procession of terrible beasts in front of our eyes all day if they so wished, and if it were their will, we would not see nor hear any of it.'

Honkensby blinked, taking this in. The guard was right, of course.

'Why, they could be doing it right now for all we know,' added the guard, cheerfully.

Great. That was all Honkensby needed to hear.

'Thank you for your time,' she sighed, and with a flap, hopped over the gate and began to descend the tube tunnel.

'Does this mean we're relieved of guard duty, Captain?' the second guard called after her. 'My claws hurt.'

The guards watched the flap of her feathers as she disappeared down into the tube, and exchanged a glance.

'Best take that as a "no", then.'

*

Amber had not been exaggerating about the length of the walk to Redthroat's Embassy. The light filtering through the sky holes from Upper London was starting to dim as they passed beneath the Thames into Deep Blackfriars and Tem was drooping in Fang's arms. None of them had any idea how well she'd been able to rest, locked in that disgusting crate like an animal. Fang seemed tired as well, he hadn't been able to shake that hungover air to him all day. The bandage on his injured leg had developed a dark, wet spot on it and he was limping considerably, even after letting Lazare carry the child for a while. Lazare could feel his own injuries from the fight earlier that day beginning to really throb. Worse still, passing vampires were starting to give them very unsettling glances. Many of them were giving the group lingering sniffs of appraisal, and Lazare swore he saw one smack her lips while looking at Fang's wound. 'Slightly off' or not, Lazare worried that the smell of his and Fang's blood was painting an increasingly large and vibrant target on them all. He had no way to know how well Nell's decoy scent would hold up against so many scrutinous vampire nostrils.

'Gentlemen,' said Nell, 'I'm calling it. You two need to have those wounds re-dressed, and I need to sleep off last night's intensive fact finding.'

'You mean, your night of passion with the docker,' grumbled Fang, still trying to limp on.

'Same thing,' Nell told him, cheerily.

Fang continued to dogmatically hobble along, stubborn as a particularly beautiful mule. 'If you guys want to rest, carry on but I'm getting this little girl home to her mother.'

'Fang, stop,' called Nell. 'You're being ridiculous, what use are you to Tem if you give yourself a fever or can't walk past Holborn?'

Fang came to a ragged, grudging halt.

'Fine. We can take a short rest. Amber, where can we sleep for a few hours?'

'We're actually pretty close to my nest,' Amber told them, yawning.

'And that has room for all of us to tend our wounds and rest up, does it?' Fang asked.

'Not even close, it's a five-foot hole in a roof,' said Amber. 'But the building it's in has lodgings for visiting undead and the like. They'll do you a deal if you're only staying overnight – most of their clientele only want to sleep mornings. You know, because they're vampires.'

She led them towards a rather shabby building, built at around twice the usual dimensions of an Upper London house. It dwarfed Amber's stunted stature even more than usual. There were deep gouges a third of the way up the wooden door, which at first seemed troubling until it became clear they were Amber's own scratch marks, to get attention from the people indoors. After a few seconds of the dragon scratching at the door, it was opened by an ogress in patched-up clothes. She gazed wearily at the exhausted, bleeding group at her door.

'Amber? What waifs and strays are these?'

'Some friends, Chicory,' said Amber, hurriedly. 'Recently turned.'

Chicory noted their wounds with apprehension. 'You in trouble?'

'A little, Madame,' breezed Lazare, 'but we are on a mission to put said trouble to an end, and will certainly be too busy sleeping in your beautiful home, should you allow us, to create anymore trouble here.'

'They got in a fight,' added Nell. 'I patched them up, I need to re-patch them. You clearly understand the art of good stitching yourself.' She indicated to Chicory's hand-patched skirt. 'Beautiful needlework from a beautiful hand – may I ask if there's a Mister Chicory? Or are you… self-sufficient?' Nell waggled her eyebrows in a way that made even Lazare feel out of his depth in the flirting department.

'Stop it, the pair of you,' grumbled Fang. 'I'm surrounded by libidinous idiots.' He addressed the ogress. 'We have a child, she needs rest. We'll pay you. Well – Nell will pay you. And we'll be gone by dawn. I trust that's acceptable.'

Chicory visibly relaxed at somebody being forthright with her, instead of trying to flirt their way in. It was only at that point that Lazare noticed the copper wedding band on the ogress's finger.

'Fine,' she sighed. 'For Amber's sake, and the kiddiewink. But,' and here she addressed just Fang, indicating to Lazare and Nell, 'could you get those two to be less… weird?'

'I would if I could,' huffed Fang.

Chicory's lodging house was basic, but it was clean and it was warm. Nell grumbled and got out a few extra pennies that nobody had asked her to pay, so that as well as board for the night they could have hot water for their wounds, and a hot meal. None of them had to pay for the ink, quill and paper Chicory set down in front of Tem as they waited to eat. They were merely gruffly told it was to keep the child busy so she wouldn't 'cause havoc' and an adult was to ensure she didn't spill anything.

Tem scratched away carefully at the paper until a bowl of pottage was put down in front of her. She gazed at the steaming bowl warily.

'It's good,' Lazare told her. 'Mostly vegetables and barley. My daddy used to make something similar in winter months, growing up. Only, it was better. Because it was French.'

'What's "daddy"?' asked Tem.

Oh. Lazare's heart hurt for the child a little more.

'Is it like a mummy?' she added.

'That depends. But, mine was. He looked after me just like *Mamman*. Cuddles. Stories.'

'Licking you clean after you've hatched,' added Amber through her fish heads.

'If I got scared at night he'd hold my hand til I fell asleep,' Lazare continued. wistfully. 'I should write to him more.'

Tem started eating. 'I would write to my daddy if I had a daddy,' she announced with a full mouth. 'And, if I could write. I do good drawings, though! I drawed this.'

She held up the piece of paper. On it were four stick figure people, one with wings, and something that looked like a dog but was probably meant to be a dragon. The three big stick people were all holding hands and the big stick person with long dark hair held the fourth, tiny stick person aloft. Everyone in the picture was smiling a wide, wonkily inked smile. It made Lazare feel warm, in a sad sort of way. He wished they could all smile those big smiles in the real world. The adults passed the paper around and agreed loudly that it was indeed a *very* good drawing.

By the time they had finished eating, Tem had already started to nod.

'There's two rooms,' Chicory told them, getting on with a pile of sewing as her silent husband cleared up the dishes. 'Top floor. We'll have no funny business between the unwed though, so it's ladies in one room, gents in the other.'

The stoic ogre husband gave a small grunt of affirmation, which was the most Lazare had heard from him all evening. Lazare and Nell exchanged glances. None of them wanted to say that at this point, putting Fang and Lazare in a room alone was an invitation to funny business akin to greasing them both up and tying them naked to a tickling stick. Lazare was just going to have to behave. Hopefully Fang snored or was prone to nighttime wind or something equally offputting. He glanced at Fang who was barely paying attention, cradling the drooping child on his lap. The candlelight danced off the various angles of his ridiculously well sculpted bone structure and the silly curves of his silly silly beautiful arms and chest. His eyes were soft as he gazed down at Tem, and there was that smile again, that sincere little smile he seemed to reserve for the child alone. He looked aggressively pretty in the candlelight. God's Pecs, why did Fang always have to make everything so difficult?

Amber, seemingly oblivious to the charged atmosphere, was the first to announce she was off to bed, meaning that Lazare and the others really couldn't put the troubling inevitability of the coming bedtime off any longer. Nell took Tem, now fast asleep, out of Fang's arms, and swished past to the stairs, shooting Lazare a little glance of concern as she went. Fang yawned, got up, thanked both ogres and headed upstairs after them. Lazare offered to help with the washing up, in the hope of delaying going upstairs himself until Fang was asleep, but Chicory's husband was having none of it and since he could barely sew a stitch, he couldn't offer Chicory any help with her own chores for the night. Lazare steeled himself, told himself to stop being such a baby and show some bloody restraint, and went up to the upstairs lodging room.

He found Fang standing just inside the doorway, looking at the bed with a faint frown.

The bed. Singular.

'There's only one bed,' noted Lazare, needlessly since Fang had already spotted that.

Fang cleared his throat. 'Standard practice in many lodging houses. It's for warmth.'

Neither of them moved towards the bed.

'Are you going to make another sad-eyed move on me to "get the sex out of the way" again?' Lazare asked.

Fang glared at him.

'That's not a "no",' said Lazare.

'The "no" was heavily implied,' Fang told him.

'Fine,' Lazare sighed. He broke the impasse, and walked over to lie on the bed facing the wall, as comfortably as his poor, injured wings would allow. After a few seconds, he felt the other side of the bed depress beneath Fang's bodyweight. Lazare noticed that the other man smelled different, now. He smelled... floral.

'Fang?'

'Mm?' Fang sounded bone tired and wary.

'Did you put on perfume?'

There was a pause. Lazare couldn't help but smile fondly at the wall over the other man's obvious embarrassment.

'I had to clean my injuries anyway. And, everyone kept complaining that I smelled bad, so I used Tem's soap. You only have yourselves to blame.'

Lazare grinned. 'I have a spare pomander, you know.'

'That won't be necessary.'

There was another pause. Lazare shifted a little in the bed, sucking in breath through his teeth when the action caused the pain in his injured wing to flare up briefly.

'You didn't fly away,' Fang mumbled.

'What's that?'

'At the docks. I told you to take the crate, fly away. She could have been freed sooner. You wouldn't have been injured. Amber and Nell wouldn't have had to get involved.'

'And Avis Hapenny would have captured and tortured you,' replied Lazare, still talking to the wall. 'Or traded you to that contact she was talking about. Who knows what they'd have done to you, and you wouldn't even be able to die from it. I was never going to let that happen.'

'Because of the attraction.'

'No – because I'm not a thundering arsehole!' He turned in the bed, annoyed, to face Fang. 'You hesitated when they threatened me, too. And I know damned well you'd never let harm come needlessly to Tem, Nell or Amber, either. You got beaten almost to death stopping harm coming to some stray cat, for pity's sake. Are you attracted to a little pussy cat? No! You do it because you're…' Lazare hesitated, he knew Fang wouldn't take the rest of his statement well. 'You're a good person.'

Fang's expression twisted back into that miserable, haunted rage again. 'Shut up. Just shut up! You know nothing about me! You didn't fly away because you have this ridiculous, romanticised, *actor's* idea of what I am, and I'm not, and because of your stupid mistake you could have got us all killed at the dock, Tem included. *And* you could have ruined your career at the inn. Why did you throw your drink at Christopher Marlowe?'

'Because he *is* a thundering arsehole.'

'Was it because he was trying to sleep with me?'

'No,' lied Lazare.

'I should have slept with him.'

'Don't do that to yourself, he's terrible in bed.'

'Maybe *I'm* terrible in bed.'

'I find that incredibly hard to imagine. And we actors are great at imagining things.'

They were nose to nose. Lazare's pulse was racing. In the dim light, he couldn't tell if Fang's pupils were blown wide or if it was just the dark ink brown of his irises. Fang's eyes danced with something Lazare couldn't quite pinpoint. There was desperation there, but also a spite. Lazare's mind flitted so fast between '*uh oh*' and '*oui merci*' that it all merged into one big Danger-Yes. They were only a barleycorn away from one another – their thighs, fingers, lips.

'I'm not what you think I am.' Fang's voice had dropped to a whisper. 'I'm not worth risking the lives of others for. I think you know that, deep down.' Fang reached out a couple of fingers, and breached that last tiny gap, gently brushing against Lazare's chest. All of Lazare's physical sensation rushed to those two, tiny, feather-light points of contact between them, his nerves forgetting the stitched-up musket and knife wounds, in favour of a hyper-awareness of two fingers resting gently, unmoving, in the valley of his chest.

Fang smiled, but it wasn't the soft, fond smile he gave to Tem when he thought nobody else was looking. It was a cruel smile, carved onto his mouth while his eyes were still filled with spite, and desperation, and pain.

'Just take what you came here for,' he whispered, and leaned his mouth into Lazare's just that whisper he needed for their lips to touch, 'you only really want one thing. Stop trying to fool yourself that this is anything but – you're not fooling me.'

Lazare pulled away, angrily.

Fang's eyes still danced with desperation, pain and now humiliation and rage. 'Again?' He seethed.

'I could ask the same of you,' whispered Lazare. 'Didn't you say less than ten minutes ago you weren't going to try it on again?'

Fang rolled onto his back, angrily. 'What was wrong with it this time? I'm sober! You can't tell yourself you're just being gentlemanly around a drunk.'

'I keep saying, I won't sleep with you if you're sad about it. Sleeping with me is a treat, and you should be duly delighted. You deserve a treat, Fang of Cathay.'

'No I don't! And I'm *not* "good" like you say, and we're not going to fall in love and live happily ever after if you can only wait for me to kiss you with a smile.'

'So you keep saying.'

'Because this?' Fang indicated at the foot of empty bed they had now created between them. 'Is not love. Don't be under the illusion that it could be.'

'Oh, I am getting extremely sick of getting told how I feel about you, by people who barely know me. It is extremely patronising, and neither you nor Nell can even make up your minds about *how* you're going to patronise me. At any given moment I'm either a naive, lovesick fool or some shallow popinjay who thinks with his codpiece. I am a grown man with a career and a curse and I get to decide how I feel for myself!' Lazare folded his arms, furious and upset that all of this was coming out while he wasn't able to raise his voice any louder than a whisper. 'I *know* our days are probably numbered, and I know you've got all this weird self-loathing self-sabotage nonsense going on and your big "mysterious grump who ran away so far from home he ended up running halfway round the world" woe-is-Fang poppycock. And, Lord help me, turns out I'm extremely into you anyway, because there's treasure under all your layers of crap. You did a lousy job of burying the treasure, Fang. I can see it glinting. So, there!'

Fang looked startled for the briefest moment, then covered the expression with a sneer. 'You *do* think you're in love with me.'

'I told you to stop patronising me!'

'Have you ever *been* in love?'

'Of course.' It was another lie, spoken as smoothly as a soliloquy.

'Really?' Fang's eyes had that desperate, spiteful glint to them, again. 'Because I've been in love. And that's how I know just how shallow and fruitless this is.' The space between them on the bed widened again. 'True love felt nothing like this. It was pure, and it hurt. This is just… something to pass some of whatever time we have left.' The horrible smile was back. 'Still think I'm "good"? Still think I'm full of treasure?'

He didn't wait for an answer from Lazare. He grabbed one of the blankets and deliberately slid off the bed, onto the floor.

'Take the bed, sleep off your delusions,' he said from his ridiculous heap on the floor. 'I'll be just fine down here.'

Even after all the unkind things Fang had just said, *that* was what took the cake for Lazare. Fang didn't get to throw a strop after his kiss was rejected, say lots of mean, patronising stuff and sulk on the floor while trying to act like he had the moral high ground. Fully enraged, Lazare snatched another of the blankets and a pillow, and got out of bed himself, hunkering uncomfortably on the floor on the other side of it.

'Seriously?' Fang snapped.

'I'm as serious as you are,' Lazare told him.

'You're trying to be gallant. Again. Well, I'm not getting back in that bed just because you've decided to act the martyr.'

'*I'm* acting the martyr?' Lazare snorted. 'I'm not sleeping in a bed while you pout on the floor.'

'Well then we'll *both* pout on the floor all night and waste a perfectly good bed, shall we?'

'Looks like it, Fang.'

'You're ridiculous.'

'You are.'

It was hard on the floor, and his injured wing hurt again. But there was no way Lazare was getting back in that bed, now. He closed his eyes and tried to make sleep come and take away the aching injuries and the thrumming anger. Fortunately, his exhaustion was so heavy that it sank him into sleep within the hour. As he descended into the sleeping world, his thoughts were of reverse fae glamour, and when he dreamed, he saw Fang, with that same desperate sadness in his eyes, deliberately burying himself under an illusion of filth; waves of fake sewage rising over him, covering his heart, his face, all the way up over his head until Lazare couldn't even see a glimmer of him beneath the festering mess.

He was still dreaming fitfully when he was awoken a few hours later by the sound of the bedroom shutters being smashed in.

CHAPTER THIRTEEN
THE SLEEPLESS MARKET

Fang was very used to rude awakenings. You spend over a decade on the road, making the sort of enemies Fang had made in his life, waking up ready to fight becomes as customary as an early morning wee. Usually though, said violent awakenings happened while sleeping rough, not in an ogress's lodging house. And they certainly didn't happen while he was taking care of a stolen fae child. The thought that Tem was in danger shot a wave of anxiety through Fang, the moment he realised what was happening. Another worry ran through him – Nell. Nell was in the other room with Tem, he'd put her in danger, too. And then a third – Lazare. He'd already put Lazare in danger twice, and now it was going to happen again.

Fang scrambled to his feet as Lazare too hauled himself upright. Two vampires – one male, one female – were already climbing in through the bedroom window. Fang noted the little hand-embroidered sampler above the window, with the word 'Welcome' neatly cross stitched inside a floral border. In retrospect, a boarding house that invited in vampires might not have been the safest place to sleep.

'Why are they on the floor?' asked the male vampire.

'Doesn't matter,' snapped the female. She lunged at Lazare. Fang launched himself over the bed, his own blanket in hand,

and threw it over the attacking vampire's head. Fang kept his body's momentum going and hurled both himself and the entrapped vampire to the floor, accidentally knocking down Lazare in the process.

'Bertha?' called the other vampire, worried.

'Just get them,' called Bertha, struggling to fight her way out of the blanket. 'Grab the Turk and Jim said the French one will surrender.'

Jim. Jim Custard? These vampires were with the Custard gang? It did make sense, thought Fang as he battled to keep Bertha subdued – why shouldn't Upper London gangs have a Deepside division? All you needed to do was have a handful of members get turned undead and a crimelord could easily expand down below.

'He's not Turkish.' Lazare tried to get back onto his feet as Fang and Bertha struggled against each other, still half on top of him.

The male vampire made a grab for Fang, but seemed squeamish about the task. He hesitated and flinched a little, giving Fang room to kick him in the shin.

'Get him, Drust!' Bertha called. 'What's the matter with you, man?'

'He's got no drawers on, Bertha.'

Lazare finally managed to make it to his knees, and took one look at Fang before looking away again, his mouth open.

Bertha had managed to free one hand from the tangled blanket and tried to make a grab at Fang, only to get a handful of buttock.

'Eurgh, you're right, what foreign devilry is this?'

'Less xenophobia, *merci*,' called Lazare, grabbing a candlestick as a makeshift weapon.

'I got hot in the night,' explained Fang, even though he really didn't need to explain himself, there was nothing wrong with sleeping in just a shirt and a blanket, none of this would have been an issue if the two vampires hadn't broken in. He could use the vampires' distaste over his level of dress to his advantage, though. He got up, planted his feet on the blanket at Bertha's sides and stood up, straddling her cocooned form, fists bunched and raised, with no care over how high it caused his shirt to ride up. Another male vampire was already crawling in through the bedroom window. He had no idea how many more of them there were.

'Good Lord,' cried the vampire at the window, horrified.

Fang made use of the distraction. He swung a high kick at the head of the troubled Drust, causing the vampire to stumble back.

'Good *Lord*,' echoed Lazare, shakily.

'Good Lord,' moaned Drust, clutching the side of his head, 'eurgh, I saw right up.'

The bedroom door slammed open.

'What's going on?' cried Nell from the doorway. 'Are you two o— Good Lord, Fang, there's kids here!'

'What's wrong?' came Tem's voice from the landing, sleepy and worried.

'Nothing, go back to your room,' shouted Fang, Nell and Lazare at the same time.

'Get her out of here, we'll catch up,' added Fang to Nell.

'Guys,' called Amber's voice from outside the smashed shutters of the window. The little dragon tumbled and flittered outside in mid-air, trapped in an in-flight fight with another stunted urban dragon, 'we're under att—good *Lord*, Fang, I can see your whatsit.'

Nell scooped up Tem, and Fang heard the reassuring sound of her thundering down the stairs with the child, followed by the much less reassuring sound of the front door being kicked in and shocked screams downstairs.

Drust, still rubbing where Fang had kicked him, went to help the third vampire, who'd got a boot buckle caught in the window frame.

'I just wasn't expecting that *angle* right in my eyeline,' Drust mumbled.

Fang bent to scoop the captured Bertha up off the floor. Vampirism, Fang had found, was not at odds with any human faith. Vampires were, after all, merely a particular type of undead human, many kept their faith after turning. Certainly, no vampire ever hissed or shielded their eyes from a cross. Therefore, Fang had no frame of reference for the way that both of the vampires struggling at the window cried out, shrank back and tried to cover their faces at the sight of him bending over to haul up Bertha.

'Save Bertha,' called the vampire struggling at the window.

'I don't want to touch his bits.' Drust closed his eyes miserably and tried lunging at Fang with his fists raised far too high, giving Lazare the chance to leap forward and wallop the vampire on the head with the candlestick. The vampire crumpled and fell on top of the half-dragged Bertha, who reacted with a pained 'oof'. Fang dropped her, eliciting another grunt, and ran the three paces over to the window. The third vampire still cringed.

'Oh, it's bobbing around,' he complained.

Fang reached out and pulled the 'Welcome' sampler off its nail. The third vampire, still halfway through the window, sighed unhappily, and was thrown out into the street below by the sheer force of a rescinded invitation, ripping the caught boot off his foot in the process, and leaving it dangling forlornly from a splinter. As the vampire fell, he hit the dragon engaged in the mid-air fight with Amber outside.

'Cheers Fang,' called Amber. 'Not going to lie, I was losing that fight.'

With one vampire thrown out, one unconscious and the third pinned, Fang and Lazare exchanged the briefest of glances before hurrying downstairs to the fracas at the door. Both Chicory and her husband had ragged zombies in headlocks. A third zombie was passed out at the bottom of the stairs. Tem was on the second to bottom step, cowering behind a banister. Between Tem and the foiled zombie attack, Nell stood firm in her petticoats, fists tightly bunched, trembling. Blood ran in a thick, dark rivulet down her arm, staining a red line onto her underskirts and dripping to the ogres' scrubbed wooden floor.

'Nell,' called Fang, horrified.

'Is this your doing?' demanded Chicory, hotly. 'My door! My windows! A zombie attack of all things, in this day and age!' She shook her head down at the zombie struggling in her grip. 'For shame!'

Fang grabbed Nell's arm. 'Did they get you? Why didn't you use your potions?'

'There wasn't time,' Nell told him, dreamily. 'They broke down the door. I just… I…'

'He wanted us all to come with him,' whispered Tem.

'I punched him,' said Nell, looking at her fists. She laughed a little. 'I looked really cool!'

'Did he bite you?' Fang tried wiping away the blood on Nell's arm.

'No, it's fine,' Nell told him. 'He just stabbed me.'

Fang wiped off enough blood to see that it was indeed a knife wound, and not too deep, at that.

'There's no biting without permission down here,' said Chicory, as her husband grabbed both head locked zombies, knocked them together and threw them out into the street. 'Capital offence. You should know that. And why would you be worried about a zombie biting her, even if they had? Are you not both zombies already?'

'Er,' replied Fang.

'Get out,' Chicory barked. 'Whatever you are – get your stuff and get out of my house!'

'Of course, Madame, we're terribly sorry,' said Lazare. He pulled off one of his rings and offered it to her. 'For the damage. I'd hate to see poor Amber get evicted over this.'

'I'm not blaming Amber for this – she took her fight outside!'

'Still, though – please accept it. The ruby is fake, but the gold is not.'

Chicory allowed him to place the ring on the mantelpiece. She glanced again at Nell's wound. 'Bandage that, immediately. You reek of mortal blood and I'm not having a feeding frenzy on my doorstep. And then, all of you out.'

'Of course.' Lazare bowed and hurried back upstairs to collect their bags and Fang's breeches. 'By the way, there's two vampires and an abandoned boot in our room, sorry about that too!'

Fang hurried to rip away the human blood on Nell's petticoat and tightly bandage her arm as instructed.

'I punched a zombie,' smiled Nell, still shaking with adrenaline.

'After getting stabbed by one,' Fang reminded her, 'which means it's *my* turn to patch *you* up and give you a hard time over it.' The bandage secured, he sat down next to Tem. 'Are you OK? Sorry that scared you – let's get you home, now.'

'Fang,' Tem told him, seriously, 'you've got no pants on.'

'Urgh,' cried Chicory shielding her eyes, 'Out! The lot of you!'

They hurried through Deep London's wide streets. Fang felt more exposed than ever, and that was with his breeches back on. Every passing glance from a Deepsider made him worry that he hadn't dressed Nell's wound well enough, that she'd be sniffed out and attacked, or that the next vampire or zombie or werewolf walking towards them was another gangster out to get them. The Custard gang knew who they were, and were still chasing them on the Deepside. Likely, that meant that any Deepside factions of the Hapenny gang would be chasing them, too. They were even less safe down here than Fang had initially assumed.

'I liked that ring,' muttered Lazare as they hurried away from the lodging house. 'Won it off William Kemp in a game of dice.'

'Nobody made you give it away,' Fang huffed.

'What was I supposed to do?' Lazare asked. 'Leave a poor Deepsider out of pocket after *we* brought trouble to her door?'

'Was it our fault, though?' asked Fang. 'How did that gang find us? They even knew what bedroom we'd be in.'

'You think Chicory could have tipped the gang off?' asked Nell.

'Hey,' said Amber, hotly, 'Chicory's a good person, a nice landlady.'

'I'm not saying she'd have done it maliciously,' said Fang, 'she could be buried in debt to them – she looked like funds were really tight. That's how these gangs work – they're parasites feeding off the most vulnerable…'

'Chicory would never,' interrupted Amber. 'I've known her for years!'

'And, if you'll pardon the further insinuation, we've only known *you* for a couple of days.'

'Wow,' breathed Amber. 'Just, wow.'

Lazare and Nell's expressions echoed that of the dragon.

'Amber's nice,' said Tem.

'Yeah,' grunted Amber. 'Amber's nice. Thank you, Tem.'

Fang looked down at the cobbles, and tried to dispel the voice inside of him screaming that the gang knowing exactly where to find them meant they probably had an informant. He had to trust this little group if this was going to work. 'Sorry, Amber. I'm not used to working in a… team.'

'That's true,' huffed Nell. 'It took him two months to stop accusing me of stealing his stuff, and that's when he was free-loading off me.'

'You were stealing my coffee supplies, though. And my saffron.'

'Only to sample them as means of establishing a trade deal through which you could pay for your board,' replied Nell, primly.

'There's plenty of ways the gang could be trailing us,' said Lazare, without adding actual suggestions to back that up.

'In which case,' Fang reasoned, 'we should try to shake them.' He looked down at Amber. 'Any idea how we go about doing that?'

'Oh, you trust me again, do you?'

'I said I was sorry!'

'I do have one idea,' said Amber, shooting an impish grin up at Fang. 'But you're not going to like it.'

'What?'

'Hey, kiddie,' said Amber to Tem. 'How would you like to go shopping?'

'Where's shopping?' asked Tem.

'Deep Covent Garden,' Amber told her. 'It's where grown-ups get you dolls and pretty things.'

Tem's big eyes lit up. 'I want to go to shopping!'

*

The Sleepless Market in Deep Covent Garden was thrumming – it was always thrumming, that was the point of it. It was just about beginning its diurnal shift when Fang and the others reached it, with nocturnal stallholders and customers flying off to rest up. This wasn't to say that there weren't any vampires or other traditionally nocturnal beings about – the torchlit square was perfectly safe for them to get out and about during the day. The market was loud with a hubbub that made all voices fade into a sort of white noise, although Fang could pick out bits of Old English, Modern English, Arabic, Turkish and Ethiopian amongst the babble, along with other languages even he wasn't familiar with. It had, Fang had to admit to himself, a surprisingly cheerful and vibrant atmosphere to it, and it was certainly bustling and busy enough for them to feel they could easily lose anyone tailing them in the crowd.

Fang did not enjoy bustling, busy crowds, or cheerful and vibrant atmospheres. The others, frustratingly, seemed to love it. He knew Nell liked her lotions, potions and imported ingredients, and he had correctly assumed that Lazare's gaze would be turned by flouncy accessories and shiny geegaws. Amber's chops drooled at every wafting smell of meat, and

Tem's eyes were wide at stalls selling stereotypically fae-friendly trinkets – porcelain saucers, dried flowers, acorn necklaces and the like.

Fang had precious little he could trade, but thankfully Tem had very cheap tastes. For a couple of his few remaining pennies, he bought a ribbon for her hair and a little felt dollie of a dragon that looked like Amber, both of which made her smile with a delight that he hadn't seen in the little girl before. Seeing her happy somehow made his heart feel lighter and heavier at the same time. The flittering of joy's wings, along with the burden of knowing how delicate those wings were, and the likelihood of those iridescent, gossamer wings fluttering away.

Lazare looked around at the jostling crowds, all buying, selling, eating and drinking. 'We'll blend in even better with some food to hide behind,' he noted. 'Who's hungr—?'

'Me,' shouted Amber, before Lazare could even finish his question.

The others also raised a hand, and that was fair. They'd been too busy fighting and getting thrown out to have any breakfast.

'Yeah,' mumbled Fang, 'I could also murder a coffee.'

'I know just the place,' called Amber, happily waddling off in the direction of some food stalls selling hot meat straight from the spit, 'this stall over here is really goo— ah.'

She stopped suddenly in her tracks.

'What?' Fang scanned the way ahead for whatever looming danger the dragon might have spotted, but saw none. 'What's wrong?'

'Nothing,' replied Amber nervously, 'just... you people don't want breakfast meat, do you? It's too early for meat, let's find a baker or something, get you a croissant, ever had a croissant?'

'Yes, I've had a croissant,' said Lazare, 'but I'm fine with breakfast meat, whereas I'm pretty sure dragons can't eat gluten.'

'I'll be fine,' panicked Amber, 'I'll have a sausage roll or something.'

‘That’s still gluten,’ Nell told her. ‘Amber, what are you so worried about?’ She pointed at a joint of meat sizzling on a spit nearby. ‘Why can’t we just have some of that… oh.’

Nell realised why Amber was trying to steer them away from that joint at the same time that Fang did. The realisation was to do with the spit turning slowly so that the end of it rotated into view, through wavering heat lines and applewood smoke, slathered in honey and studded with cloves. The juicy roast joint ended with what was now obviously a human foot.

‘When I said I could murder a decent breakfast, I meant it figuratively,’ said Fang, transfixed by the spit.

Amber cringed. ‘Sorry. Just, Deepside market, y’know. They’ll have been killed legally and ethically, if that’s any consolation?’

Fang couldn’t think about whether it was a consolation, at that point. At that point, all he could think about was the leg. It had been marinated and spiced beautifully. It smelled, to his abject horror, absolutely delicious.

Amber took a sharp left, and tried leading them away from the monstrous rotisserie. ‘There’s a guy down here sells buns and such, assuming you haven’t all lost your appetite?’

‘I’m actually hungrier than before,’ admitted Nell, guiltily.

They got buns, and all told themselves that it was fine that they were salivating so much, and they’d just been really hungry for carbs. They even managed to source some coffee, although Deepside coffee wasn’t half as good as the stuff from Nell’s. Nell tried to pass on her business card to the vendor to set up a meeting about becoming his coffee wholesaler, before Fang snatched the card off her and explained quietly that when one is going incognito on a secret mission one does *not* hand out one’s card with one’s personal details on it. Amber, on learning that yes, the sausage rolls did have gluten in them, scurried off and reappeared moments later chewing on something that she swore blind was a chicken foot but looked a lot like a human hand.

Still munching on their breakfasts and trying to ignore the delicious wafts coming from the nearby rotisserie, they set off following Amber again.

'Might we find some fae-folk right here at the market?' Nell asked Amber.

Amber shook her head over her shoulder. 'They really don't leave their enclave these days, not even to shop.' She thought for a second, as they passed another stall selling fae-friendly trinkets that made Tem's eyes go wide. 'There are some Deepsiders that are close enough to the fae to be allowed in and out, though. Púca, brownies, hobgoblins. Sometimes they can get jobs doing deliveries for them and suchlike. There's a chance we could find one of those here.'

'Would that be better than going to the embassy?' Fang asked.

'Not sure,' Amber admitted. 'It'd be more hush-hush, but it'd involve us being able to trust some random delivery guy. Worth keeping our eyes, ears and nostrils open for one, at least.'

Fang already had his eyes peeled, thank you very much. He'd noticed a few Deepsiders were beginning to give Nell hungry looks. He stopped her and checked her bandage. His breath hitched when he noticed a dark red spot on it. Human blood. He knew enough about vampires' sensitivity to the stuff to be aware that even a stained bandage could overpower Nell's cover scent at any moment.

'You need to get that stitched up straight away,' he whispered to her. 'You'll get sniffed out, and then—'

He looked around himself, anxiously. There had to be hundreds of vampires, dragons and zombies here. If they were to turn on Nell, he'd have no chance of protecting her.

Nell silently followed his eyeline. Worry flitted briefly over her expression before she swiftly buried it in superficial bravado. 'Clearly you didn't do a good enough job dressing it,' she huffed.

'Because *you* got yourself stabbed.' He turned to Lazare to tell him they needed to get Nell out of there to patch her up, only to discover Lazare was wandering off, straining his head to peer through the throng like a dog that had caught scent of a squirrel.

'Lazare!'

Lazare turned, briefly. 'I think I can find us some help. Or, a hindrance, I'm not entirely sure, yet. Just wait there a moment.'

Amber immediately trotted after him. 'Oh no you don't.'

Nell quickly followed the dragon.

'No splitting off from each other,' seethed Fang, annoyed that they were all now following Lazare instead of trying to leave the market.

As Fang followed Lazare, he became aware of what it was the Frenchman was following – a voice cut through the clamour of the market. The voice was familiar, loud, obnoxious and, for some reason, speaking in verse. Lazare led them past stands and stepped over a row of benches, when they found themselves in an opening amongst all the stalls and carts. Large lamps lit the space from on high. It looked like it could be used for eating, or meetings, or, on this occasion, as a performance space. A small crowd of Deepsiders had gathered to watch the performance in the centre, by a man who Fang unfortunately recognised.

'And meet me in my study at midnight,' cried the zombie of Kit Marlowe, his stance all puffed up like a silly bird in the middle of a mating display, his voice booming, his cape and voluptuous hair billowing dramatically in the breeze. 'And then resolve me of thy master's mind.'

There was something not quite right about the scene, realised Fang. They were Deepside. Down here, there was no dramatic breeze in which Kit's hair and cape should be able to waft. Fang only had a second to wonder how the zombie was managing to summon up just the right amount of waftage before the solution presented itself. Little Wulfric stepped forward. He'd been obscured by an audience member up until that moment, and was still gently flapping a slight breeze into Kit's hair, with one wing.

'I will, Faustus,' said Wulfric, woodenly, reading from the top of a large stack of papers in his hands.

Lazare let out a despairing little wail.

CHAPTER FOURTEEN
The Globe Hopper

The group all gazed with concern at Lazare's audible distress.

'That's my line,' Lazare breathed.

'How so?' asked Amber, 'sounded like Wulfric's line to me.'

'I *know*,' Lazare replied, 'and he's *murdering* it.'

Wulfric spotted them, waved and ambled over as Kit continued to perform to the small crowd.

'And now he's coming over?' complained Lazare. 'You don't just go over to talk to the audience while the scene's still happening. I can't look!'

'Actors talk to the audience all the time though,' whispered Nell, 'to tell us what they're thinking or explain a pun or something.'

'That's soliloquies and asides,' Lazare hissed, 'there isn't a soliloquy here. Well, there is, but it's not Mephistopheles'. He's just breaking character, I would *never* break character… oh, hi Wulfric.'

Wulfric finished picking his way through the audience. 'So you made it Deepside.'

'Is your inn OK?' Nell asked. 'Are *you* OK?'

'Oh, that's all fine,' he told them, cheerfully. 'I've got great lawyers, they made the guards tidy up after themselves and everything. I was up and trading again by suppertime.'

'How did you get here so quickly?' Fang added.

Wulfric pulled a confused face. 'It's only a few miles and I can fly. How did *you* guys take so long to only get this far?'

'A few different spots of bother,' admitted Nell, showing Wulfric her bandaged arm. 'Slowed us down.'

Wulfric began to drool a little at the wound. 'That'll do it, all right,' he replied. 'You're going to need that arm stitched by the way, Mistress Nell. It smells delicious, if you don't mind me telling you so. Properly cutting through your zombie perfume.'

Fang raised an eyebrow at Nell. 'Told you so.'

'I can do it now, if you've got a mo,' smiled Wulfric. 'Little fingers and centuries of practice – I'll get the stitches lovely and small for you.'

'Much obliged,' smiled Nell. 'I'm sure it'll be better than what this hack can manage.'

'Hey,' huffed Fang.

Kit finished his soliloquy with a flourish and bowed deeply to modest applause. Wulfric led the group past him, shoving a stack of the papers into Kit's hand as he did.

'Wulfric,' whispered Kit, still deep in the bow. 'I do the charming, you do the flyering, remember?'

'Something's come up,' Wulfric told him.

Kit stood up out of the bow, took a brief glance at the group, his eyeline sliding from Lazare's furious, accusing glare as easily as a greased mermaid falling off the ocean's slipperiest iceberg. Annoyingly, said greasy gaze settled on Fang instead.

'Oh! Tis the jewel of the east.'

'Eurgh,' groaned Nell.

'Please don't call me that,' added Fang.

'Just need the costume cart for a tick, OK?' Wulfric said. 'Flyering not flirting, Kit!'

Kit shrugged, turned, stopped and did a double take at Tem, who he seemed to have only just noticed.

'Flyers,' Wulfric reminded him, hurriedly, before bundling the group into the small covered wagon they'd been performing in front of.

He got out a needle and thread, and started making short work of Nell's injury.

'You all right there, Lazare?' he asked of the still furious Frenchman.

'Fine,' seethed Lazare. 'You enjoying the acting gig?'

'Oh, that. I'm just doing Kit a favour, really. He's been talking of setting up a Deepside theatre company ever since he died, and it'll be nice for Deep London to have a bit more culture. I'd tell you guys it's nicer down here than you'd think, but I am aware I'm patching up a fresh stab wound so that you don't get eaten.'

'To be fair,' said Nell, 'people get stabbed a lot in Upper London, too.'

'Speaking of Deepside businesses,' added Fang, 'do you know of any Deepside factions of the Hapenny boys? Or Custard's gang?'

'Oh, every Upperside gang's got a Deep counterpart,' Wulfric told them, breezily. 'And the other way round. I suppose Upperside and Deepside being different states with different laws doesn't make much difference if you're criminals to begin with. You'd be surprised how many demographics operate in both Londons. It's not just us undead. Admittedly, most humans who venture down here get killed sharpish, but I saw an alchemist wandering round the market this morning, happy as Larry, swishing his silly cape. Must've had a protective amulet or something.'

'Oh for pity's sake – I could've got us protective amulets?' Nell sighed. 'Sorry, gang – that's my oversight.'

Fang shrugged. 'You're the one who got stabbed.'

'Also, nobody's actually eaten you yet, so it's not the end of the world,' added Amber.

Wulfric finished the stitching and began ripping a fresh strip of petticoat for a bandage.

'Thanks, Wulfric,' sighed Lazare. The rage and prickled ego had already left Lazare's tone. Now, he just sounded sad. Unfortunately, that was the moment that Kit poked his head through the wagon's opening, and Lazare bristled all over again.

'Just so you know,' Kit told Fang, 'you having a daughter isn't a turn-off for me, as long as she stays out of my hair. Happy to be a homewrecker, but stepfathering isn't my scene. OK, hot stuff?' And, with that, he was gone again.

Fang blinked at the empty wagon entrance where Kit had been, then at Tem, who fidgeted with the ribbon in her hair, looking as confused as he felt.

'What did he mean?' squeaked Tem.

'He must think Fang's your d—'

Fang interrupted Amber, hurriedly. 'He never means anything – he's a poet.'

'What's a poet?' Tem asked.

'A very silly man,' Fang told her. Nell cleared her throat meaningfully, and Fang sighed. 'Or, a very silly woman.' Amber then cleared her own throat meaningfully, and Fang sighed again. 'Or, a very silly dragon.'

Tem nodded, satisfied by this explanation.

Wulfric finished up with Nell's arm. 'You're done. Let's get you out of here before Kit decides to bother Fang some m—'

Kit stuck his head into the wagon again. Lazare managed to huff at his reappearance even louder than Fang did, which was impressive.

'Few notes, Wulfric,' said Kit. 'Everyone out there's loving a wingéd Mephistopheles, what are your thoughts on a long term role?'

Lazare actually growled at Kit.

'Can we discuss it later?' replied Wulfric, breezily.

'Yeah, yeah.' Kit wafted his hand around, as if swatting away his own comments. 'Secondly – Mr Fang, Fang Junior, Lazzers, dragon I don't know and sexy lady from the pub, I apologise for my earlier rudeness, it was very good of you to come all the way Deepside and support the Deep Players, I assume you want an autograph?'

'Oh, that's not why we're down h—' began Amber, before being nudged into silence by Lazare's foot.

Lazare painted on a bright, angry smile. 'Please, Kit. Not for us, of course, for the child.'

Kit nodded, and scribbled with a quill on the back of one of his flyers. '"For the brat... standing in my way... of her father's splendid arse... Christopher Marlowe; Poet, Playwright, Lover and Cad".'

He held out the flyer and Lazare took it, his smile as transparent and brittle as glass.

'And, one more thing,' said Kit, 'I think there's someone outside the cart waiting for you.'

'What?'

'There's a ghoul woman outside. Looks like one of your lot, Mr Fang.'

'What?' repeated Fang.

'If it's Mrs Fang, I'm not fighting her, I don't fight women unless we're both armed, fair and square. She's welcome to join us, or just sit in a corner and watch if she prefers.'

Panic and hope and fear welled up in him, all at the same time. No. No, it couldn't be. Could it?

'What does she look like?'

Kit shrugged. 'Undead and east Asian?'

Well, that wasn't helpful.

'Did...' His mouth felt dry. 'Did she have a tail?'

He noticed the strange looks Lazare, Nell and Amber were giving him. He ignored them. It couldn't be her. Not her. Not after he'd been made to watch as they'd... but what if by some miracle...? What if it was her, somehow? What if she had the cure for this curse, what if after all these miserable years, his troubles were over? What if...'

'See, I want to say "hard to tell, under the ghoul-shrouds",' said Kit, breaking Fang out of his spiralling thoughts, 'but honestly, it's a pretty tight fitting little number she's got on, leaves nothing to the imagination, so if she had a tail adding to the shape of a very nice bottom, I'd have seen it.'

And just like that, all those feelings jangling Fang's nerves died again, and the weary hollowness rushed to take their place once more.

'Gang member, you think?' Lazare asked the group.

'Let's get out of here,' said Nell. 'Er… if we're being followed, we could use a distraction.'

'Lucky for you, Kit Marlowe's in town,' Kit beamed. 'I'm *extremely* distracting. Wulfric? Act One scene five?'

'Fine,' replied Wulfric, clambering out of the wagon.

'Good lad.'

'Older than you,' Wulfric reminded Kit, 'by a considerable amount.'

Outside, the sounds of Kit and Wulfric's wildly different approaches to acting started back up once more.

Amber poked her head outside the cart. The ghoul woman was, sure enough, watching Kit and Wulfric intently. 'OK. This way.' She led them around the back of the wagon, where they could squeeze past a couple of stalls and get back into the market while avoiding attention from most of the gathered crowd.

'Lazare,' Nell hissed, 'stop reciting all Wulfric's lines along with him, it's weird.'

'But I'd be *so* much better at Act One Scene Five than him!'

They hurried out of the clearing and back into the winding, cluttered pathways of the market, and set back to the task of trying to head northwest as quickly as possible while also not drawing attention to themselves and trying to lose anyone who might be tailing them. And looking out for brownies and hobgoblins. So far, so difficult. At least nobody had accosted them yet.

'Hello? Hey? Hey!'

Fang snuck a glance over his shoulder at the sound of the voice. The ghoul was barely a few feet away, gaining on them in steady, well-paced leaps.

'*Nǐ hǎo xiānshēng*?' called the ghoul.

She was indeed from the Ming Empire. He recognised this type of ghoul. Clad in tightly wrapped off-white shrouds, leaping tirelessly with pinned arms and legs. A Jiangshi. Of course, he'd seen a few about outside of the empire, but Fang had hoped that England was far west enough to avoid magicals and humans from his homeland altogether. He had hoped wrong.

'*Nǐ shì na guó rén*?' called the ghoul, loudly. '*Nihonjin desu ka? Kon'nichiwa? Hangug-in?*'

'If she were with a gang,' muttered Nell, 'would she be drawing this much attention to herself?'

She really was drawing far too much attention, and not just to herself. Fang sighed, stopped and turned to the Jiangshi, who hopped right up into his personal space before stopping.

'What do you want?' he asked. 'In English, so my companions can understand. And for crying out loud, keep your voice down. We're in a cavern. Voices travel.'

'I just didn't think I'd see anyone else from back home this far west,' beamed the Jiangshi. 'You *are* from back home, right? Great Ming? Like me?'

'How did you get here?' asked Amber, impressed.

'Hopped,' she told them, proudly. 'Something to do, isn't it? Name's Hue Susu, just call me Susu.'

'I'm Amber, that's Lazare, Nell, littlun's called Tem and Fang is indeed from the Ming Empire,' said Amber cheerfully before anyone could suggest to her that maybe it would be best not to tell strangers everyone's names.

Susu gave them all a stiff little bow. 'I know a Fang family in Guizhou, any relation…?'

'Well, no, since I'm from Shangdong province…'

'Ooh, yeah, that's the opposite side of the Empire. Still, you never know, might be a distant branch of the same family…'

'Fang isn't my family name.'

'Ah! Yes! Good for you!' The Jiangshi didn't seem in the slightest bit embarrassed. 'Using your given name in Europe. That's what I'm doing too! Comes across friendlier! What's your family name, then? I did travel through Shangdong on the way to Korea, maybe I met your folks.'

'Very doubtful. I'm from the countryside.'

'I love the countryside! Which village? Which family?'

'It doesn't matter.'

That at least wiped the grin off Susu's face. Fang was almost pleased he'd managed to bring a frown to this latest noisy pain in the arse. But he could see from her expression that she wasn't upset for herself, but troubled for him, and the others were picking up on it.

'You think your family name "doesn't matter"?'

'It doesn't. "Fang" works just fine, and I am extremely busy right now, I don't have time to nitpick about whether a ridiculous ghoul thinks she might have hopped at one of my distant cousins.'

'What happened?' asked Susu, seriously.

'A long story that I am *trying* to end,' Fang told her. 'So, unless you can help us right now, I'm going to have to cut this chat about the old country short.' He addressed the others, trying to ignore the concern in their own eyes. 'Come on, let's go.'

They tried to walk away from the Jiangshi, but she hopped along after him.

'Did your family denounce you?' called the Jiangshi. 'Fang, that's terrible. It might help you to talk about it. You know, my family weren't happy about me becoming a Jiangshi, but I didn't lose my name, my identity.'

He tried speeding up. She sped her interminable hops to keep perfect pace with him.

'Did you bring great shame on your community?' she continued. 'You can tell me, I'll understand. I never thought I'd see someone in pauper's clothes all the way from Shangdong this far west, are you running from the shame, Fang?'

He tried leading the group through a narrow walkway, with boxes to clamber over. She continued to follow easily, leaping over the boxes in single bounds.

'You do realise,' she called, 'that there's only so far you can run west before you end up back on the shores of the Empire again? Fang! Fang! Fang, what happened? Were you tricked? Seduced? Is that your daughter with you? She smells strange, was she the product of some cursed union? Did you tup with an undead, Fang? Some of us magicals can have kids with humans, you know, like Huli Jing. Was it a Huli Jing? Those fox spirits can be really tricksy...'

Fang stopped and turned again. The Jiangshi was right up in his face.

'Will you stop? What do you want?'

'Just to help,' Susu told him, innocently.

'I feel there may be better ways to help, Madame,' said Lazare, attempting to disarm her with charm.

'A Jiangshi,' muttered Nell, thinking. 'There's a couple of things she might want from us.'

'I just want to talk,' repeated Susu, hopping up and down right in front of Fang.

'She may actually want us to poison her with rice so she can find peace,' suggested Nell.

'No,' replied Susu hotly. 'I don't want that.'

'But it's the only way to free you from a thousand years of undead torment, isn't it?'

'I'm enjoying my thousand years of undead torment. I'm seeing the world, learning new things. I've taken up tennis – I have to hold the racquet in my teeth, but it's still hugely preferable to being dead.'

Nell leaned in to Fang. 'It could be part of the Jiangshi curse that she's not allowed to ask us to end her suffering.' Fang could tell from her tone that Nell was teasing. It was the sort of detail that would probably go right over the head of an undead traveller who had only known Nell for a couple of minutes.

'It is not! I do not want you to set me free! Setting the undead free without their say-so is strictly against the rules of Deep London… I think.'

'Or,' continued Nell, 'maybe she's just winding you up because she wants to feed off your qi.' She smiled primly at Susu, who exhaled in a light, self-effacing laugh.

'Ah, you got me. Irishwoman, right?'

'Welsh,' Nell told her, 'but the education in magicals from around the world is similar to the kind they get in Ireland.'

'Fair enough. Yes, I was totally feeding off my countryman's qi. And Lazare, is it? Yours too, since you get as angry as Fang does when I upset him.'

Lazare smiled a greasepaint smile. 'Madame is mistaken, I'm sure.' He faltered. 'Um. What *is* my qi, exactly? And how much did you… eat? And will I miss it now it's gone?'

'Just your life force, don't worry. I was expecting you both to collapse, amount I was trying to digest, but… it's strange. You have normal amounts of qi, but it's not depleting. It feels like I keep eating the same one morsel, over and over again.'

Fang just scowled at her.

'Oh come on, I didn't do you any harm,' Susu told them. 'And just so you know, your qi tastes weird, the pair of you. Might want to get that looked at, I don't know what it means for your souls, but I doubt it's a good thing to be walking around with funky tasting qi. Reckon it's got something to do with whatever you're running from back home, Fang?'

'You're feeding off them again, aren't you?' asked Nell.

'Sorry, what can I say? I'm still not full.'

'And you're *still* doing it!'

'Yeah, OK, OK, I'll go.' Susu didn't go at all. She just stayed there in Fang's personal space.

Nell grabbed both Fang and Lazare by the shoulders and pulled them away. 'Come on, she's a vulture.'

'She's right. I can't help myself, can I? What am I like?'

The group followed Amber northwest through the market again. Susu hopped happily after them. They sped up. Susu's hops sped up along with them. They began to run. Susu's hops grew bigger and faster. A quick glance over Fang's shoulder showed that the Jiangshi was smiling widely, likely feeding off their annoyance at being chased and the general alarm it was causing amongst the crowds.

Fang concentrated, and rotten, maggoty meat tumbled from a stall as they passed, causing Susu to stop, gagging, wriggling as her long-constricted hands tried to cover her mouth. Amber took advantage of the distraction, hurrying them around a winding route of very narrow passages, at one point squeezing through the gaps between the backs of two stalls. Eventually they crashed out of the market and came to a ragged stop, puffing and panting, next to the northwest gate. Susu was no longer behind them. Perhaps they'd cunningly lost her trail. More likely, she'd just found another meal who wasn't already wise to her.

'Are you all right?' Lazare asked Fang, getting his breath back.

'Fine,' huffed Fang. 'Not feeling drained or anything. Infinite qi. That's… that's weird. Must be the curse.'

'I didn't mean your qi, I meant the things she said,' added Lazare. 'She got really personal, you seemed upset.'

'I'm fine,' lied Fang. 'She was just fishing.'

'You need a rod to fish,' Tem said. 'Or a net. Mummy said so.'

'She was fishing for bad feelings,' Fang explained. 'Her rod was made of unkind words, disguised as kind ones.'

Tem's eyes lit up, understanding. 'Like you disguise the hook as an insect!'

'Yes.'

'*Your* words aren't disguised, though.' It wasn't a question. Tem seemed sure about this statement. 'Cause you said you'd buy me Little Amber and then you did buy me Little Amber.' She showed the tiny felt dragon doll he had bought the girl for a penny, by way of explanation.

'Aww,' cooed Amber. 'That dollie looks like me! Does that make me Big Amber, then?'

Tem nodded a serious affirmation.

'You are not "Big Amber" by any stretch of the imagination,' Fang told her.

'But I'm bigger than Little Amber.'

'She is,' Tem reminded him, still petting the three inch long felt dragon.

'Fine. You can be… Mediocre Amber.'

Amber nodded, pleased. 'I'll take it.'

*

Honkensby hated the Sleepless Market. Every roast human on sale was, while legal down here, a slap across the beak to her. An Upper Londoner who should have been protected by her laws, but had somehow slipped through the cracks, to be dragged down, one way or the other. She flapped towards the market's eastern entrance gate and contemplated what to do next, as Deep London residents pushed past her with shopping bags and cups of coffee and suspicious cuts of meat. To think, were it not for the generosity of the Upper English Crown, Honkensby and her kind would have to live down here with the rest of the magicals, like that dirt-poor ogress Chicory.

Honkensby was certain that her suspects had been at Chicory's boarding house only hours ago. It wasn't just a case of trusting her instincts. The reports of a serious fracas at a vampire-friendly boarding house a walking distance from New Cross tube had been enough to make her hurry there immediately, and to find there the proprietors dealing with unconscious undead members of the Custard gang – well. She didn't believe Chicory's story that it was an attempted burglary one feather. The boarding house was poor and cheap, not worth breaking in for, and the 'burglars' had left a golden ring glinting on the shabby mantelpiece. Payment, no doubt, for Chicory's silence, and while Honkensby welcomed the chance to have her sergeants arrest even more Custard boys, she had no jurisdiction to haul the civilian ogress in for questioning. Her true quarry had eluded her again.

Though Chicory continued to swear blind that her guests that night had been zombies who she hadn't recognised and hadn't seen which way they'd gone, eyewitnesses spoke of a group with a dragon, a vampire, a woman with a bandaged arm and a very good looking man clutching a child, running northwest. While that largely matched the descriptions of the mysterious group that seemed at the centre of this trouble with the stolen fae goods, the 'child' aspect of it was new, and concerned Honkensby greatly. Could the child be an illusion, to invite pity and try to secure a safer passage? If so, it clearly wasn't working. No, she had a feeling it was something far more troubling than that. No wonder Her Majesty had ordered her to intervene. If they were headed northwest, they could be headed to the embassy. If they reached Redthroat's ambassadors before Honkensby caught them… since she was not a diplomat, she couldn't say for certain just how problematic it could become, but Honkensby did know that it would mean she had failed. Failure was not a concept that Honkensby liked to countenance.

She knew that it would make sense for fleeing criminals trying to make it to the embassy to cut through the Sleepless Market, to try to lose any gangs or guards on their tail. There was another reason the suspects may have fled to the Sleepless Market, which bothered Honkensby even more than the thought of them running to Redthroat's Embassy. They could be looking to make a quick sale of whatever stolen items they had.

Honkensby decided not to walk through the market, but to take flight and view it from above. She was going to stick out like a sore wing whatever she did, and she'd rather view the whole market with her own eyes than rely on Deepside witnesses, who were generally even more useless than their Upperside counterparts. She was just giving herself a run-up when a very odd looking undead bounced over to her.

'You're a swan!' called the undead, unnecessarily. Honkensby was aware that she was a swan. 'Oh, you're like in the travel guide, aren't you? One of Elizabeth's guards? What're you doing down Deep, then? Thought you guys got to live in palaces and towers in the Upper city, all posh. Why're you slumming it? Did you do something wrong?'

The undead bounced right up to her. Honkensby felt a strange combination of annoyance and exhaustion.

'I am allowed to pursue Upperside suspects who flee Deepside,' Honkensby told her, 'by special order of Queen Elizabeth—'

'Well, that sounds very complicated,' interrupted the undead, 'you must be kicking yourself that you allowed suspects to get away, if the Upper Queen's involved it must be a serious matter, too.'

Honkensby felt as though she was made of lead. She wanted to take off and get on with the pursuit, but she wasn't sure she could.

'What do you want?' mumbled Honkensby.

'Just to help! Why don't you talk through your problems with me?'

Honkensby suddenly felt too tired to do anything.

'We've all got problems, swan – like me, less than an hour ago, ran into this couple with the weirdest qi. Like the same bite kept getting yanked out of me and fed to me again. It was really unpleasant.'

'Qi…?' croaked Honkensby. She was sure she should know what qi was, hadn't a Ming ambassador warned her about qi vampires once or something? She couldn't remember. She was too tired.

'And the kid with them was all strange,' continued the undead, 'might have had something to do with her.'

'Kid?' managed Honkensby, flomping down as her legs gave way under the sudden terrible weight of her body.

'Mm, reckon the dad was seduced by a fox spirit. He seemed their type – insanely good looking.'

'Was…' Honkensby could barely keep her eyes open. 'Was one of them a vampire?'

'Yes and no,' grinned the undead, 'it's a long story, so yeah, you go ahead and get comfy.'

CHAPTER FIFTEEN
CLIFFHANGER

'Are we nearly there, yet?'

It was Nell complaining, not the child. Fang reminded her yet again that nobody had forced, or even asked Nell to come with.

'Good news is, the embassy's just the other side of Cliffcaves,' Amber told her.

'And what's the bad news?' asked Fang. 'You always give us bad news straight after the good news. Sometimes before *and* after the good.'

'I do not,' argued Amber. She paused, cleared her throat and continued. 'Anyway, the bad news is, we still have to get to the other side of Cliffcaves.'

'What's Cliffcaves?' asked Lazare.

Amber just nodded ahead. They were on a wide thoroughfare, which they were used to by now in the Deep, but usually one could see an intersection at the end of roads like that. Fang could see that this road ended with seemingly nothing. As they got closer to the end of the road, the nothing began to stretch out, until it became clear that in front of them was a vast, sheer drop.

'Cliffcaves,' announced Amber, indicating to a street sign. 'High density housing for cave-dwelling Deepsiders – dragons and vampires, mostly. Built really deep – we call 'em corescrapers. Usually I just fly over it, but since only two of us have wings, we'll have to go round the long way.'

Over to their right, Fang saw half a dozen ogres turn a corner and start walking towards them. It was a worryingly intentional walk. The others spotted this, too.

'Let's take a left,' said Amber, as calmly as possible, but from the left, a different group emerged from a building. A combination of ogres and zombies.

'Should we turn back and find a different way?' Lazare suggested, but behind them, a couple of werewolves had appeared, and they didn't look to be off shopping.

'Are we just being paranoid?' asked Nell. 'These are their streets, they have every right to be here.'

Fang noticed the weapons that the three different, very determined looking groups were holding.

'Not paranoid,' he pointed out.

'Run?' asked Nell.

'If we run,' reasoned Fang, 'they'll just chase us towards the gorge, and then what?'

But the werewolves behind them started running towards them anyway, prompting the ogres and zombies to join in too, so Fang and his group ran and they were being chased towards the gorge. Sometimes Fang hated being right.

'How did they find us?' puffed Nell. 'I thought we lost them in the market.'

How, indeed? Someone out there was clearly far better at tracking them than Fang had accounted for. Someone who could keep watch over them without themself being seen, with some uncanny power. That was one of only two explanations he could think of for how they kept getting found so easily, in spite of all their efforts. And, since the other potential explanation was that they had a spy in their midst, a supernaturally clever and hidden hunter was the only one he was prepared to accept. He was aware that his preferred answer was the less likely of the two, but he was determined to cling to it while he could.

There was, after all, a more pressing problem at hand. They were being chased, there were too many well-armed pursuers to fight off, especially with Tem to keep safe, they were flanked on all sides and they were rapidly running out of road. Fang tried using his illusions, tried making Amber appear bigger, tried throwing the image of silver spikes in their wake, tried flooding the road behind them with a vision of sewage, but the gang were onto him, they shouted to one another to ignore the obstacles, they weren't real. Amber got airborne and tried to breathe her little plumes of flame on them, but they were puny and the muskets some of the pursuers were carrying meant she couldn't get close enough to ward them off. Nell tried fumbling in her bag for something to use, but it was hard to mix potions and run, and the cliffside was almost on them now.

He was just trying to think of a plan when Lazare grabbed him around the waist.

'Wha…?' He realised what Lazare was going to try to do, and held on tight to Tem.

Lazare grabbed Nell in the other arm, opened his wings and flapped with a mighty swoosh, once, twice, and Fang's toes were lifted off the ground… and Lazare faltered, and landed heavily back on the road, dropping them both.

Lazare grabbed Fang and Nell again and tried to take off once more. He managed to lift them all about a foot this time, before plummeting back to the ground again. Nell swallowed a yelp as she landed awkwardly, turning an ankle.

They were too heavy for Lazare to carry them all. Amber turned back and grabbed Nell's bag and carried it in her claws. The weight made the little dragon dip lower and her wings flapped more slowly. Lazare tried holding onto them a third time, but Fang knew it would be no good. Carrying Fang was one thing, but trying to carry two adults and a child was another. And the cavern was so deep, and they were almost upon it. If Lazare was to falter and fall over Cliffcaves, they would all plummet for hundreds of feet.

Fang grabbed the arm Lazare had around him. Nell was the first to realise what Fang was about to do.

'Don't you dare.'

'Don't dare what… *Ow*!'

Fang dug his nails into the Frenchman's arms.

'Let me go. Take them, I'll find my own way round.'

'No,' whined Lazare. 'You said, no splitting up on the mission!'

'Fang, don't be so *Fang* about this,' shouted Nell, angrily.

Their pursuers were yards away. The drop of Cliffcaves was dead ahead. They didn't have time to argue. Fang concentrated on Lazare's hand. The skin on it began to blister and rot and crawl with worms. Tem screamed, and Lazare let go of Fang on instinct, flexing the horrific looking fingers as the illusion swiftly dissipated again.

'You want to look worse?' threatened Fang. 'Want your face to melt off?'

'God's Farts, Fang!' And, there was that look in Lazare's eyes Fang had been waiting for ever since they'd met. The anger and hurt of yet another would-be suitor as Fang Fanged it up again. They should have just slept together on the first night and got it all out of the way, spared him his ridiculous notion that they could ever be some sort of wonderful romantic partnership, that being carried once – against his will – meant that Fang would fall into his arms forevermore, allowing Lazare to put himself and Nell and the child in danger just so he could act the brave knight. This was where the partnership ended. Not with kisses and speeches, but with pain, and fake rot, and furious glares. Fang shoved Tem into Lazare's now normal looking hand.

'Get her to her mother.'

'Fang?' Tem clutched her toy dragon. Her eyes were full of tears. OK, Fang admitted to himself, now *that* was upsetting.

'I'll be fine without you lot holding me back,' called Fang. 'Can't die, remember? I'll find you!'

'You'd better,' called Nell, 'you and I need to have words!'

Lazare said nothing more. Just gave him another of those horrible, disappointed stares as he took off, successfully this time, right at the edge of the cliff. There was the crack of a musket behind him, and Lazare swerved and ducked out of the way of the shot.

'Go,' screamed Fang.

Lazare and Amber flew off, wheeling away from a second musket shot. Good. Good. This was for the best, Fang told himself, they were safe. None of their pursuers could fly, and they would be out of range of any further musket shots in seconds. As for himself, he'd run out of any ground ahead of him, and so feinted left. He'd been in scrapes like this before on his travels, it was fine, he'd be fine. Better than fine. He was at his best when he was on his own.

There was a narrow outcrop of rock jutting from the Cliffcaves' edge. Could be a chance to lose the tail of some of the larger ogres and clumsier zombies. He leapt the three foot chasm onto it and ran along it. There was the top of a huge stalagmite fairly close to the end of the outcrop. He jumped to it and balanced on its tip for a second, looking for his next move. Only the three werewolves and two of the zombies were daring to scramble along the outcrop after him, the rest were watching him from the edge, which would have been more encouraging were one of the watching ogres not reloading his musket. Honestly, it was fine, not a problem at all, he could outrun this, he could outrun anything as long as he wasn't having to watch over a cat or a kid or a dragon or an apothecary or some ridiculous popinjay actor.

The cliff edges of Cliffcaves were, true to their name, peppered with cave entrances big and small. Many of them had landing ridges in front of the cave entrances. There was one close by – well, close enough. It was carved into otherwise sheer rock around five feet away from the small jag of stone on which Fang was perched, and a few feet down. It would be quite a leap, and if he missed, there was nothing he could see between himself and his intended grab-hold but air and darkness flecked with dwindling torchlight flickering deep, deep down. One of the werewolves was close. The ogre levelled his musket.

Sod it, he thought. Fang jumped, stretched out and managed to grab the landing ridge just as the point of the stalagmite he'd launched himself from shattered from the impact of the musket ball. He scrambled up onto the ridge. There was another one a few feet along he could jump to, and another, and another. Just keep running, Fang. Just keep running and jumping and fleeing, like always. He tried not to think about the fact he was intruding on the front porches of multiple innocent Deepside residents. Just keep running. Just run, jump, run, jump, run.

Two of the werewolves were still chasing, and he was fast coming to the end of the row of large caves. He could make out a narrow gangway below, but it was too far to leap to. At the end of the large caves were a set of much smaller caves. It felt like even more of an imposition on whoever's homes they were, but in a pinch, they would do as hand and footholds. He leapt, and grabbed the nearest one, muttering apologies to the residents as he went, and clambered down them until no matter how much he reached, his foot could find no more purchase. He glanced down. The gangway was still several feet down, and was further away from the caves he was clinging to than he'd initially judged. He glanced up. One of the werewolves was clambering down the small cave system after him.

Just keep running, Fang.

He took a deep breath, and shoved himself away from the cliff edge as hard as he could. He flipped in mid-air, reaching out his hands to grab the edge of the gangway.

And missed.

Just the tips of his fingers hit the gangway edge. Even as he tried to grip, he knew it wasn't enough. He slipped off, towards the vast chasm below.

Strong hands caught him by both wrists. He dangled for a second, legs kicking helplessly against the hundreds of feet of shadow beneath him, before he was pulled up towards the relative safety of the gangway. Dangling as he was, he couldn't see the identity of his saviour. He really hoped it wasn't one of the gang chasing him, rescuing him from the void only to take him captive. He *really* hoped it wasn't Lazare and Nell, landed in the middle of danger to act the big heroes after he'd made himself very clear, setting them all back at square one just so they could shout at him. He was pulled up high enough to get both arms on the gangway and drag himself the rest of the way, finally getting a look at who had saved him.

It wasn't Lazare or Nell. Well. Good. That was good. Fang wasn't disappointed by that at all, actually. It wasn't one of his pursuers, either. He frowned with faint recognition at the man who had hoisted him up.

'You're… do I know you?'

'Now, there's a simple question with a rather complicated answer,' smiled the man.

He was a deeply average looking human. Middle aged, blandly handsome, his safe presence Deepside explained by his protective amulet and alchemist's robes, including a particularly sparkly cape.

'Were you at the pub, the other night?' Fang asked. 'In Deptford. An actor threw your drink at Christopher Marlowe.'

'Yes,' smiled the alchemist, politely. 'I was there for Lazare's hot-headed little display.'

Ah. That explained it, thought Fang. 'You're a friend of Lazare's.'

'Again,' replied the alchemist, 'it's complicated. I doubt Lazare sees me as a friend.'

There was something about the alchemist's tone that Fang really didn't like. There was something else, too – he noticed he was no longer being chased. None of his pursuers were anywhere to be seen.

'Why did you catch me?'

'Because you were going to fall.'

'How were you… right here? Right where you needed to be, right as I fell?'

The alchemist smiled that bland smile again. 'I'm always where and when I need to be, Fang. Just like you and Lazare are always where and when I need you to be.'

Fang really didn't like this. 'Have you been following us? Are you working for the Hapennys? The Custard boys?'

The alchemist laughed a light, polite laugh that in other circumstances might have passed as pleasant. 'Again, Fang, that first question is a tricky one to answer. You're going about asking them all wrong. I can at least answer your follow up question plainly. No, I do not work for Avis Hapenny or Jim Custard. Quite the opposite, in fact.' He leaned in close to Fang, and lowered his voice conspiratorially. 'They both work for me. They just don't know it.' He smiled again. 'I'm Avis Hapenny's main client. And also, Jim Custard's main client. I've been having a lot of fun playing them off against each other, getting them to steal and trade magical weapons back and forth, making money and most importantly, getting them under my control and getting all the pieces where I need them to be.'

Fang stared at the man. 'You're the one who had Tem kidnapped? Kept and carted around in a box like an object?'

'Just part of the process,' smiled the alchemist.

'What are you? You're no alchemist.'

The alchemist feigned a hurt expression. 'Of course I am. Got the robes to prove it. Look at this cape, this is a good alchemist cape.'

'Alchemists are ten a penny, they scratch around making copper and bronze, they'd never have the power to control two gangs, or to steal a fae child.'

'Clearly, you haven't yet thought hard enough about the basics of what an alchemist actually does,' the alchemist told him. 'But no matter, you have time for that.' He laughed again, as if he'd just said something terribly clever. 'So much time. At least you worked out that the fae daggers weren't the point of all this. Controlling the gangs wasn't the point either. It's just mixing ingredients to create something incredible, and deliver it to me. The ultimate magical weapon.'

It was Fang's turn to laugh – a joyless, derisive snort. 'Well, you're too late, there. That poor child is already being flown to safety. They'll be the other side of Cliffcaves by now. They'll see her delivered back to her mother.'

'Oh!' The alchemist chuckled but there was a horrible look in his eye, as if he found Fang's ignorance adorably helpless. He made Fang feel like a little kitty cat about to get tormented for fun. 'Oh, that's too much! You're still not thinking it through at all, are you? Let me help you, by asking you the right sort of question.' The alchemist put a hand on Fang's face in a hateful pantomime of tenderness. 'Do you have any idea how valuable it would be to own a personal guard who cannot die?'

The bottom fell out of Fang's soul and tumbled down into the depths below. 'What, me? All this time, we thought the gangs were trading and chasing Tem, but you were actually just chasing me? To be some sort of bodyguard?'

'Yes. And no.' The alchemist didn't remove his hand from Fang's face. 'Before you go blaming yourself for putting the others in danger, it isn't just about you. You're just one delicious ingredient. Like I say, you've got to think about the big picture, the process. Think like an alchemist, if you possibly can – I know that's difficult for someone of your position and upbringing. Now, the whole mixture hasn't quite finished cooking yet, but

I do believe that you, at least, are pretty much ready. I thought I'd do something nice for you, and offer you answers and an off ramp right now.'

Fang frowned. '"Off ramp"?'

'Yes! Just slide on over to my side instead of delaying the inevitable. After all, you've already burned through so much goodwill with the Welshwoman, and dear Lazare. You'll join me sooner or later, no matter what. Wouldn't it be lovely to do things the easy way, for once?'

Fang grabbed the alchemist's hand and pulled it from his face. 'I would never work for someone like you.'

'But, you will. I know your weaknesses, Mr Liu.'

The breath caught in Fang's throat. He dropped the alchemist's hand. 'Where did you hear that name?'

'You're still asking all the wrong questions,' said the alchemist, gleefully. Fang tried to run again, along the gangwalk, but his path was blocked on both sides by the assorted Deepsiders who had been chasing him. That didn't make sense. How had they got down there so fast? Not that it made any difference now. He was trapped. He had no direction left to escape.

Well. There was still one direction left – down, very far and very fast.

'And,' continued the alchemist, 'blessed with answers as I am, I know your answer to my proposal already, but I will offer it to you again. I'll leave it up to you to decide whether I'm being magnanimous or needlessly cruel in doing so. You are at a dead end. Are you going to come along with me nicely, or are you going to be difficult?'

Well, obviously, Fang thought, he was going to be bloody difficult. Still one direction left. One direction, and it couldn't kill him because he couldn't die.

'Drown in a sewer ten thousand times,' Fang told him, and jumped.

CHAPTER SIXTEEN
CAUGHT

Down, very far, very fast. And after about three seconds of falling, Fang realised that even though it was unlikely to kill him, he was going to smash like a dropped pudding and he'd just pushed away everyone who might have been willing and able to come to scrape him up off the ground.

Oh, no, thought Fang. This was going to be worse than dying. He was just going to be left there, a broken lump on the rocks, alive and helpless.

Was this the worst idea he'd ever had? He'd had, he admonished himself as he fell, a *lot* of really dreadful ideas over the years but yes, this might be the worst one yet.

He could hear Nell's voice in his head, talking about how 'self-sacrifice' was just self-sabotage wearing flattering makeup, and no more helpful to anybody. That alchemist was going to keep following the others. He wanted them for something, maybe wanted to hurt Tem even more than he already had, maybe he'd hurt Lazare, Nell and Amber as well, and how was Fang supposed to warn them or help them as a mushy puddle at the bottom of a ravine? Why did he only ever regret these sorts of decisions when he was already falling? When it was already too late? Stupid! He was just as useless as he'd always been, and now more people were going to get hurt because of his mistakes and because he let himself get too close, and… and…

And, he was caught, in mid-air, by something large, and feather-soft, and shrouded with red livery.

'Are you the Cathayan known as Fang?' asked a voice.

'*Ái*?' squeaked Fang, winded and surprised.

'Occasionally goes by "John"?' the voice continued.

'Wuh?'

He was on the back of a giant white swan, around the size of a large human man. She wore the ruff and tabard of Queen Elizabeth's Royal Guard.

'I am arresting you,' announced his saviour, 'on suspicion of fae kidnapping.'

'Uh. Wait. What? No.' Fang tried to get some spit back into his mouth and make it work properly again. 'Who are you? How did you find me?'

'Captain Dame Isobel Honkensby, but you can call me "Captain Honkensby", "Ma'am" or "your worst nightmare". I followed your lead to Cliffcaves where I noticed a significant disturbance of the peace…'

'That was the kidnapper attacking *me*!'

'And several residents of Cliffcaves in some distress due to a trespasser matching your description…'

'Ah. OK, that was me, but I was trying to escape a gang, who…'

'So where's this "gang", right now?'

Fang clutched desperately to Honkensby's back and looked around for the alchemist and his gang. They were nowhere to be seen.

'Vanished,' he admitted. 'Must be another of the alchemist's powers.'

Honkensby snorted, derisively. 'What did this alchemist do – turn some lead into brass?'

'He's behind all of this, he's dangerous! I just… don't know how or why, yet.'

'You're saying he kidnapped the child *you* were seen in possession of?'

'Yes! I was taking her home! I wasn't kidnapping, I was doing the opposite. Kidreturning.'

'Where is she?'

'Being returned, safe and sound.'

'By whom?'

'By none of your business.' Fang really hoped that Honkensby wasn't the sort of guard who'd drop a fellow down a chasm for not complying with an airborne interrogation.

Luckily for him, she wasn't. She just sighed. 'You are so very nicked. Perhaps you'll be more talkative under proper interview conditions at the Tower. Can't really fit thumbscrews to you mid-flight.'

Very briefly, Fang thought about jumping off the back of Honkensby to escape. He quickly put it out of his mind. He couldn't just get out of every difficult situation by jumping down a ravine. And, he thought to himself, he probably wasn't the only one reaching for an impossible solution on instinct.

'You can't,' he told her. 'An agent of the Upper Crown can't arrest a foreign national on the Deepside and take him to Upper England for processing without special dispensation from the Deep Court. You wouldn't want to overreach the limited remit of your dispensation down here, it'd put all future Deepside operations in jeopardy, for your whole department.' Fang had absolutely no idea whether any of that was remotely true or not, he just hoped that it had enough accurate elements to it and that he sounded confident enough to sow doubt.

Honkensby went quiet for a moment.

'Fine,' she huffed. 'We'll go to the Deepside Embassy and get the paperwork, and *then* you'll be nicked, having wasted a couple of hours of our time and thoroughly annoyed your captor, if that's what you really want?'

It bought him time, and it was preferable to falling down a really big hole.

'Yes,' Fang told her, 'that's what I want. Rules are rules.'

The great swan dipped a mighty wing, and turned in flight. They soared up out of Cliffcaves, and flapped towards a huge, ornate building in the distance.

'All right. It's your eventual funeral.'

Chance would be a fine thing, thought Fang.

*

The Deep London Embassy of Redthroat the Invincible was not Fang's first visit to an embassy by any count, but it was definitely one of the grandest and finest he'd seen. The Great Ming Embassy in Upper London was just a house with a couple of bored bureaucrats who stamped his papers and sent him back out into the streets without so much as a cup of tea. By contrast, this building was as grand as a Royal Court in its own right. Statues of Queen Redthroat and her ruling ancestors proudly snarled forth from intricately carved stonework everywhere he looked.

An Ethiopian sphinx passed, speaking seriously with a jinn and a chaneque. Fang stared down at the floor and tried to make himself small when a loong walked by, pressing himself against the far wall to give room to the Asian dragon's huge silver body, supple as an eel, shimmering like a fish. So, there were magicals from the Ming Empire here, too. That, as well as needing to find a way to avoid arrest and surreptitiously find and warn the others, added up to a situation that was not at all ideal.

'Fang?'

Oh, no, Fang thought.

'Fang! Fang, *tu connard*!'

Well, at least that solved the problem of finding the others. He raised his head and glanced over to the other side of the hall, where Lazare was standing with Nell, Tem, Amber and the new addition of a bewildered, well-dressed magical – most likely a púca, judging from the magical's tiny stature and black fur.

Lazare looked as furious as he had the last time Fang had seen him. The actor was officially causing a scene.

'Pardon my French,' Lazare told the assorted magicals startled by his outburst. He marched over to Fang, as Nell, Amber and the púca all tried to tell him at the same time that maybe that wasn't the best idea, considering Fang's feathery escort.

'What the Hell's bells was that nonsense?' Lazare snapped, even as Fang waved his arms at Lazare to try to make him stop talking. 'I was so worried! We're supposed to be a team, we're doing this together...'

'Ah,' interrupted Honkensby, 'so you *are* this man's accomplice. I thought so. I've been looking for you for some time.'

'"Accomplice"? What do you... oh no, you're a Royal Guard.'

'I'm under arrest, Lazare,' Fang sighed.

'As are you, right now,' announced Honkensby, 'and the woman. I'll thank you to come rather more easily than your friend has done so far, making me file paperwork and catch him falling down Cliffcaves...'

'You fell down the cliff?' asked Lazare.

'It was more of a jump,' Fang admitted. 'But I had good reason, I can explain everything. I found out who's behind it all. He chased me onto a walkway to gloat and tried to make me a sort of enslaved bodyguard.'

Lazare blinked. 'You managed to get chased, almost abducted by some evil overlord, jumped down a hole and got arrested? We've been separated less than an hour!'

'Yeah, see that's why I don't like leaving him to his own devices,' said Nell. 'Good day, Officer.'

'Captain Honkensby,' the swan corrected her, gruffly.

'Sorry for wasting your time, Captain, but you can't actually arrest us.'

'I can! If you will follow me to the Upper London attaché, I can get the paperwork signed off and whop you all on the racks before suppertime.'

'Ah, beg pardon, Captain, but you really can't,' said the púca, quietly. 'These people are under diplomatic protection until the fae child they have safely delivered to us has been returned to her mother. Orders of the Deep Court.'

'Safely delivered?' huffed Honkensby. 'They're the kidnappers.'

'They're not.' Tem's voice was a tiny, timid squeak. She pulled away from the púca's hands, and latched herself onto Fang's leg. 'He got me Little Amber.' She caught Honkensby's eye and nodded meaningfully down at the little felt dragon still clutched in her hands. Fang could feel that she was shaking. Tem hadn't spoken up against the word of another before, let alone an authority figure.

'Kidnappers do sometimes buy trinkets for their victims, you know,' Honkensby said, addressing the púca. 'And their victims can sometimes side with them. Stockholm Syndrome.'

'Stockholm Syndrome isn't real,' said Nell. 'The Swedish court made it up because they couldn't believe a girl would outwit a troll on her own.'

'They were nice to me,' trembled Tem. 'Even when we had to sneak past guards and run away from the men with knives, they didn't ever put me in that box.'

Fang put a reassuring hand on Tem's head, and mentally praised her for her bravery, even though the way she was phrasing things really wasn't good at all.

'The fae raid is an internal matter for the Deep Court,' the púca told Honkensby. 'Assuming you didn't lose the stolen weapons that Mistress Amber and her companions left for you at the dock?'

Honkensby sighed, again.

'We will thank the Upper Crown for those back, by the way,' added the púca. 'Be pleased with the arrests of the Upperside gangs you were able to make, Captain. Everything else involving this unpleasantness is now out of your beak.'

'Except, it isn't,' attempted Fang. 'That alchemist was from the Upperside...'

'I'm demanding duplicates of all the paperwork on this,' Honkensby told the púca, over Fang's head, 'and to be informed the instant this silly "diplomatic protection" is over, at which point, the Upperside Court would very much like to speak to the... whatever it is those three actually are. There are further investigations that we would love you to help us with. Something about a vampire attack above Blackfriars Bridge, a stolen dockyard cart and, and I quote, "these two guys with weird tasting qi".'

'And in the meantime, if you could look for this alchemist who's the *actual kidnapper*?' asked Fang.

'And apparently now I've also got to go around investigating every sad sack I see in swirly robes trying to make copper, in case he's a mysterious vanishing criminal mastermind,' added Honkensby, wearily. 'Terrific.'

'Thank you, Captain.' Fang picked up Tem, who hugged him.

'It would be extremely premature of you to thank me right now, Mr Fang,' Honkensby told him. 'You'll be seeing me again, very soon.'

The group watched her waddle off.

'I was scared you were gone,' mumbled Tem into Fang's hair.

Nell and Lazare still looked absolutely furious with him.

'Well. It all worked out just fine,' Fang declared. 'The others did very well getting you to the embassy and finding ambassador... uh...' he nodded to the púca, realising he didn't know his name.

'Grubble', the púca told him, 'and, they didn't exactly "find" me. They were intercepted just after Cliffcaves, by dragon guards who had smelled through their disguises.'

Fang cocked an eyebrow at Nell. 'Zombie scent wasn't that effective after all, then.'

'Worked well enough to keep us alive,' huffed Nell. 'Anyway, turns out it was a good thing it couldn't get past the dragon sniff test. The dragons took us straight to Grubble and he's been really helpful. See what happens when you work together and trust people, Fang?'

'You said an alchemist confessed to the fae raid?' asked Grubble. 'And had the gangs chase after you and the child?'

Fang nodded.

'Could be a warlock in disguise, or even a renegade fae casting a glamour,' pondered Grubble. 'Whoever it really is, they're clearly very powerful and have an interest in young Tem, here.'

Tem clung harder to Fang, miserably.

'We're not going to let him bother her again,' Fang assured her. He frowned at Grubble. 'Are we?'

'Indeed not. It would be prudent to put together an escorting party of goblins to take the girl back to the fae enclave safely. You should all rest under our protection in the embassy tonight. I'll get a security escort assembled by morning. And then, you can go home, little Tem. Won't that be nice?'

Tem managed a small smile. 'Will you come with me?' she asked Fang and the group. 'And then visit? I want to show you my house...' she trailed off, frowning at a memory. 'And Mummy was hurt, Nell can bandage her up.' She gave Nell another shy smile. 'Please? You're all so nice, Mummy needs a nice friend, too.'

Nell and Fang exchanged concerned glances.

'Who hurt her?' asked Fang.

'Hurt how?' asked Nell, over him.

'I'm afraid your friends can go no further than the embassy,' Grubble told Tem. 'Only fairie folk are allowed to visit your home.'

The tentative hope on Tem's face crumbled away into disappointment. 'But why?'

'It's just to keep you safe.'

'But I wasn't safe, before.'

'Well...' Grubble's furry little face bristled as he struggled for an answer. 'It's my job to make sure you and your neighbours *are* safe from now on.' He turned to the others. 'Thank you for bringing her this far. Please take tonight to say your goodbyes. I'll show you to the guest rooms.'

So this was it? Fang thought. They'd come to the end of their quest… hadn't they? Fang respected the privacy of the fae, of course he did, but… it didn't feel right, leaving Tem with a stranger before she was home. And if her mother had been injured somehow, how did they know what sort of a home Tem was going back to? From what the girl had said, her life amongst the fae seemed horribly lonely.

The púca rattled on about protocols and regulations as he led them through the massive embassy, talking constantly but saying little that was of much interest to Fang or the others. After a short while, Tem wriggled out of Fang's arms and walked ahead with Amber, pointing out dragon statues.

'Do we trust him?' asked Fang quietly, falling into step with Nell and Lazare.

'Do we have any choice?' asked Nell. 'We're here now, this is her best and safest way home.'

'Couldn't you have got past those dragons somehow? Just flown her straight home?'

Lazare glared daggers at him. 'We followed the plan. You don't get to complain that we didn't change the plan at the last minute, because at that moment, *you* weren't there. *You* had run off like an idiot, because you're obsessed with playing the hero.'

'There was no other way,' Fang reminded him.

'We could have found a way,' argued Lazare. 'You could have let me try to fly you again.'

'And let us all fall? *Now* who's the idiot obsessed with playing the hero?'

'If we can agree that you're both idiots, will you stop arguing?' sighed Nell. 'I get it – we're all tired and we're all going to miss Tem something horrible. And, it's a pisser for you two that we're still no closer to breaking your curse…'

'But we are,' interrupted Fang. 'That alchemist, I swear it's all connected, he just wouldn't tell me how.'

'This wretched alchemist of yours,' sighed Lazare.

'He… knew things, Lazare. And he's still out there.'

'And,' replied Nell, 'the embassy is taking it seriously.'

'Tem wasn't safe from him in the fae enclave,' argued Fang. 'Why not? And, how are a few goblins supposed to keep her safe from him tomorrow? It doesn't make sense.'

'Who said everything had to make sense?' sighed Lazare. 'Who said everything had to be fair?'

'Ex*cuse* me, Monsieur Smiles And Frou-Frou? Are *you* lecturing *me* on the unfairness of life?'

'Fang!'

Fang looked over to Tem, who was staring at a landscape painting, beckoning him over. She pointed at the painting.

'It's a picture of town!'

It was indeed a large painting of a Deepside town square. The fae enclave. Even in the rendering, it shimmered with pristine marble and popped with swathes of bright bluebells, daubed here in expensive ultramarine. The architecture in the painting was achingly beautiful, impossibly intricate – all fluid, delicate curves that seemed unperturbed by the rules of engineering or physics. The fae in the painting looked just as delicate, just as impossible. They didn't look much like Tem.

'Yes,' said Grubble, proudly. 'A lovely painting of your home.'

'My home's not here though,' said Tem. She pointed a line far beyond the frame of the painting. 'Home's over there. They don't like us to be too close.'

Another strange expression crossed Grubble's face. It seemed pitying.

'Can you *please* ask if Fang and Amber and everybody can visit, please?' Tem asked. 'Or I'd miss them too much.' Tem grabbed Fang's hand. In the other hand she still cradled the little toy dragon. 'Dragons are cute,' she stated, with a rare tone of certainty, 'and Fang's like a... blanket. All cosy and safe.'

Grubble still pulled that sorry face, looking at the painting. 'Hey – who wants some honey milk?'

Tem gasped. 'I do!'

*

They'd won, hadn't they? Beaten the odds, braved the Deepside, saved the girl, and now this was their reward. A fine meal, which only Tem and Amber had had much stomach for; a whole evening of peace together with which to say fond goodbyes, in which Lazare and his friends kept going from long periods of unhappy silence to whispering animosities at one another. Board for the night in one of the embassy's beautiful guest suites. He opened up the gorgeously carved door for him and Fang to freshen up before saying goodnight to Tem. He sighed.

'There's only one bed, again.'

'Typical,' added Fang wearily.

Neither man made a movement to claim the bed, nor offered to sleep on the floor again.

Here he was, with a big, soft, clean bed and an extraordinarily pretty man. An extraordinarily pretty man who was a colossal pain in the derriere.

'So, you threw yourself off a cliff,' huffed Lazare.

'Good grief, are you still upset about that? We have bigger problems here.'

'We could have lost you! We thought we had! And now you say the guy who abducted Tem was trying to abduct you, too?'

'And he failed because I jumped off the cliff, but that's not even important anymore.'

'Yes it is! Of course it is! Why didn't you trust me to find another way? Why haven't you trusted anybody, this whole time?'

'Because.'

'Because?'

'Because I work best alone.'

'*Connerie*. I have never seen a man get stabbed and shot more than you do, you need almost constant help, you could at least stop being such a dick about it. It's not fair on Nell or Amber...'

'Oh, now you're playing the white knight for Nell and the dragon as well?'

'And it's not fair on me! We all came down here and risked our necks to help Tem of our own free will because it was the right thing to do, we are not here for you to protect while wailing "woe is me" like the big tragic hero. I don't even know who it is you're performing this for!'

'I do not perform, Monsieur Lazare, we're not all actors.'

'Oh, you are an actor, sir!' Lazare jabbed a finger at Fang, getting up in the other man's face. 'You put on an act all the time, you even act for your own reflection.'

'You don't know me, stop behaving like you know me.'

'I see when the act stops. When you're with that little girl...'

'You don't know what you're talking about.'

'When you look at her, the mask comes off. I *see* you, Fang.'

'Shut *up*!'

'You're so easy with her, it's like you can finally exhale. And then, all the rest of the time, I see you putting *so* much effort into acting the asshole, it looks like such hard work.'

Fang snorted. 'Says you.'

'I beg your pardon?'

'You work so hard to make sure everybody likes you all the time, Lazare. People whose opinions don't matter, like that idiot Marlowe. I bet with your curse, you don't even care that much about how badly it hurts to get stabbed to the edge of death and then get shoved back into life again. I bet that all you really care about is how your wings mark you out as different, so you can't fit in Upperside anymore.'

Lazare instinctively wrapped his wings a little tighter around his shoulders. That wasn't true! Perhaps it had been, once, back at the start, and good grief, he was allowed to find the wings awkward, wasn't he? They were six foot wings. They'd got him in trouble with that Swan Guard. What would Fang know? He still looked exactly the same as he had done before, with his silly gorgeous face and body that he was always hiding away and taking for granted. Fang didn't have to worry about someone assuming he was a monster just by looking at him. Fang just got handed out drinks and acting roles for looking hot, he didn't even have to try.

Fang watched his defensive reaction, and shook his head, derisively. 'Why are you *so* desperate to be liked?'

'Why are you so desperate *not* to be liked?' countered Lazare.

'Shut up!'

'You say that a lot.'

'And yet, you never do! Just… just stop it. I know what you're doing, you're still acting like this is a great romance, even though I've told you it isn't.'

'I didn't bring romance into this!'

'Yes, you did!' Fang pointed at the bed. 'There's only one bed!'

'How is that my fault?'

Fang clearly had no answer to that, and so he changed tack. 'You treat me like a project. Like something you can clean up and fix until I turn into a boyfriend, and I'm not.'

'Good,' shouted Lazare. 'I don't need another project, I already have a quest. Two quests, in fact. Save the girl, end the curse. So pardon me for trying to have a little fun and kiss the boy as well before we both die.'

'OK, first of all, not a "boy", second, I am the one who tried to initiate both kisses, *you* turned me down.'

'Because you were sad, and I'm not being part of your little narcissistic tragedy complex.'

'Narcissist? This coming from Mister Centre of Attention?' Fang poked Lazare in the chest.

'Yes. Narcissist.' Lazare poked Fang back. 'Everything you do is about you and your self-pitying nonsense, and you never think about how much it hurts the people who love you.'

'Nobody loves me.'

'See? Stuff like that. Whining. Self-pitying. Coward! You know Nell loves you.'

'I...' This threw Fang, a little. 'I know I don't deserve a friend like Nell, OK? But someday soon I'll move on one way or the other and be out of her hair.'

'More cowardice. Did you think about how much you frightened Amber when you made us leave you on that cliff? Or Tem?'

'I...'

'You don't think that child loves you to pieces? That little stick man Fang she drew was smiling the loveliest smile.'

'What's a child's drawing got to do with any of this?'

'She wants you to smile, she loves you, people love you, Fang. Like it or not.' Lazare paused. 'I...'

'No. Don't you dare.'

'You're not even going to let me say it?'

'You don't love me, Lazare.'

'*Va te faire foutre.*'

Fang shoved Lazare a little. 'We've only just met.'

'So what? You don't get to tell me how I feel.'

'You're just... confused, because we haven't had sex yet.'

Lazare pushed him against the wall. 'You patronising ass. How about I pin you against this very expensive looking wallpaper and make you scream my name right now, and still love you like crazy afterwards? That'll show you.'

'About time, I've been trying to get this tension out of the way for days now.'

Lazare's chest was right up against Fang's, his hands on the man's shoulders. He was suddenly very aware of the half a foot height difference he had over Fang. He loomed over the other man, and found he enjoyed it. Enjoyed Fang's head tilted upwards to face him, belligerently. That flush was back to his nose, and that very particular darkness was back to his eyes, glittering with rage. He knew they were dangerously close, that this was the point where usually he would back off, but here was the thing – Fang didn't look sad about it, this time. He looked angry. Lazare could work with angry. It made sense to him that Fang could be angry and still genuinely want him, because at that point Lazare wanted Fang very much, and he was absolutely furious.

'Thinking up another excuse to turn me down?' Fang sneered. 'And you call *me* a coward. You silly, preening, pretty sack of feathers and fluff.'

'You *are* a coward. You stage-hogging sad clown.'

They were nose to nose. A little of Fang's long hair was caught up on the edge of Lazare's beard. He wondered if anybody was about to burst in and catch them like this. It was usually their luck that someone would burst in at a moment like this.

'You noisy parakeet,' continued Fang, his expression a dare that Lazare really shouldn't give in to, 'you prancing pony.'

'You self-worshipping monk,' whispered Lazare. 'You howling, haunted peat bog.'

'Capering jester.'

'Shambling fool.'

'*You're* the fool.'

'I am a fool,' replied Lazare. 'Because, I love you.'

Fang grabbed the back of his head, and kissed him. For the briefest moment, Lazare counted it as a win that the other man had caved first. This time, Lazare didn't pull away. It was, Lazare quickly realised, not so much a passionate kiss, as… desperate. Fang clung to Lazare's head like a shipwrecked man clings to ballast. He drank in Lazare's kiss as if Lazare was a tankard of water in the middle of the desert. And, it made Lazare feel the same thirst. Lazare had kissed so very many, all the prettiest lads and lasses he could get his lips on in London, but he had never been kissed like this before. He felt as though he had spent his whole life living off thin broth and this was his first meal of bread and meat. This had substance to it. This had weight. This was solid. This kiss filled the core of him. His stomach, liver, lungs and heart.

At some point, he was vaguely aware, the kiss was going to have to end. A part of his mind was already wandering to the next things he should do after the ending of the kiss, all of which involved both of them wearing far fewer clothes. His fingers did not move down to begin undressing either of them, they were instead contentedly threaded through Fang's hair. Another part of his mind wondered what on earth Fang did with it to get it so soft. The surprisingly good condition of that man's dark hair, considering the horrible state of his clothes and the callouses and scars all over his skin, was like a punchline to a joke Lazare hadn't realised he'd been told.

Fang shifted his weight onto one leg and ran one foot lightly up Lazare's ankle in what Lazare understood could mean, what with Fang being smaller and pushed hard against the wall, that Lazare was welcome to pick him up. Maybe it didn't mean that at all, maybe Fang just had an itchy foot, but Lazare was deep enough into the kiss now to give it a go. If it ended up offending Fang, they could get back to arguing, which was cathartic enough. If it worked out the way Lazare wanted, however, it would turn into something even more cathartic. Lazare finally made his hands leave the mysteriously soft hair and hoist Fang up from beneath each thigh. This was happening, it was actually happening, it was actually going to happen, it w—

The door burst open. *Merde!*

Lazare meant to drop Fang, turn around, shield him with his wings and question the intruder. He didn't get to do any of this. There was no time between the door being kicked in and his getting grabbed. The door was several feet away, he should have had a second or two, heard running footsteps across the floor, but he didn't. He just heard the door and then immediately felt a hand on his throat and a knife against the thin skin of his wing.

'Good evening, gentlemen,' cooed a voice right by Lazare's ear. 'Were you in the middle of something?'

Still pressed between the wall and Lazare, still being held aloft by the thighs, Fang's face was a frozen picture of shock, dismay and rage. His lips still glistened from the horribly cut-off kiss, his face was still flushed, but now the pinkness on his nose made Lazare's stomach knot in distress. He could feel the intruder's leer over his shoulder. Lazare let go of Fang.

'You. How did you get here?' Fang breathed, hotly.

'I can do anything,' said the voice against Lazare's ear. 'But please, no more barked questions. You continue to labour under the impression that the power balance here is very different to the reality of the matter. Even after our little chat, earlier.'

'You're not taking her,' Fang snarled. 'You can't!'

'Of course I can, I can do anything, as I said. I just need to get one more piece in place. And you're not going to stop me, because you would never allow your boyfriend to suffer painful mutilation for your pride. You've already caused enough of that sort of thing to last an eternal lifetime, haven't you, Fang?'

Lazare hated that he was still pressed up against Fang, facing him instead of his attacker. He felt helpless, humiliated. And having to see Fang's expression at that comment was the worst of all. The wonderful spark of wilful belligerence was drained from Fang's eyes and he looked down, ashamed. Horrible! Terrible!

'You may turn around now, Lazare,' said the voice at his ear and Lazare obeyed, pressing himself against the wall next to Fang. He wanted to take Fang's hand, but Fang wouldn't let him. He found himself looking at the alchemist from that night at Wulfric's inn. The same alchemist, he realised now, who had caused a scene at the New Cross tube and allowed them to slip past the guards.

The alchemist had drawn the knife back a little to give Lazare room to turn, and now that the blade wasn't pressed directly against his skin, Fang lunged forward to try to grab it off their attacker. As before when the door was kicked in, Lazare wasn't quite sure what happened. One moment, Fang's hand was about to wrap around the alchemist's wrist, the next, it seemed that Fang had horribly misjudged where the alchemist was standing by several inches. The alchemist stood serenely, holding the knife as Fang entirely missed him, lost his balance and stumbled to the floor. Lazare could have sworn that Fang was lunging at the right spot – the alchemist had been right *there*, and then he was a sidestep to the right, without ever having taken the sidestep.

Lazare called out Fang's name as he fell.

'Still haven't learned to behave, then?' smiled the alchemist.

'You're not taking her,' growled Fang, rolling to his feet, 'or him, or me, you're not taking anyone!'

Lazare tried grabbing the knife at the same time that Fang made another dash for the man, and suddenly Lazare and Fang crashed into one another painfully as the alchemist watched, amused, from the side. Fighting the man clearly wasn't going to work. If he could move faster than the eye could see, Lazare reasoned that trying to outrun him wouldn't work either. This creep was here for Tem, and he'd threatened to enslave Fang, so Lazare couldn't just let him have his way. Lazare went for the next logical step.

'Help! Somebody help us! Intruder!'

'Oh,' beamed the alchemist, 'this is too perfect.'

Lazare realised, too late, that he'd made a terrible mistake. The closest person would be Nell, in the guest suite next door. Indeed, she appeared now in the doorway at his cry.

She glanced at the alchemist, and his knife. 'I've called the guards,' she warned him.

'No, you haven't,' smiled the alchemist. 'Thank you, Lazare, that was the last piece I'm owed, for now.'

'Nell, run,' called Fang. 'Get Tem, get Amber and get…'

But Nell gasped, cutting him off.

The alchemist held up a large glass bottle of a sickly yellow liquid. Lazare didn't remember seeing that on him before.

'This is one of your nasty little potions, isn't it, apothecary?'

'Where did you get that?' asked Nell, horrified. 'Did you loot my shop? It mustn't be kept in that kind of volume! It's dangerous!'

'Why would you make a lethal potion, apothecary? I thought you wanted to use chemistry to help people? Isn't that what you gave everything up for? Isn't that what you left home to do? Or is it that your community saw how dangerous your mixing of magic and science was, and drummed you out of town before you could poison the kingdom of Wales with deadly tinctures like these?'

'It does help people, in the right doses.' Nell was trembling. Lazare realised he'd never seen Nell look truly shaken before. It made him feel sick. 'But that much in one go… please. Just hand me the bottle? And let the boys go? I'll give you anything you want. OK?'

The alchemist smiled, blandly. 'I want you to die.'

He dropped the bottle.

'No!' Nell dived to catch it, and somehow fell awkwardly into Fang instead, even though Lazare was sure that was the opposite direction to the one in which Nell had leapt.

The bottle smashed. Nell took a deep breath and indicated for the others to do the same. Lazare held a gasped breath but wasn't sure how long it would last. The spilled liquid bubbled and boiled in connection to the air, and in under three seconds, the room was filled with an acrid yellow gas. It burned Lazare's eyes. He could barely see. Nell grabbed his and Fang's hands and tried to lead them both to the door…

Which was suddenly shut. Not only that, but the bed and a heavy chest had been pushed against it. Lazare scrabbled and struggled blindly to pull the heavy furniture away from the door as the stinging smoke filled his vision and a growing, aching desperation to breathe filled his lungs. All three of them desperately heaved without being able to take a breath. They eventually managed to move the chest away, but when they went back to move the bed they found another chest in its place. Lazare could have sworn it was the same chest. There was a thump, next to him, as Fang collapsed. In the yellow gloom, Lazare saw Nell rip off another of her petticoats, but she fumbled her attempt to wear the rag as a makeshift mask. Lazare tried to pick up Fang and found he was too weak. It was too much. His lungs were fit to bursting. The breath heaved out of him in a hopeless wail, and then his body gasped to inhale automatically. The pain of that was worse than the asphyxiation of before. His lungs burned, but his heart... his heart...

He saw the shape of Nell collapse, and realised he was already lying on the floor. He found Fang's hand. It was slack and cold. It all hurt so much. The darkness rushed in, the way it had that night a month ago, bleeding out in a filthy alley.

CHAPTER SEVENTEEN
ALL WRONG

Nell's lungs were on fire. Her heart was agony. She felt as if her chest was exploding and being crushed at the same time. As much as it hurt, as much as she worried about the boys and what would become of Tem now, as unfair as it was to have her life snuffed out so young when she relished the joy of being alive so much, the thing that upset her the most was that she had been ended by one of her own potions. She'd been proud of that concoction. How dare this stranger use it as a weapon against her and her friends!

Nell had always assumed that when she died, it'd be as an old woman, in bed with at least two hotties over-exerting her and feeding her pie. She'd never imagined she would die on a hard floor somewhere in Deep London, frightened and angry. Darkness rolled across her vision like thunderclouds. The pain in her chest began to dull. The fire in her lungs and heart was replaced with something cold, heavy and still. She knew that this was death. Whatever this stranger's horrible plan was, at least the boys couldn't die. Maybe the others would come up with some way out of this and get Tem home safe and sound after all. But it would have to be without Nell. As awful as all of this was, she didn't regret coming along to help that sweet little girl. It had been an adventure, up until this part. She wished she could have done more, given more, instead of dying from her own potion like a sadly ironic little footnote.

It wasn't fair. She wanted to live.

In the darkness, there was a spark. And then there came a new pain, even sharper than before. Sharper and… wrong. It was a new fire, but burning backwards, somehow. Nell's lungs heaved, on instinct, and she gasped in a noisy, excruciating breath before coughing out a thin cloud of poison. She became dimly aware of more coughing, and the sound of a panicking dragon.

She was aware of something else, too. It wasn't really something she could sense in any traditional way. It wasn't heard, nor smelled, nor touched, nor seen through her fluttering eyelids. She could just… feel it. Her nerves jangled with it in a way she couldn't explain to herself. Her blood, newly pumping once more, jumped with it. The hairs on her arms stood up with it. It was magic.

She opened her eyes, and found herself looking at the upside down face of Tem. The child stood over her, looking down with a horribly distressed expression. The child shuddered with sobs. Magic poured from her. It was a flood. A torrent. It was cascading out of Tem, and it was… weird. All back to front.

A panicked thought hit Nell, distracting her from the unfamiliar magic. The alchemist! The smoke! She painfully propped herself on her elbows and looked around the room. The yellow smoke had cleared. She saw Grubble at the fireplace, his snout covered, still desperately holding open the damper and wafting air up into the flue. His eyes were fixed on Tem, his own, half-masked face a picture of alarm at the girl's strange magic. The alchemist was nowhere to be seen. How long had she been out? How long had she been… well, there was no point beating around the bush, she'd been dead for a bit, hadn't she? Or very nearly dead, at least. And then she'd just come back. Pulled back into life, just like the boys had described. Oh, Fang wasn't going to be happy about this.

'Nell!' Fang coughed and spluttered and crawled on his elbows over to Nell.

'Still here,' croaked Nell.

Fang didn't seem to be able to hide the expression of relief that flitted over his face for a split second. He quickly, deliberately replaced it with one of grim frustration. 'You too, huh?'

'The curse got Nell?' Lazare asked. Nell noticed Lazare and Fang were holding hands. *Aww*, she thought, in spite of everything.

Fang noticed Nell looking at his hand, and let go of Lazare like he was a hot coal. Nell and Lazare rolled their eyes at one another.

'All three of us,' muttered Fang. 'The final piece... It was him. The alchemist. This was all part of his plan. But how...?'

'Guys?' said Amber. 'I don't know about any alchemist, but I think we know where the curse comes from, now. And it's not some fella who can make copper.'

Fang looked at the child. 'Tem. Tem, it's OK, we're fine.' He reached out to touch the child's shoulder. She still wept, horrified, and that strange magic still cascaded out of her. Tem was consumed by a self-fulfilling spiral of panic and fear.

'What's that girl doing?' Grubble demanded, his voice quavering. 'Her magic's all wrong, stop her!'

Well, thought Nell, that was absolutely the wrong thing to say about a terrified kid, Grubble. Tem began to wail. The magic was a tsunami. Grubble cowered away from it, hiding inside the fireplace. Amber nudged Tem's legs with the top of her head, like a cat affectionately butting, attempting to bring the child a bit of comfort. Still, the girl cried. Still, the magic poured, but Tem was able to rest a couple of fingers on the dragon's head, feeling the dry smooth scales, grounding herself just a smidge. Fang pushed himself onto his knees and wrapped Tem in an embrace. She let go of the dragon and clung desperately to his hair, buried her face in him, sobbing out her wordless terror.

'We're OK,' he whispered to her. 'We're still here.'

Next to her, Lazare also painfully sat up so that he could hug the child as well. Nell did the same, the three of them wrapped around the girl as she wept out the unspeakable.

'You,' Tem managed after a while. 'You were... it was like... You were hurted.'

'But now we're all right,' Fang told her. 'Was that you, Tem? Did you make us better?'

'I don't know!' Tem wailed again, but it was short-lived, this time. She was able to speak again a moment later. 'I didn't mean to. I saw you and... I wished you to be all right. Are you angry?'

'Of course not.' Nell and Lazare cooed gentle affirmations at her along with Fang. Nell could feel the magic was beginning to peter out, along with the child's frightened tears.

'He said... he said it would be my fault,' stammered Tem. 'That I was going to do something bad to people, that I had already done something bad to people in the future. That it was my density.'

'Destiny,' corrected Amber, gently.

'Shush,' Fang told the dragon. He turned his attention back to the child. 'Who told you this? The man who took you? A man in a silver cape?'

Nell felt Tem nod against her shoulder.

'The alchemist,' Fang explained to Grubble, still hiding. 'You said we'd be safe from him here – you were wrong. Or, you're working with him.'

'How dare you,' squeaked the voice from the fireplace.

'He said I'm a weapon,' said Tem, miserably. 'A special weapon who makes other weapons. He said I was going to mess up and do it really soon. Did I just mess up?'

She cried one more time, but it was even shorter than before. She was calming down, and as she calmed, so did her magic.

'You didn't mess up,' Fang told her, 'and none of this is your fault.'

With the strange magic abated, Grubble emerged tentatively from the fireplace. He looked Nell up and down, his expression still etched with fear. 'You're like them, now,' he noted to Nell.

Nell nodded, smoothly. She felt oddly calm about being under the curse. She'd have to process the crap out of it once the shock had worn off, but at least it was better than being dead. And anyway, didn't this mean she'd have some sort of cool magic power, now? She wondered what it would be. She supposed she'd find out. She had potentially the rest of time to do so.

'That magic,' continued the púca, 'it's like no magic I've ever experienced before, not even from high-ranking fae.'

'Me neither,' added Amber. 'It wasn't even like that the first time Fang died.' She paused. 'Although,' she added, 'with Fang that first time, it was like an… aftertaste of tonight. You know like when you eat mutton and then you burp three hours later and you can still smell mutton on your breath? Only, it's happened days before you've actually eaten the mutton. And instead of mutton it's magic. Does that make sense?'

'Not really,' said Lazare.

'I need to summon an emergency council,' muttered Grubble.

'Fine,' replied Fang. 'While you do that, we're getting Tem home. Right now.'

'But you're not allowed,' Grubble protested. 'The goblin escorting party…'

'…will not be able to keep her safe,' interrupted Fang. 'You aren't even able to keep the alchemist from entering and escaping the embassy building at will. The longer we stay here, the more we risk another attack. Rules be damned – the fae will just have to put up with three lowly undead and a dragon bringing their child back to them.'

'But how are you supposed to keep her any safer? Doesn't this alchemist keep attacking you?'

Nell noticed Tem's miserable, guilty expression. It was like a wet flannel to the heart.

‘True,’ admitted Fang. ‘But we have leverage.’ He smiled encouragingly at Tem. ‘That means, we’ve got something he wants. And we’re not going to give it to him until he’s let us take you home in peace.’

Tem nodded at Fang, her face still worried and guilty.

None of them asked what it was Fang believed the alchemist wanted from them enough to let them take Tem back to the fae enclave. The alchemist wanted Fang. There was a good chance he wanted all three of them.

*

‘I’ll cover for you as well as I can from here,’ Grubble told them, opening a side door down a barely used service corridor. ‘I can stop others raising the alarm that you’ve gone, but I can’t protect you from anyone who may be on your tail, so, you know. Chop chop.’

‘*Merci*,’ said Lazare with a small flourish, although Fang could tell from the púca’s demeanour that he wasn’t helping them out of the kindness of his heart. Grubble seemed absolutely terrified of Tem’s magic and most likely wanted to get her as far away from him as he could, as quickly as possible.

Fang carried Tem as they slipped out, into a long tunnel, through which flowed the Westbourne river. According to Grubble, the Westbourne ran to the fae enclave. All they had to do was follow it upstream. It only came up to the adults’ knees, and Amber was able to fly along with them at head height to keep herself out of the dark, cold subterranean water.

‘We were just looking at all the dragon statues, weren’t we, Tem,’ gabbled Amber, flapping around Fang’s ears, ‘and we were coming up to meet you when we heard the commotion. Thought some sort of bomb had gone off, at first.’

Tem clutched onto Fang a little tighter, still traumatised by what she’d witnessed.

‘It’s a good thing you came when you did,’ Fang told her, smoothly. It was certainly a good thing that she and Amber hadn't arrived a few minutes earlier and seen him and Lazare having their… their moment of mutual weakness. Now, *that* would have traumatised everyone involved. 'You saved us, Tem.'

'I just wish I'd have been more help,' sighed Nell. 'I mean, that's why I came with you. To help. Instead, I barged in and got taken down immediately.'

'You helped us plenty already,' Lazare told her. 'None of this is anybody's fault.'

'Oh, but it is,' said the alchemist, smugly.

Fang stopped and stared. The alchemist stood only a foot away. There was nowhere he could have stepped out from. He was just… *there*, when a moment before he hadn't been.

'You all made choices,' smiled the alchemist. 'At least, looking at it from your angle, you did. From my angle, the question of your autonomy gets a little more… complicated. If it makes it easier on your hearts, I will happily take the lion's share of the credit for this situation – although even then, we get into a bit of a tangle over which "me" we're talking about.'

In Fang's arms, Tem cringed with fear. There was something about the alchemist's easy, smiling confidence that made him feel sick and helpless.

To Fang's surprise, it was Lazare who stepped forward angrily to address the interloper. 'Why are you doing this? Why are you following us around? Terrorising us? What did we ever do to you?'

'It's not about what you *did*, Monsieur, but what you are *going* to do. Well – you're all here now, I may as well explain.' The alchemist folded his hands peacefully, like he was about to tell a story to a group of children. 'Some years ago now, I was visited by a very powerful sage, who promised me an army. Living weapons, with brand new magical powers that would be the envy of every empire on and under earth, under my total control. All I had to do was to follow his instructions, and I did just so. It involved rather tormenting all of you. Chasing you about, or setting my gangsters on you. I'd apologise for that, but if I said I was sorry, that would be a lie, and we couldn't have that now, could we? It was all necessary to get us to this point. The Welshwoman was the last piece I was promised, and now I can collect the fruits of my labour.'

'Promised by whom?' Lazare demanded. 'Who is this "sage" you speak of? Whose wicked plan is all of this?'

The alchemist laughed a soft, patronising laugh. 'Why, myself, Monsieur. Myself, from the future… or, I suppose, by now, the present.'

Suddenly, it all made sense to Fang. The alchemist's ability to seemingly appear and disappear at will, the way he always seemed to know where they would be, his ability to get past the defences of the fae enclave and the embassy.

'You can manipulate time,' he breathed.

The alchemist smiled an affirmation.

'That is in itself a powerful magic barely seen before,' noted Nell, her tone somewhere between impressed and horrified. 'Far more power than a mere alchemist would possess.'

The alchemist pulled a whimsical expression. 'Is it, really? Actually think about alchemy for once. It is merely turning one thing into another. Metal is the most common medium in alchemical magic, but not the only one by any means. We all go through the process of temporal transmutation without even giving it a second thought. All of us are turning our futures into our pasts as naturally as we turn water into piss. But, I found a power to exert control over that process. I can twist and shape all the time of my own lifespan like a goldsmith making filigree. I can reach forward to the last moments of my life – wretched, decrepit, stooped and wheezing moments no doubt, that my frail and elderly future self will never miss – and use it as extra time in the here and now, while the clock is stopped for the rest of you.'

'So that's how you appear and disappear from nowhere,' said Amber. 'You just freeze time for the rest of us and wander in?'

'Indeed, so don't think about trying to escape,' smiled the alchemist. 'You will be blocked, and to you it will feel immediate.'

Fang had a feeling this was a sign the alchemist was about to monologue at them. He was correct.

'I used my powers to get up to some absolutely delightful mischief in my youth, as I'm sure you can all imagine,' monologued the alchemist, clearly enjoying himself. 'Accrued considerable wealth with it, not to mention wealth's more delicious companion – power. It's one thing being the best paying client that *one* Upper London gang bends over backwards to accommodate. It's altogether another thing to have *multiple* gangs scrapping over one another to please you, especially if none of them know they're all actually working for the same paymaster. They can be played against one another no end, not to mention that, once they've served all other purpose, they can be used to test the powers of my new weapons.'

'You set all those gangs on us,' breathed Fang, 'just to see what we'd do about it?'

'Ha! Yes!' The alchemist looked like the cat who'd got the cream. 'Must say, you exceeded my expectations neutralising Avis Hapenny as swiftly as you did. No doubt, I can concoct a similar end for Jim Custard and the kingpins of all the idiot gangs who unwittingly work for me, if I please. You should be proud! You're helping me make both Londons safer!'

'What,' asked Nell, 'by bringing every street gang directly under your control?'

'Well, yes,' the alchemist told her, 'but I'm not myopic enough for all this to just be for control over some petty street gangs. I can use time skimmed from my silver haired years to go back to my own past and tell myself pertinent information. I can be my own source of nigh-on omnipotent knowledge. I told myself how to do all of this, how to turn my powers for transforming time into a power for transforming mortal immigrants into immortal weapons. I have known every step I've needed to take, right up until the event in the embassy. As soon as that was done, I fulfilled the debt owed to myself. I skimmed some end-of-life time, went back ten years and told myself the plan, completing the other end of the time loop. And so, here we are! Destiny fulfilled for all of us! From here on in, unless I get visited by another future self, everything's a surprise to me. Take the dragon, for example.' He grinned at Amber, who shrank back behind Nell's skirts, self-consciously. 'I wasn't expecting the dragon. She doesn't really fit into the plan, she's just a nice little extra, who I'm afraid won't be allowed to go free, considering what she's seen. Maybe the dragon's destiny was to get Tem to the right place at the right time for the event – bearing witness to the Welshwoman falling foul of her own medicine along with the boys. For you see, it was Tem's destiny to use her half-fae magic in a panic, accidentally cursing you all.'

In Fang's arms, Tem whimpered, miserably. Fang bunched his fists.

'You all felt it, didn't you?' continued the alchemist with a smirk. 'Her magic's backwards. The cursing event only just happened tonight, but her magic reached through time, cursing both gentlemen with immortality at the moments you first needed it to survive, when you first bled out. Her magic works by recycling life. Think of the old cliché that life is measured out in grains of sand in an hourglass. My magic works by skimming the sand off the top of my own hourglass, but *hers* is so much more impressive. She can take the same final grains of sand in someone else's hourglass and make them keep repeating, over and over again, I don't know how long for – possibly forever. The same little chunk of life, constantly regurgitated, so that you can't die. And, even more impressive, she can cast that spell backwards through time so that it activates in your past. Before she'd even met you! Now, *that's* power. Obviously, I had to mould her a bit to get it just so. Removing her from the fae, who never appreciated or deserved her in the first place, concentrating that power by keeping her in the box, then giving all of you all those little scares during your quest together, to ensure she was properly motivated to let that strange, wrong magic flow free once she thought she was going to lose you all again. I know you were looking for answers around the curse – searching for who cursed you. Now, you know. You're welcome. How does it feel, knowing you hold your own curse in your arms, Fang?'

'I think there's only one curse here,' replied Fang, as levelly as he could. 'One blight upon the world. And it's you. We're taking Tem home to the fae, to her mother…'

'The fae won't take her back,' the alchemist told them, with a sickening matter-of-factness. 'I saw to that. Just as I saw to her mother.'

At hearing this, Tem began to wail again.

'The fae made Tem and her mother live alone at the edge of the enclave, because she's a half-human with twisted up backwards magic, and her people found her very existence offensive,' said the alchemist, 'so when I sent some Hapenny boys to collect the girl, no fae came to help. Her mother put up a fight, of course, but she was weak, and alone. I instructed the Hapennys that they could do whatever they wanted to the mother in self-defence, as long as the child didn't see her mother's fate – in case she tried to bring her back. Tem's magic wasn't ready yet so the spell might have failed, but still, the last thing I wanted was an immortal fae wandering around, even if she *was* a weakling. The mother was only able to kill two Hapennys before they ended her. Honestly, three times that many were killed just trying to steal the weapons as cover. So I'm afraid your quest has been for nought. Tem has no home in Deep London to go to.'

'Then we will find a new home for her,' announced Fang, no longer able to dampen down the fire of rage in his voice, 'with people who do love her. We'll find her human family, her human father…'

He trailed off at the look on the alchemist's face. The realisation made his stomach feel as if it was plummeting down a dark, cold ravine with no end. No. No. Her magic, reaching backwards through time. Re-using their life energy, just as the alchemist re-purposed time from the end of his life. No, no, no…

'Then good news,' said the alchemist, 'your quest is already complete. Now hand her over, like a good immortal supersoldier. She's mine.'

'She is not your property,' interjected Lazare, hotly. 'You don't get to own people.'

'Lazare, she's his daughter,' said Fang, quietly.

'I said what I said,' huffed Lazare. 'So you sired this child, Monsieur. What other claim do you have for her? Have you ever cared for her? Ever shown her love? Held her hand when she was scared? So much as combed the tangles from her hair?'

'I brought her into being using my powers, as is my destiny,' explained the alchemist, calmly. 'When one is able to keep going back in time, one can apply this power really rather well to finding out through trial and error exactly what a potential mate wishes to hear, how best to manipulate them, and one can make it look like all your designed meetings are either by star-crossed chance, or down to some buried desires of the quarry. The poor fae thought *she* was the one seducing *me*. She also thought it was her idea to raise the child as I waited for the right moment to collect her. In fact, all of it was timed and planned quite carefully by myself, with help from… myself.'

'You're horrible,' seethed Nell.

'And you're being very rude to someone who has outwitted you at every turn,' smiled the alchemist. 'It was so funny watching all of you scrabbling about, thinking you'd lost the tail of the gangs pursuing you, when I always knew where you'd be in advance. And all that desperate clandestine nonsense, thinking that Tem's abduction would cause a diplomatic incident – even the swan guard and the púca ambassador were taken in by that one. The fae don't care! They care about the weapons, but hardly some messed up half-breed with twisted magic. Nobody's going to stop me. Not Redthroat's dragons, or Elizabeth's swan guards. Not the fae, not púca or goblins. Certainly not you. You're mine, now. All of you. So, you'll be coming with me.'

'Obviously, we're not,' replied Nell.

'Yes you will, eventually,' countered the alchemist. 'Perhaps you haven't yet been fully motivated to do so, but I thought I'd at least offer you an easy out – kind of like the one I offered Fang before, only this time, I actually mean it, I absolutely was just toying with you at Cliffcaves, Fang, you've probably worked that out by now.'

Lazare took an angry step towards the alchemist, who vanished from his spot and reappeared instantly a little to their left.

'I've gone to all this trouble after all,' continued the alchemist, as if the interruption hadn't happened, 'years of planning, making sure Lazare and Fang got stabbed and beaten to death so that Tem's curse would reach backwards to them. And more besides. I have taken a long time spinning this intricate web you little flies are tangled in now. Struggling's only going to make it harder for you. Now come along.'

Fang concentrated, and the clean flowing waters of the Westbourne began to swim with sewage and viscera. Tem noticed, and squeaked with horror. Fang pulled her face closer into his hair to try to stop her seeing the limbs and entrails that bobbed obscenely in the now red-brown sludge.

'You're not impressing anyone, Fang.' The alchemist himself had begun to rot. Skin peeled, fat ran down as a lumpy liquid, flesh sloughed off him in festering chunks. The alchemist just looked bored. 'It's your own time you're wasting – although I suppose you have plenty to waste.'

'We are taking the girl to safety,' insisted Fang. 'Leave us in peace to do so, and then you may do with me as you wish.'

'You will *not* be taking any of us, actually.' Lazare opened his wings with a single, aggressive flap. They almost filled the tunnel. 'Not even the self-sabotaging fools. We're getting out of here. All of us. Come.' He took Fang's shoulder and tried leading him away from the alchemist.

'Still trying to deny destiny, and rob me of my dues. I had a feeling you'd be like this,' sighed the alchemist.

The alchemist blinked.

And horrible sudden memories filled their minds.

CHAPTER EIGHTEEN
HISTORY

CARMARTHEN, 1593

Nell looked up brightly as a potential customer entered her apothecary. Not just any 'potential customer' either – she'd known Gwen verHywel ever since girlhood, and she knew Gwen had money to spend now she was betrothed to the son of a Town Councillor – money, and influence to encourage more of Carmarthen's residents to give the apothecary a try. All Nell needed was a decent chance to prove her products worked. She just needed to get over these early teething problems and she was sure the business would become sustainable. Just, she could really do with it becoming sustainable sooner rather than later, because the bills kept coming in while the customers resolutely continued to stay away.

Honestly, she got it. Carmarthen trusted magic, they had done for centuries, even before Redthroat had saved Wales from the English. She just needed to help her neighbours understand that her apothecary didn't seek to replace magic with science, but to combine the best parts of both worlds, to complement, work in tandem for better results. Thank goodness for Gwen! Gwen would trust her, right? Whatever was ailing Gwen, Nell would ease it with a potion, and then word would spread. Nell's heart leapt as a second customer walked in mere seconds after

Gwen. It was working already, and she hadn't even sold Gwen anything yet! She never usually had two customers in at the same time – people must be walking in just because they'd seen Gwen enter the shop. She allowed the man to browse the shelves and addressed Gwen cheerfully.

'*Bore da*, Gwen. What might I help you with today?'

'Nell.' Gwen gave her a small, respectful nod, and lowered her voice to a mumble. 'I was told you may have some herbs to assist with the... monthlies.'

'Irregular or painful?' asked Nell, smoothly.

'Painful,' Gwen explained, quietly. 'They're getting worse, and the charms and spells my mother gave me aren't working.'

'Let's try the tea first,' said Nell, heading to her boxes of dried herbs to mix it up. 'It's mostly dandelion, chamomile, pine bark and I got some ginger from a travelling loong. If that doesn't work, the loong traded me samples of some of the mixtures women use in Cathay, but that's more expensive and harder for me to restock...'

There was the sound of a man sucking through his teeth. Nell looked around. The second customer was right next to Gwen at the counter.

'I'll be with you shortly, sir,' she told him in a friendly voice. 'Perhaps meanwhile you'd like to browse the Gentlemen's Specialties?' She indicated to the small, curtained off alcove where she kept the more delicate products for marital assistance. That would keep him nicely entertained and out of the way while she sorted out Gwen.

The man didn't move. He retained his worried expression, and made sure Gwen could see it.

'Herbal teas? To interfere with matters of the womb? Were I married, I'm not sure I'd entrust the very womanhood of my wife to newfangled drinks and physick.'

'I am not your wife, sir,' replied Gwen, defensively, but Nell could hear a worrying little edge of hesitancy creep into her tone. 'Indeed, I am yet no man's wife, I wed in June.'

‘Then you must trust this apothecary very much indeed with something so important,’ said the man. ‘Were something to go wrong, leaving you incapable of providing your young groom with issue, well.’

Nell flitted her glance from the stranger to Gwen. She saw the doubt and the worry in Gwen’s eyes.

‘Forgive me,’ said the stranger. ‘I practice some magic myself – I’m an alchemist by trade. I find that most women struggle not with pain but with a monthly hysteria that deludes them into perceiving natural functions as painful. I have a charm to ease this madness. Might I suggest we try that before imperilling with strange sciences a marriage that does not yet even exist?’

Gwen opened her mouth. Nell could see the apology forming in Gwen’s mind before she even spoke it.

‘Sorry to waste your time, Nell. I should probably give magic one more try.’

Nell managed a tight little smile and nodded, politely. ‘If the pain comes back again, maybe then we can try the tea?’

‘Of course,’ lied Gwen, matching Nell’s false smile with one of her own. She left with the alchemist, and nobody else came into the shop all day. Gwen didn’t come back the next month, or the month after that. Nell ended up not going to Gwen’s wedding after all. By May, she couldn’t afford to keep the shop open anymore. She packed up, moved to London and tried again.

UPPER LONDON, 1594

Lazare walked up to the Admiral’s Men’s casting call with all the swagger of a tall, dark and handsome twenty-three-year-old Frenchman with a good grasp of English and an accent as sexy as his arse. This was going to go brilliantly, the Admiral’s Men were still smarting from the plague closures, not to mention that whole scandal with the faulty stage gunfire, they were desperate for new talent to bring in the punters and freshen up their tainted image. The first stages of Lazare’s dazzling acting career would truly be the silver lining around the gloomy clouds of pandemic and those poor kids in the audience who the special effect had killed.

He wasn't just going to the Admiral's Men because they were desperate, though. What really excited him about the troupe was their connection to Kit Marlowe. The audition was for Tamburlaine, and Lazare had a feeling that pretty soon they'd be doing Kit's newer one. The one with Mephistopheles. If he impressed in Tamburlaine, then the Mephistopheles role could be his, he just knew it. In fact, he'd quite deliberately run into Kit at a tavern the week before and spent a physically unsatisfying evening ensuring Marlowe would definitely consider him for the role. His heart lifted when he saw Kit amongst the auditioners. He walked up onto the stage, and noticed Kit nudge the man sat next to him.

'The one I was telling you about,' Kit said. 'Afternoon, Laz,' he called up to the stage.

Lazare bowed, pleased.

'Is that paint you wear to audition as Callapine the Turk, Mr Quitbeef?' called another man.

Lazare shook his head, politely. 'My mother's family were merchants of Moroccan stock.'

'Would it not save on paint money if we cast an actual Moor?' asked Marlowe. 'We could whop him in a loincloth and everything.'

'When do your characters wear loincloths, Kit?'

'I'm happy to do a rewrite.'

'I think,' said a third man, 'Kit is merely ensuring we all know he has already seen that Mr Quitbeef is naturally painted in that shade, all the way down.'

Kit laughed at that jibe. Lazare didn't enjoy having these strangers talking about him like that while he was standing in front of them trying to get work, but he laughed along lightly. Don't cause friction, don't rock the boat, be in on the joke Lazare, make sure everyone immediately likes you.

'And indeed,' added the third man, 'that he would look good in a loincloth.'

Marlowe laughed again. 'You know what I'm like with handsome young men,' he admitted, grinning at Lazare. Lazare smiled back. Stay in on the joke. All friends here, all having such fun.

'Well, not *that* young,' noted the third man. 'He looks older than you, Kit.'

'I am but three and twenty, sir,' called Lazare, playfully. 'I do believe Mr Marlowe has a few years on me, he simply retains a youthful complexion from so many days spent writing poems in his chamber, away from the sun's glare.'

'A saucy one,' beamed Marlowe.

'Is that your real accent?' called the third man.

'It is, sir. I am French...'

The third man rolled his eyes. 'A Moor *and* French. Heavens.'

'...but I can work on my diction.'

'And what of your height, sir?' called the third man. 'Can you work on that? You're rather too tall to play many of the roles, you couldn't play a girl, certainly.'

'I... do not audition for a woman, but for Callapine.'

'Please do, in that case.' The man next to Marlowe indicated for Lazare to go ahead with his audition piece, but Lazare was only a few lines in when the third man stopped him again.

'Were you at the Pegasus in Deptford last week?'

'Uh?' asked Lazare, thrown off his stride. 'Maybe?' He tried laughing, being in on the joke some more. 'I do admit I enjoy spending time in taverns with interesting men.'

'Yes,' said the third man, archly. 'Thought I recognised you. I do believe, Mr Marlowe, that I too have borne witness to Mr Quitbeef's ability to wear a loincloth.'

What? Was this man implying that Lazare had lain with him? Lazare had done no such thing – he remembered all of his lovers no matter how brief the dalliance, and this man was not one of them. Lazare didn't know what to do, so he kept smiling a desperate, painted-on smile, and hoped it was all just a big funny joke that he could play party to.

Marlowe blinked. 'Oh. I see.'

'Don't act that surprised, Kit. There's only so many parts to go around, you're the playwright, I'm a funder, young hopefuls are bound to try to maximise their advantage. As well as, ah, not-so-young hopefuls. I only hope that, if you went first, I haven't managed to catch the French Disease off you by proxy.'

Marlowe shot the man another grin, but it was colder now. There was a new cynicism to Kit's tone. 'Spot of mercury and you'll be fine. Alchemists are good at making mercury, aren't they? Please. Mr Quitbeef. Do carry on.'

Lazare did so. In spite of his confusion and knocked confidence, he carried off the rest of the audition piece with great aplomb. He didn't get the part. It went to a pasty lad who had to wear a lot of brown make-up. In the following years, Lazare worked hard to build a friendship with Kit Marlowe and the other playwrights. He was always in on every joke, even when he was the butt of them. He ensured he was always very well liked. He very, very rarely got any actual acting roles. He was never cast as Mephistopheles.

KASHGAR, 1592

'Fresh off the road, are we?'

Fang blinked up at the stranger. A middle aged European man of averagely good looks stood over Fang where he'd slumped in a quiet, shaded corner to try to get some rest. He was indeed 'fresh off the road', and he really didn't want to look as if he was. He had discovered the hard way that while using the same route as silk and spice merchants meant it was easy to pick up casual work in exchange for safety in numbers and the occasional access to transport, it also meant that robbers and bandits along the way mistakenly thought you had silk and spice money – and could get very violent if you in fact had no riches to hand over. Kasghar wasn't exactly the safest place to crash – from what Fang could tell of its recent history, it was having a spot of bother with getting invaded every couple of years, so its buildings and residents alike were scarred and frayed by war. Fang wouldn't stay here long. This city had enough problems without him adding his own to them, and besides, he was still far too close to the lands of the Huli Jing to feel he could stop running yet. Perhaps he would feel able to stop once he reached Mosul, or Constantinople, or Athens or Timbuktu. Perhaps. Kashgar was just a spot to catch his breath for a couple of days, get supplies, find a new westward bound caravan to join for the next leg of the trek and try his hardest not to get beaten senseless by disappointed would-be street robbers.

'I'd be careful if I were you,' continued the man. 'Slip of a lad all the way from the Great Ming, and all alone out here.'

'I'm eighteen, not a slip of anything,' grunted Fang, 'and I've already been doing this for six months.'

'Then you'll have the wherewithal to know that this is not a safe place for you to sleep,' the man told him, and damn it all, the stranger was right. Fang spotted a couple of large men at the end of the street sizing him up for how much they might be able to steal from him and how badly they could damage him in the attempt. Fang would have tried to find a better spot, but he was exhausted and had no funds to spare on a bed for the night.

'You're exhausted,' continued the man, as if reading his mind, 'not to mention, starving hungry and in desperate need of a drink more quenching than stagnant water. Let me buy you dinner.'

Fang frowned at him. The man laughed a light, self-assured laugh.

'Oh, don't worry, even if I were disposed to rob you, I know you have no valuables to take. You're a peasant boy, aren't you?'

Fang shrugged. It wasn't that he was ashamed of being a peasant, even in the company of fine merchants. But, the fact he was from a poor farming village only served as an unwelcome reminder of home, and the past, and the screams, and the blood, and…

'It matters not to me,' smiled the man. 'Your value is within, it's not about what trinkets you carry or what monetary wealth you hold. I merely wish to offer you succour, one traveller to another. As an Upper Englishman, I fancy I'm even further from home than you are.'

The British Island? Now, that *was* far. It was as Fang contemplated this that he realised something glaring about the man that he should have paid attention to right from the start. He was not speaking in English, nor in Urdu or Pashto or Turkish or Latin or any of the languages he'd picked up a smattering of on his travels so far, but instead was speaking in Fang's own mother tongue. He had a faint accent, but besides that, he spoke it perfectly well. Fang was about to ask the stranger whether he had spent time in the Ming Empire when the man spoke over him.

'And,' continued the man, 'I fancy as well that we are both driven by the same force. I feel a kinship with you, young man. As if we were destined to cross paths. Allow me to honour destiny by buying you supper and a good drink. Even if you believe that destiny is a farce, at least you'll have got a hot meal out of it.'

Fang sighed and got to his feet.

*

'Morning,' mumbled the Englishman. 'I'm glad I was at least able to provide you with a safe bed to rest.'

Fang nodded. 'Thank you.'

'Didn't hurt you last night, did I?' asked the man, his voice full of concern.

'No,' lied Fang.

'Good,' nodded the man, and Fang couldn't help but feel like that same edge of dishonesty was also in the Englishman's voice, even though… that wasn't right. It had been Fang's idea, after he'd been offered the bed, to thank the man; to turn over in a way that made his invitation clear. It had not been enjoyable, but the fact it hadn't been enjoyable felt correct.

This man was as sad as Fang. A widower. The mother of his child had been brutally murdered by a criminal gang, and now his own sweet little daughter had been snatched by some ghoul. Some undead creature who the girl was beginning to see more as a father than she did her own flesh and blood. Fang could imagine the pain of that. It sang to his own pain. He and the widower had eaten and drank together, and he had felt the man's sadness, and then with a clear head, Fang had gone to his room, and, well. At least it was more comfortable than an alley. They had never once exchanged names. He had felt this poor widower's misery and self-loathing with the hands on his thighs and hips and they had hated themselves together, and it had hurt and it was right and good that it had hurt because Fang was filth and it was all he deserved.

'This is what we deserve,' the man had whispered into his ear through his shudders, 'people like us, we're not normal. Love died in us, this is what remains – an empty house.'

Fang had never heard someone speak aloud the words to him before, the very same words that dripped thickly through his brain and sat thrumming, cold and slimy like a toad in his belly every day. And then, the stranger had said some things in a language Fang couldn't understand, but suspected of being in the English tongue. Afterwards, before he'd slept, he'd asked the man to teach him a few phrases.

'Shall I write some down for you?' he'd asked, causing Fang to shake his head quickly and explain he couldn't yet read the Latin alphabet, which was at least a half truth. He was, at least, very good at picking up languages orally, so the man said a couple of English greetings aloud and Fang copied them, carefully wrapping tongue, teeth and lips around the unfamiliar European sounds.

'I Su-Ren-Der' was one, 'You Win' was another.

'You're a natural at this,' the man had smiled, and then he'd gone to sleep.

And now it was morning, and Fang hurt. In the cold light of day, the bedroom made him feel trapped. He'd get out of here. Barter a day's work for provisions, then find a merchant headed to Samarkand who needed an extra pair of hands. He hoped the widower wouldn't mind. Hoped he didn't assume this was a longer term arrangement. He couldn't do that. He wasn't going to do a relationship ever again.

'I really shouldn't have done this,' sighed the man, from his bed. 'I made vows. But… I don't know, at the time, it seemed right. You really are so terribly pretty.'

Fang frowned, his face turned away from the widower, and hurriedly dressed.

'You might want to think about hiding that more,' added the widower, 'I do believe you have a beauty that could seduce good people to their graves.'

Fang closed his eyes against the memory of blood and screams.

'But then, you'd know about those perils already, wouldn't you, Liu Fangli?'

His breath caught. Who the *Hell* had told him that name?

He spun on his heel, fists clenched. 'What…?'

But the man was simply gone.

CHAPTER NINETEEN
FAIRY TALE

The three of them spoke at the same time.

'The arsehole who got my shop shut down,' cried Nell.

'The bastard who ruined my audition,' shouted Lazare over him.

'You...' managed Fang. 'You... The widower in Kashgar. You lied to me, you manipulated... all to... you sick piece of...'

'Now now, I didn't lie to you, Fang. You simply... misinterpreted my truth.'

'You lied to Kit,' grumbled Lazare.

The alchemist shrugged. 'Fair enough. And maybe I did manipulate all of you a tad. Your lives. Punishment for disobedience. You will notice that the memories are years old, but you didn't have them seconds ago, or they were fuzzy. No faces. Not until I stopped time for you and went back, just now. Took a lot of skimmed time, especially to get all the way to Kashgar, but I wanted to do something very special for the three of you.'

'You ruined my life,' seethed Nell.

'I brought you to London, my good woman,' smiled the alchemist. 'I even waited til the worst of the plague had passed. So sorry about all those debts you had to pay off for years though, that must have been hard.'

'You ruined *my*...' began Lazare, before frowning and starting again. 'What were you doing in Kashgar?'

The alchemist just gazed blandly at Fang. Fang felt hot humiliation rush through his cheeks and pound in his ears.

'If you think your angry little vagrant is pretty now, Monsieur, you should have seen him at eighteen. Fewer scars, less roadworn, the demons he was running from a little closer and sharper. Ever so willing to lie with the first person who showed him kindness...'

'*Trou du cul! Cochon!*' Lazare took a swing at the alchemist and stumbled when his fist hit mid-air.

'He did just tell me I could do with him as I wished,' continued the alchemist from his new position, a couple of feet to the right. 'I will admit it was naughty of me to deliberately find him at a low ebb, but Fang was never forced, there were no drugs or potions given to him, he made all the moves. All I did was offer him hot food and shelter, from the goodness of my heart. Have you even tried something as simple as buying him dinner, Lazare? Must sting to know that you've been mooning over someone who's anybody's for a bowl of stew and a pot of tea.'

'Nobody should be ashamed of any of this but you,' railed Lazare.

'Really? You know it would be easy for me to go back and seduce you in your past, too? Or the Welshwoman.'

Lazare and Nell flicked slightly guilty looking glances at one another. Fang knew that the alchemist was exactly the kind of gently handsome looking stranger Nell would cheerfully round off an evening with. From Lazare's expression, the same was true for the actor. The threat of the alchemist deliberately setting out to humiliate Lazare and Nell in that same way made Fang feel even worse than the sudden memory of it happening to himself. The alchemist made eye contact with Fang, and noted his discomfort with joy.

'Then why go all the way to Asia to do it to Fang?' asked Nell.

'He's the prettiest. It was more fun to just mess with your careers, for now, but the main takeaway is, I get to do what I like, I have the seeds of the immortal army I was promised – a breeding pair,' here the alchemist indicated to Nell and Lazare, who shot one another 'no offence but no thanks' looks, 'and a spare, for my own personal enjoyment.' The alchemist gave Fang a little wink full of an easy playfulness that in its context felt obscene. 'The sooner you all accept that reality, the less unpleasant this will be for you.'

Tem moaned miserably into Fang's hair. 'Leave them alone, please leave them alone.'

'I can tell this is your first attempt at threatening people,' replied Lazare with a bright, angry grin. 'You're not very good at it. Who cares who had a bad one night stand with you, years ago? And, so what if you ruined my career as punishment? At least now I know I wasn't just bad at acting.'

'And, if this is your idea of leverage, you're running out of it already,' added Nell. 'I may have only remembered you being there recently, but my Carmarthen shop failing is a fixed point, it always happened to me. There's only been so many bad times in my past – and that was one of the worst. What are you going to do to me next if I misbehave – cause that awkward date with the cute vampire back in '97? I'm not scared of that. Everything you can do to my past has already been done. Change too much, and you'll mess up your "destiny" or whatever.'

'Oh, you people still have some bad times left,' smiled the alchemist. 'And yes, the big ones have always happened, but what if you were to find out that you were right about it being your fault, Fang?'

Fang glared at the alchemist, his face still hot, clutching Tem tight to himself. The one silver lining to all this mess was that at least he couldn't remember the alchemist being there in the village, his face hadn't been one of those twisted in violent fear and rage that day. But, he knew now, that could change.

'When I went back and told myself how to fulfil my great destiny,' the alchemist told him, 'part of the plan was to travel to the Great Ming and do a little research into Huli Jing. To find some bureaucratic records on Huli Jing murders at human hands.'

Fang couldn't look at the alchemist anymore. He darted his gaze down to the dark underground river flowing around his legs.

'Took me *ages*,' complained the alchemist. 'Had to get there, sneak into a load of records offices and of course, learn the bloody language. I skimmed a *lot* from the end of my life so it wouldn't take up too much of my youth, but still. Years. Eventually, I found it, in recent records from Shangdong province. Some hick little nothing of a village. Huli Jing are fox-form magicals – not like werewolves, more akin to the fae – and like the fae, they're known to seduce humans to breed. But, something went wrong in that tea-and-pigshit-strewn village, didn't it, Fang? Because this village had a young man – just some ignorant farm boy really, but pretty as peach blossom.'

'Fang's past is his past,' blurted Lazare. 'It's neither our business nor yours, leave him be.'

'Oh, but this is a fairy tale for the ages, Lazare,' beamed the alchemist, 'so shut up and listen. When a local Huli Jing tried her succubus tricks on this pretty boy, he pitched woo, and the Huli Jing found herself entranced. Order turned upside down. The villagers didn't know what to do. This unnatural pair cavorted! Acting like lovebirds, like it was normal. And then, came the last straw. The stupid, stupid farm boy began to speak of marriage. His community, for fear he would bring shame on his family, locked him up, while they entreated to the Huli Jing to leave. But the idiot boy escaped, and was caught trying to elope with his so-called fiancée. The villagers decided they had two options to end the indecency – they could put either the boy to death, or the Huli Jing. Given these two options, humans will always kill a Huli Jing. So, they smashed her with rocks as she cursed the whole village with her final breaths – until there was nothing left but a bloodied fox pelt. The boy couldn't face what horrors he'd created, nor the consequences of the Huli Jing's dying curse that his deviancy and seduction had wrought. He ran away, never to be heard from again. Likely changed his name, fled the empire. Does that cowardice sound familiar to anybody?'

Fang cringed down at the dark water.

'You didn't,' breathed Nell.

Fang flicked a guilty glance at Nell and saw that she was furiously glaring not at Fang, but at the alchemist.

'Oh, I didn't arrange it at all, it's merely a story that I read,' the alchemist told them. 'At least, that's the case so far. But, I know where and when to go. I even know the real name of the stupid little peasant at the centre of all that shame and violence. I could skim the time to pop on over to some ratty farm village at the arse end of the Ming Empire, if I thought it would be worth my while. Whisper words in a few ears. Ensure that the poor Huli Jing's death really was all your fault for being disobedient, Fang. What do you say? Or I could change the past to have consequences you just haven't found out about, yet. I could go back and ensure that the Huli Jing's pack in their vengeful fury tear the ignorant yokels of your family apart, Fang. Or I could set magicals on the Quitte-Beuf family in Paris! Or on Nell's family in Carmarthen. Dragon, do you have family? No, don't answer, I don't really care at this point, but if you make trouble for us, I can take the time to make it my business.'

'Please leave them alone,' squeaked Tem into Fang's hair. 'I'll be good, I'll go back in the box.'

Fang took a deep breath and stroked the girl's head with his free hand. It wasn't about his feelings anymore, or his cowardice, or his failings. His past didn't matter anymore, not when this child's safety was on the line. And for now, the best thing to do was to stay together, and quietly try to come up with a plan to escape, as a group.

'We'll go with you,' said Fang. 'Just, leave Tem alone, OK? Nobody's going in a box.'

'Oh, you can all live quite comfortably, as long as you do what you're told,' replied the alchemist. He turned, and began to wade through the tunnel. 'All of you. Including my child. Come along.'

Lost in their own miserable thoughts, they waded through the freezing water after the alchemist. After a minute or two, Fang noticed Nell was staring at her hands. He realised they'd never had the chance to find out what her new magical power on being cursed by Tem might be. He frowned deliberately at her in a silent question, and by way of reply, she held out her hand to him. A viscous, dark liquid exuded from the sweat pores of her palm. It looked quite disgusting, and Nell appeared to be delighted with it. The colour and consistency of the liquid seemed familiar, but it was catching the smell of it that really brought it home. Nell's famous cough mixture. It was one of her best sellers during cold season. He'd spent weeks bottling the stuff up for her as a favour last November. Her body could produce potions. She had become her own apothecary.

Fang barely had a moment to think about the advantages and dangers to Nell's new powers before Nell rushed the alchemist, her right pinkie finger brandished aloft like a knife.

The alchemist half-turned too late. She rubbed the finger against his eyes.

'Go,' she shouted to the others. 'It's an irritant, he won't be able to see for a…'

As they all turned to run the other way, the alchemist blocked their path, his eyes reddened and streaming.

'Half an hour,' he seethed. 'How did you think that would work, apothecary?'

'I thought maybe if you couldn't see us you couldn't freeze us?' Nell replied. 'It was worth a try.'

'No, it wasn't. Your powers are a gift from me, *for* me. Use them against me, and you pay for it.'

'Oh, boo,' said Nell. 'I got a letter from Mam yesterday – family's fine. And are you really going to go all the way to Fang's old village to keep *me* in line? Or Amber or Lazare? I don't care about some Huli Jing from years ago, not compared to saving my friends here and now. I'm not scared of you. I'm all immortal and magic. And, I was right before – you're already running out of leverage.'

The alchemist regarded her with watery eyes for a moment, before laughing. It was a soft, gentle, fond laugh, like someone watching a puppy wrestle in cute confusion with its own tail. And then, in an instant, Fang was underwater.

CHAPTER TWENTY
DEATH

One moment, the alchemist was laughing, the next, Tem was in Lazare's arms and the alchemist was nowhere to be seen.

Tem stared, big-eyed, at Lazare, as shocked to suddenly be held by him as he was. 'Where's Fang?'

That was a very good question, thought Lazare, peering through the gloom. Nell and Amber were looking around themselves, surprised.

'Fang?' he called out, joined by the others. 'Fang!'

'Shh,' said Amber after a moment.

They fell quiet, looking at the dragon expectantly. Her ears flicked about like a cat's, focusing on a sound too faint for Lazare's hearing.

'This way,' she announced, flapping off. 'Quickly!'

It was easier to say 'come quickly' as an airborne dragon than it was to do for a person dealing with the massive drag factor of having to wade through thigh-deep river water. Lazare and Nell strained and struggled to keep up as the dragon led them through a branching tunnel of the underground river. In a tunnel this narrow, Lazare couldn't fully open his wings, let alone fly, and even neatly folded down his back, they only made wading harder. They were sloshing around for about a minute, but to Lazare it felt like an eternity, especially once the sounds Amber was following became close enough for him to hear. A horrible, panicked splashing. They turned a corner, and Tem screamed.

The alchemist was several feet ahead of them, too far to jump and grab him. He was bent over, his face tense with concentration, his arms in the water right up to the pits. Around his submerged arms, there were four different points of agitation in the water – the helpless underwater thrashing and flailing of a man's fists and feet, trying to fight back, but hitting nothing except more of the buried river that was drowning him. Just breaking the surface of the water were swirling patterns of long, black hair, barely visible upon the darkness of the river.

The alchemist looked up at them, the fake softness of his smile replaced by a manic, rictus grin. His eyes were no longer red. He must have frozen time for long enough to completely recover while moving Fang.

'You're immortals,' he panted, gritting his teeth against the effort of drowning the man, 'and that plays to *my* benefit. Not yours. I can punish you by death, over…'

Amber flapped over to the alchemist, her little claws bared. But then, the alchemist and Fang were another few feet upstream, and she missed.

'And over,' continued the alchemist, 'and over!'

The thrashing of the water stopped.

'No!' Lazare screamed. Tem screamed. The low, narrow tunnel echoed with horror.

With a triumphant grin, the alchemist pulled the other man out of the water. Fang's head fell limply back, water running from his slack mouth, his eyes staring out at Lazare, unseeing, frozen in the terror and pain of death by forced drowning. For once, Lazare had no words. There was nothing in the vast lexicons of his three languages that could give names to the way Fang's dead face stabbed at every part of him.

The magic poured out of Tem in a panic, as it had when they'd been poisoned, and Fang coughed agonisingly back to life.

'What was it you told me back at the cliffs, Fang?' asked the alchemist. '"Drown in a sewer ten thousand times"? I'll have to find a sewer, but for now this must suffice.'

The alchemist laughed, and pushed Fang's head underwater again. Lazare and Nell tried to grab him, but he and Fang disappeared upriver once more.

Helplessly Lazare and the others followed the new sound of splashing in the wet gloom.

'I'm the one who stung you,' cried Nell, 'take it out on me, not him.'

'Oh, but this one's my favourite,' the alchemist gritted out in the dark. 'And, more importantly, he's Tem's favourite too, isn't he, poppet? Let's really hone that power of yours, child.'

The alchemist pulled Fang's drowned body out of the river again, and again Tem's magic surged, and again Fang gasped with that forced spark of renewed life, and again the alchemist shoved him back under and disappeared upstream.

'We surrender,' shouted Lazare, desperately.

A few yards ahead, the alchemist pulled Fang up out of the water by the scruff of the neck, still coughing, not drowned just yet.

'We'll behave,' Lazare continued. 'I'll make sure the others do, I…'

Lazare noticed a mould bloom over his arms. It crept all over the alchemist too, and the river water between them was choked with scum.

'Doesn't sound like my boy agrees with you yet,' grinned the alchemist. 'No. You creatures need to be broken.'

'No! Please!' Lazare could see his arms beginning to rot with the mould, he knew what Fang was doing, he didn't care. He had to stop this. 'Fang, listen to me, it's over! We can't beat him, he has all the time in the world to play with, he won't stop until we give up. This isn't self-sacrifice, it's hurting all of us, it's hurting Tem.'

Fang blinked in realisation, and the scum and mould dissipated, insubstantial as shadows.

'I surrender,' croaked Fang, miserably. 'You win.'

The alchemist smiled fondly down at Fang. 'Love hearing you say that. But, as Lazare mentioned, I do have all the time in the world to play with, and I want to make sure you'll behave. Sorry, surrender isn't enough.' He shoved Fang underwater again, as Lazare and the others screamed. Fang was drowned again. Tem brought him back again. The alchemist moved him again. They found him again, he was drowned again, Tem brought him back again.

'You've got to break,' explained the alchemist. 'All of you.'

'No, no, no,' Lazare tried wading up to the alchemist, who moved upriver yet again. It was hard to tell who was crying more – him or Tem. 'Please! For the kid!'

'This is training for the kid! Come on, Tem! Again! Faster! More power!'

'She is your own child, Monsieur, how could you do this to her?'

'*All* of you are my own, and I'm doing this so you understand that,' replied the alchemist. 'This is our destiny.'

'...Guys?' said Amber, quietly.

'*I* followed the path of destiny, for years,' continued the alchemist. 'You're my reward. Break. Break out of thinking you can fight destiny, you can't.'

'You're right,' cried Nell, 'we'll behave! Just stop hurting him.'

'You don't believe in it yet! *He* doesn't believe it yet.' The alchemist glared down at Fang, his mouth somewhere between a grin and a snarl. 'Break.'

The alchemist moved upriver again, several yards off in the gloom. Amber didn't fly straight over, this time, but flapped in place for a moment, nostrils flaring.

'Something's changing,' muttered Amber. 'I've got an idea.'

And with that, she rushed after the alchemist, which really wasn't much of an idea, it was what they'd all been doing to no avail ever since he'd grabbed Fang in the first place. As usual, the alchemist moved himself and Fang further upriver again, but Lazare could sense it too, now – there was something strained and fragile about the alchemist that hadn't been there before. Something about him was now stretched rather too thin.

Fang, still alive, kicked and grasped automatically as he began to run out of air yet again. To Lazare's surprise, a couple of Fang's kicks actually made contact with the alchemist's legs, causing the man to stumble and wince with pain a little. Lazare saw the alchemist concentrate, but neither he nor Fang moved position this time. The alchemist didn't look worried by this. Instead, Lazare saw on the alchemist's face an even more promising expression than one of worry. It was a very specific and deliberate expression of unflapped confidence. It was acting. And, Lazare recognised acting when he saw it. Something had changed indeed, and the alchemist knew it.

Lazare handed Tem to Nell, and waded over to the alchemist. He swung a punch, still half expecting the alchemist to move again.

The punch connected.

Lazare had never actually punched a person for real before. He hadn't expected it to hurt his fist so much. In retrospect, he probably should have untucked his thumb. '*Aïe*,' he complained, shaking his fist in surprise as the alchemist fell backwards into the water, dropping Fang, who fought and gasped his way out, grabbing Lazare by the hose and using the Frenchman to drag himself wetly up to a wobbly stand, as if Lazare was a particularly well upholstered safety ladder. The alchemist, for his part, had nobody to help him up, and flailed in the water in surprise and outrage.

'How dare you,' he screamed, finally righting himself in the water. 'You *still* haven't learned. Destiny will punish you for that!'

'Let's see it, then,' replied Lazare.

The alchemist didn't vanish or shift position. Lazare's mind was not filled with a new, terrible memory. The alchemist tried to grab at Fang again, but Amber flapped in his path, nipping the alchemist on the wrist. The alchemist howled – again, more in rage than pain – and cradled his wrist.

'Your magic's gone,' Amber told him, cheerfully. 'Did you use too much of it up because you angry-fancied Fang? Whoopsadaisy!'

'Don't be ridiculous, you pathetic gutter lizard, one can't just "use up" all one's magic.'

'You can use up all your life, though,' reasoned Nell, wading over. 'It's finite. All that skimming off the top, to go to Cathay and Kashgar and Carmarthen and so on, you must have been running out by the point you kept freezing time to drown Fang over and over. You're all out of time to skim, so you can't freeze us or go back or anything. Too bad! May as well just step aside and let us take this poor poppet home in peace.'

Tem, in Nell's arms, stretched both hands out for Fang to take her, sopping wet as he was. Fang gladly received her in a tight, dripping hug.

'You're all wet and icky,' she whispered into his drenched hair.

'That, I am,' replied Fang, gently.

Amber's ears twitched. The little dragon landed on Lazare's head, stiff with alertness, staring far upriver.

'And I can't just "use up" all my life either, idiots,' shouted the alchemist. 'I still have my greatest weapon – Tem. If I have run out of lifetime to skim then she will just put it back for me. It's my destiny.'

He tried to make a grab for Tem, but Nell tackled him, clutching the protective amulet around his neck to drag him backwards away from the child.

'Or else what?' Nell grunted as she fought him. 'You can't hurt us anymore, that was the only way you could make her do anything for you. None of this was "destiny". It was just you abusing your own kid.'

The alchemist elbowed Nell off himself, snapping his necklace and sending his amulet plunging into the dark cold river water in the process. 'She doesn't put life back on purpose.' He grinned a grin devoid of any warmth or joy. 'It's an automatic reaction for the little bastard, the moment she sees anyone she's close to run out of life – and I am her *father.*'

'I don't think it works like that,' Lazare told him. He didn't know for sure, of course, but he had a hunch he'd figured out what Tem's magic needed to work – and it was something that the alchemist did not have.

Lazare's vision was suddenly obscured by the upside-down face of a small urban dragon.

'We have to go,' Amber told him, urgently.

As if to back Amber up, there came a strange and unsettling sound from far along the tunnel. In the gloom, Lazare noticed the dark wet smear on the bitten wrist the alchemist was clutching. Amber's bite had drawn blood. Nowhere near enough to badly injure the alchemist per se, but enough to cause small globules of his human, mortal blood to drip into the river water. Human blood, in Deepside water.

The sound was coming from downstream the direction of the embassy – of Cliffcaves, of the Sleepless Market. Hungry dragons and vampires, with a taste for human flesh and the scent of it in the Westbourne, where they were absolutely allowed to kill and devour.

'You need to run,' Fang instructed the alchemist, in spite of everything.

'I will do no such thing,' snarled the alchemist.

'You're human, you're bleeding and you just lost your protective amulet – you are officially dinner.'

'Good job I have an undead army to protect me, then!'

Nell scoffed incredulously.

The alchemist pointed at Tem. 'She's got my blood too, you don't think they'll go after her as well?'

Fang darted a worried look at Lazare. 'Can you fly, here?'

Lazare shook his head, unfurling his wings until the tips hit both sides of the tunnel, by way of illustration. Amber took off from atop his head, flapped over to Fang and indicated for him to put the child on her back.

The sounds of approaching Deepsiders were getting closer. Fang put Tem on the dragon's back. 'Get her home.'

Tem gripped Amber's neck anxiously, and gazed across at Fang. 'You're coming too?'

Fang nodded. 'Right behind you. Love you, poppet.'

Amber flapped away upstream, in the direction of the fae enclave.

'Bring her back,' shouted the alchemist to the departing dragon, even as the splashes and roars grew closer.

'Come on,' Fang instructed the others – including the alchemist. 'We'll get out of the water, bandage that wound.'

'Get that dragon, and make her bring my daughter back,' fumed the sodden alchemist. 'Tem,' he screamed at the vanishing child, 'your magic! Do your spell! Change Daddy! Make Daddy immortal!'

Fang lashed out a hand and grabbed the alchemist by the cape. 'You're not her daddy, you piece of shit. Now, will you let me save what little life you've left yourself?'

The alchemist slapped Fang across the face. 'Don't you *dare* talk to me like that!'

Lazare had seen and heard enough. Clearly, so had Nell. They grabbed one of Fang's shoulders each and started dragging him away from the alchemist.

'Don't just *leave* me!'

'You're out of lifetime, Monsieur,' Lazare reminded him.

'Running away again, then? You cowards! You horrible little foreigners...'

'You're a foreigner down here too, mate,' Nell reminded him.

The coming stampede of dragons and vampires became visible in the dark tunnel. Luminous eyes and ember-bright nostrils danced as the Deepsiders hurried on foot, all of them too large to fly… *Most* of them too large to fly. One vampire was tiny enough to fully open his short wings and flap ahead of the competition. Wulfric soared out of the shadows and into view; his childlike, friendly face twisted with hunger and the scent of a fresh kill ahead. Not a little boy, Lazare was reminded. Yes, a fine upstanding innkeeper on the Upperside, yes a valued ally and a terrible actor, but not a little boy at all. An ancient undead being of fangs and claws. Wulfric bore down on the alchemist, his mouth and wings and fingers impossibly sharp.

'You'll see,' the alchemist screamed even as Wulfric tore into him. 'She doesn't need to be present for her magic to work! I was destined greatness, I was promised, I worked for this! When I come back as immortal as you, you'll see! You'll be sor—'

Wulfric bit into his throat, cutting off the word 'sorry', as two more vampires and a dragon descended on the man. He collapsed into the river under a growing pile of Deepsiders. Still, Lazare and Nell dragged Fang away. In retrospect, even if the alchemist had agreed to go with them from the start, Lazare wasn't sure they'd have been able to outrun the Deepsiders. They certainly couldn't outrun them now. One giant silver loong thundered past the feeding frenzy, straight up to Lazare, Nell and Fang, and gave them a long, deep sniff. Fang froze, rooted to the spot, and Lazare found himself and Nell doing the same. The loong opened their massive, sharp-toothed mouth a little to take a second sniff, catch the scent of them on their gums. The loong then raised their head and sniffed the air in the direction Amber and Tem had just flown. There was an incredibly long and horrible pause that probably only lasted a couple of seconds, and then the loong turned their shimmering body and headed over to the pile of feasting Deepsiders, to lap at the blood pooling in the water.

'Go.' Lazare wasn't sure whether he was instructing the others or himself, to make his own legs work. They waded as fast as they could through the water, with Lazare's wings half-outstretched as a shield, just in case. No Deepsiders came after them. Nor did they hear any victorious cry from a reanimated alchemist. Tem was never going to bring the alchemist back. Lazare believed she couldn't even if she'd tried.

They followed the river upstream. Lazare wasn't sure what else they could do. After little more than a furlong, they came to a gate, beyond which the tunnel opened into another underground town, carpeted with bright bluebells and full of shimmering, beautifully carved houses. There were three fae at the gate – all male, with long, pointed ears and hair and bone structure that put even Fang's to shame. One was pointing the glowing tip of a spear at a cringing Amber, with Tem still clutching onto her back.

They had reached the fae enclave.

CHAPTER TWENTY-ONE
HOME

'Tem!' Lazare and the others hurried over.

'I got her home, guys,' Amber told them, unhappily. 'But, there's a new problem.'

She nodded up at the tallest fae at the gate. He had no spear, but wore finer, floatier clothes than the other two fae men, and a circlet of perfect bluebells that seemed to grow and intertwine through his long, diamond-bright hair.

'He's not a problem.' Tem clung to the dragon. Fang noticed that she kept her eyes low, didn't look directly at the fae in the bluebell crown. 'He's the Fae Lord.'

Yeah, he looked like a Lord, thought Lazare. And in his experience, somebody being a Lord didn't exclude them from being a problem, it actually upped their chances and the scale of the problems they could cause.

'We'll stay outside your boundaries,' Fang assured the Fae Lord. 'You can take her from here. We heard about her mother. Our condolences.'

'If you know about her mother,' said the Lord, 'then you know the child's a half-breed, and how dangerous she is.'

'Yes, but this was her home, she was kidnapped,' Nell argued. 'Her father was human, but she's a child of the fae. Isn't she?'

'Not anymore,' replied the Lord, impassively. 'She's tainted.'

Fang scooped up the upset child. 'Don't be ridiculous. Tainted by what?'

'By you,' the Lord told them, with distaste. 'We put up with the child before, even though her magic was half-human and strange. But, a spell fell over her mother when she was killed by those human crooks. A weird, unnatural spell. We suspected it was coming from Tem, even after the humans had taken her.'

Lazare's breath caught on the gossamer threads of hope in his chest. Tem's magic had worked on her mother! Even though she hadn't seen her get killed, perhaps her magic had been able to push through time and bring her mother back to life after all.

'It took all of our powers combined to put a stop to the spell,' continued the Lord, and the threads of hope snapped. 'We would never tolerate twisted half-human magic polluting the fae, turning one of us into wretched undead. The power of it was horrific. If we'd allowed the spell to be completed and the fae in question to be reanimated, we don't believe we'd have been able to undo it – which makes the appearance of the three of you even more unfortunate. What *are* you, besides abominations?'

'We were rather hoping you fae could tell us that, *Mon Seigneur*,' replied Lazare, as lightly as he could.

'Dirty, is what you are,' the Lord told them. 'Dirty, and you make her magic too dirty for us, since it's tied to you Uppersiders now. Perhaps if you could undo the spell that bonds her magic to you we may consider taking her back, but until then, she's too impure. She would infect us, and likely not survive here herself.'

'But if *you* don't know how to undo the spell, who does?' Fang asked.

The Lord just shrugged.

Amber flew up to hover nose-to-nose with one of the guards. 'Can't believe you proved that alchemist right about what a bunch of stuck-up snobs you are.'

The guard merely arched a perfectly groomed eyebrow at her.

'Is that supposed to guilt my guards into allowing infected magic inside?' sneered the Lord. 'Even though guarding the enclave against the likes of you is the whole point of their job?'

'Yeah, well whose fault is it that the alchemist got in in the first place?' Amber grumbled. 'Twice. And you can drop the attitude with me, "My Lord" – I'm a dragon. Mightiest of the Deepside beasts.'

The Lord chewed the inside of his chiselled cheek, clearly annoyed.

'Well, why don't you take your complaint to Redthroat, then?'

'Well, maybe I will.' Amber huffed. 'Come on guys, we don't need to talk to these beautiful rude dickheads.'

Lazare turned to follow the dragon. 'You're not even my favourite beautiful rude dickhead in this tunnel,' he told the Lord.

'What's a dickhead?' asked Tem, quietly.

Fang kicked Lazare on the ankle.

They walked back downstream in the cold and the dark.

'Mummy's really gone,' said Tem, quietly. 'I can't go home.'

'Not yet,' said Fang, gently. 'We'll find a way. We just… get to spend a bit more time with you. Have a longer adventure.'

Tem nodded, clinging to his neck and cradling the dragon dollie in her free hand. She wasn't even crying anymore. The poor little thing just looked exhausted. Fang shifted her to the other hip as they approached the spot where the alchemist had been descended upon, so that she couldn't see the remaining skeleton, with a couple of small dragons and vampires picking the last morsels from the bones, the flamboyant swirly alchemist's cape drifting forlornly downriver towards a new life as particularly sparkly flotsam. Wulfric, his youthful face calm and innocent looking again – or at least, as innocent looking as the blood smears allowed – waved at the group as they passed.

'Amber! You missed out! But there's still plenty of marrow in the bones!'

'Nah,' sighed Amber, 'I'm all right, thanks.'

*

Back at the embassy, Grubble was waiting for them. He was still wary of the child, but had a new, apologetic look of pity in his eyes. He had held an emergency council in their absence, where he'd learned of Tem's banishment, and he had not been able to successfully plead her case. Dry clothes, warm milk and a soft bed weren't going to bring Tem's home or mother back but they could at least offer some physical comfort to the child. Lazare was also glad of the chance to get the river water off himself, and change into dry clothes. He found Nell sitting on the bed in her guest room, sniffing patches of skin all over her hands and arms, and scribbling words down, furiously.

'Lazare, tell her,' begged Amber, watching the apothecary with concern. 'She needs to sleep.'

'I got turned like the rest of you,' explained Nell. 'Every potion I've ever made can seep out of my pores, and I had to compartmentalise it at the time, because that bugger kept menacing us and drowning Fang. So now Fang's stopped getting murdered, it's my chance to actually deal with this new situation. Or at least find out what bits of me leak what.' She sniffed the inside of her left elbow. 'Wart remover,' she muttered to herself, writing it down.

'You don't think your mind will be clearer after some rest?' Lazare asked. 'We have time now, Nell.'

Nell sighed, with a slump. 'I suppose. He's definitely gone, right?'

'Oh, definitely,' replied Amber. 'Those bones were picked clean. We won. Kind of.'

Nell shook her head. 'We didn't defeat him. The alchemist just lost all by himself. At one point or another, all of us were willing to give up before he ran out of time, but he just carried on because – I don't know – he thought it was his destiny to break us, or because he had that angry creepy attraction to Fang, or maybe because he was just enjoying it too much to stop.'

'Do you think he was ever... normal?' asked Lazare, feeling prickly under the skin all over again at the reminder of the alchemist's particular interest in Fang. 'Do you think, if he hadn't been told he had this big powerful destiny to fulfil, he wouldn't have even imagined being capable of all that cruelty?'

'Does it matter?' asked Amber. 'He *was* capable of it. Extremely so.'

'Fair point,' replied Lazare.

'But, besides the sudden dramatic reduction in attacks on our person and sadistic drownings, his death didn't fix anything.' Nell paused. 'I wonder why there's so many tales where a villain creates and controls loads of monsters and when he dies, all the monsters drop down dead too, or get turned back to normal. Easy ending, I suppose, but it doesn't work that way. Didn't happen after that old Emperor Qin created the undead, did it? And, hasn't happened now. We're just left behind, not dead but not really alive either.'

'All half-way and strange.' Lazare nodded. 'But, now we know the alchemist was not our creator. Tem was.'

'Poor little dot,' frowned Nell. 'How could they turn her away? How could they call her "tainted"? They even stopped her magic from bringing one of their own back to life.'

'The fae must have seen Tem's spell as worse than death,' said Lazare.

'Well,' replied Nell, forcing the tired melancholy from her tone, 'we had better prove them wrong.'

'We will,' added Amber with a similar false, bright, fatigued cheer. 'And we'll seek counsel from Queen Redthroat. Queen of the dragons'll untangle this trifle like a shot.'

'Can one "untangle a trifle"?' asked Lazare, quietly, but Amber carried on talking to Nell, over him.

'Grubble wants to send an envoy, but we are a dragon and a Welshwoman, that's all the "envoy" we need to deliver Tem and the gentlemen to the Lost City of Llanelli in person.' She turned to Lazare. 'It isn't even really lost, you know.'

Lazare gave them an excellently executed hopeful smile, even though he honestly had no idea whether Redthroat would be willing or able to help them. It was a plan at least, and that was more than he'd been able to offer since the fae enclave. It was something they could focus on to keep them going for now. 'I am certain that you will both be wonderful guides on our next adventure – once you have rested. Mesdames, I bid you *bonne nuit*. I'm off to do the same for the exhausted little girl in our care.'

Lazare went next door to Tem's room and found Fang snoring on the floor next to her bed; wet, reeking of river water and still holding the girl's hand as she slept. Lazare gently nudged him awake and helped him to his feet. Tem mumbled a wordless fret at the loss of Fang's hand, at which Fang leaned over and put the dragon dollie in her arms.

'Night, Tem,' he whispered. 'I'll be here tomorrow.'

He allowed Lazare to help him out of her room.

The girl sleepily mumbled back, 'Night, Daddy.'

Lazare was sure that Fang had heard it too, but neither of them mentioned it as they went two doors down to their guest room.

Lazare tossed him rags to dry himself off and yet another spare shirt. 'Before you get sick.'

'*Can* we get sick?' Fang asked.

'You had a hangover, so let's not hedge our bets. Especially since soon we will be travelling west. And we all know how much you like to travel west.'

'It is rather my default, isn't it?' replied Fang, with a rare lightness.

Lazare wondered whether that was half a self-deprecating smile on Fang's expression, or whether he was just tired. Fang's usual frown returned as he rubbed the water from his hair.

'You know, I keep wondering – why didn't the alchemist come back? You seemed so sure before he was killed that Tem's magic wouldn't work on him, even though she can't help when it happens. It seems triggered by closeness, and he was her father. How did you know it wouldn't work?'

'It isn't triggered by closeness, or blood,' Lazare explained, 'but by love. Whether she loves you now, or will love you in the future, her magic brings you back from death – or in the case of her mother, it tries to. The alchemist may have been her father by birth, but he never gave her cause to love him, nor did he have the potential to do so in the future.'

Fang blinked. He looked confused. 'You're making that up. You're trying to flirt again.' He took off his wet shirt. For pity's sake, Fang.

'Not making it up. It's just a hypothesis, but it's rung true so far. It's not flattery to think the girl could love me, or Nell. It's not shallow flirtation to say I believe she already loves you. She's also crazy about that little dragon, so we'd better keep Amber away from sharp implements unless we want to see what happens when her spell transforms a dragon. And besides, I'm too tired to try to flirt with you, at present. You should know damn well by now when you're being flirted with by Monsieur Lazare de Quitte-Beuf.'

Fang carried on drying his torso. Lazare didn't deliberately avert his eyes anymore, but neither did he stare. Yes. Fang was pretty. This had been established. There were so many more elements to Fang that Lazare found beautiful – hidden things, like the soft smiles he gave Tem, like the gentle care for an injured cat – which others tended not to see, but Fang's superficial prettiness was as glaring as a peacock at a chicken farm. He had a feeling this prettiness was why the alchemist had exhibited more obsessive possessiveness and cruelty towards Fang than the others, which was a detail that made Lazare's stomach twist. Lazare certainly wasn't going to try to go back to their interrupted kiss right now. He was exhausted, and they'd been through so much awfulness since the kiss. Getting gassed to death and reanimated, seeing his vampire friend rip an admittedly evil man asunder, learning that the child in his care had been orphaned and banished and having to watch the man he loved get humiliated and repeatedly drowned as torture all conspired together to form a mood killer too strong even for Lazare's ardour that night.

'Lazare?' Fang looked odd. Lost. 'What… *are* we?'

'In general? Or we as in you and me?'

Fang shrugged. 'Either? Both?'

Lazare thought about this. 'Something new. Something strange. Something neither one thing nor another. Something that I don't think we have the answers to, right now. But, I meant what I said, about love. You are loved, Fang, and not by me alone.'

God's Thighs. Yes. Lazare loved Fang. Was in love with him. Argh. The drownings had cemented that knowledge, but that hadn't been the moment he had known. It hadn't been at first sight – that had just been an attraction. Nor had it been any of those moments at Wulfric's inn, the mopey shambling fool getting drunk and trying to kiss him and acting all gruff and embarrassed, or the charged morning after, on the roof. That had merely been the thrill of lust reciprocated, with pangs of genuine, soft affection, but not love. Not *love* love. *Love* love had hit him the moment he'd found Fang sitting cross-legged behind Tem, using Lazare's own comb to check the child for fleas and lice. That he had thought to perform such a disgusting act of care, which would never have even crossed Lazare's mind… that was the moment Lazare had fallen truly in love. And he knew, he *knew* Fang had the capacity to love still, even after all the hurt.

Fang retained that lost expression. 'The love was dead in him, that alchemist. He saw that it was dead in me as well. This is what remains.'

'But…' attempted Lazare.

Fang abruptly pushed all the lost vulnerability from his demeanour, and the shutters to the haunted house Fang built around himself slammed shut.

'Doesn't matter. I'm in poor spirits right now, but then I did get murdered multiple times tonight.'

They were both distracted by a soft meowing. They looked in the direction of the sound and saw a familiar cat walk around the corner of the corridor. She had a docked tail and only walked with a slight limp now.

'Mimi?' called Fang as the cat ambled over to him. 'What are you doing all the way down here?'

Lazare was similarly confused. 'Did… you follow us?'

'There you are!' Wulfric trotted around the corner after the cat and scooped her up. 'Sorry about that, she escaped my room. I should put a protective amulet on her down here, really.'

'You've got a room at the embassy?' asked Lazare.

'You brought Mim… the cat Deepside?' asked Fang, over him.

'Yeah, you asked me to feed her while you were gone, didn't you? And I couldn't remember how often cats need feeding and I thought "well, if I'm off Deep to help Kit with his play I may as well bring her in my jerkin so she can get used to my scent". And she's *so* warm and fluffy, aren't you?' Wulfric snuggled the cat, who rasped at his nose with her scratchy pink tongue. 'Did you say her name was Mimi? I've just been calling her Cat.'

'It's not her name! It's just… a word…'

'Mimi she is! Thanks, Fang.'

'And I didn't ask you to adopt her.'

Wulfric shrugged. 'Tavern could do with a resident mouser. And I *wuv her.* Yes I do!'

'Sometimes people just adopt someone,' added Lazare, 'or love someone to pieces, and there's nothing you can do.'

'Nothing you can do,' beamed Wulfric in agreement, feeding the cat a little morsel of raw meat from his pocket.

'Where'd you get that meat?' asked Lazare.

'I think you both know,' Wulfric told them.

Sometimes, people just adopt someone, or love someone to pieces, and there's nothing you can do.

*

Fang took a while to find dry breeches and set everybody's wet boots in front of a fire. He pulled a soggy mess that had once been carefully folded paper out of the pocket of his soaked jerkin and tried putting the sodden remains of Tem's drawing out to dry, but the paper had mulched and the ink run so much that it was barely a picture anymore. The only part of it that was even faintly recognisable was the wide smile Tem had drawn on Stick Fang's face. Fang gazed at the lopsided, dribbly smile for some time. Stick Fang looked so happy.

By the time he turned away from the hearth, Lazare was already asleep, spread-eagled on the one bed. He looked really very lovely in the flickering firelight. Perhaps... No. Lazare himself had said, they were something strange, not one thing nor another. It wasn't love, the love in him was dead. It wasn't the same as those dappled afternoons beneath the peach tree. Nothing ever would be.

Fang saw Lazare had left a cloak folded neatly on a chair, with a note on top of it, which Fang set aside immediately, unread. It was a good quality cloak – warm, sturdy and soft, if an unnecessarily garish shade of popinjay green. It was a very Lazare cloak, and, as he had mentioned at the warehouse, it absolutely did not fit the Frenchman anymore. Fang silently thanked Lazare for the gift, and left the room. He went past the ajar door to Nell's room and spotted Nell was also asleep, curled on the bed with Amber. Tem was still asleep where he'd left her, the toy dragon still tight in her hands. He lay on the floor next to her bed, wrapped himself in warm soft garish green, closed his eyes, and allowed peace to descend. He did not dream of the peach tree at all, that night.

*

In Upper London, Captain Dame Isobel Honkensby waddled solemnly through the hallways of Whitehall Palace. A fellow swan guard nodded her through to the chamber where the Queen sat, flanked by the two cephalophore Ladies in Waiting who, to Honkensby's knowledge, followed the monarch everywhere. It said much for Queen Elizabeth's presence that she still managed to be the most intimidating person in the room while sitting next to two undead beings who carried their severed heads in their hands. Her Majesty's small white regal face watched Honkensby calmly from a sea of gold silk, glittering jewellery and bright auburn wig, and nodded for the swan to speak.

Honkensby bent her head low in a bow of greeting. 'Your Majesty. It is with a glad heart I inform you that the diplomatic and criminal incidents regarding the stolen fae weaponry have been resolved. The items were collected, the perpetrators have been arrested, and two well-established criminal gangs have been dissolved as a result…'

'Yes, yes, I read your report, Honkensby.'

Oh, quack. So, that meant she'd read about the foreigners who'd made it to the Deepside Embassy.

'The Deep London Embassy is also assisting us in some matters,' added Honkensby as smoothly as she could, 'including the return of a kidnapped fae child to her people, and investigation of a handful of foreign suspects, all of which are currently accounted for…'

'Tell me more about the hopping zombie,' demanded the Queen, suddenly. 'The undead witness from Cathay, she mentioned something strange about the foreign suspects'… "chee", is it? Their life energy.'

'…yes,' replied Honkensby, trying not to get flustered. 'I will admit, I'm not fully familiar with the concept…'

'Well, since you are, as you've stated, in close communication with the Deep London Embassy, I suggest you request an audience with a loong or an undead from the Great Ming to have them enlighten you on the matter.'

Honkensby didn't understand why Her Majesty wanted to hear all about east Asian measurements of life energy all of a sudden. Of course, she would never dream of questioning the Queen. She tried bowing again in lieu of saying anything.

'It is wise,' continued the Queen, 'to listen to a Cathayan who speaks of irregularities amongst mortal and undead life energy, since it was their Emperor Qin in the first place who created the undead races. It has made that culture more wary of it happening again. Your report also states multiple Deepsiders claimed that the foreigners smelled "off"?'

'Aye, Majesty.'

The Queen turned to the cephalophores. 'Ladies, kindly summon my Deepside Ambassador.'

The cephalophores swished out of the chamber, carrying their heads. As they went past, Honkensby noticed one of them catch her gaze and roll her eyes irritably. Honkensby did her very best to pretend she hadn't seen it.

'I should like to hold an audience with these three foreigners at the earliest convenience, Honkensby,' continued the Queen, 'and with whatever or whomever has caused their "chee" to seem… "off".'

Honkensby bowed her neck again. 'I shall attend to it personally, Majesty.'

'See that you do,' replied Elizabeth.

Honkensby left the chamber, leaving the Queen alone. Only then did Elizabeth allow herself to slump, to feel the weight of her huge, heavy dress and wig on her old bones. Could it be that these three foreigners had accidentally stumbled upon the solution to all Elizabeth's problems? Could it be that they had somehow found what old Emperor Qin had tried and failed to find all those years ago? She had to pursue the chance, the stakes were too high not to at least try. Not if the answer was right there beneath her feet – the secret to eternal life.

Also available

Wish You Weren't Here

(The Rooks series, Book 1)

The Rook family run a little business: ghost hunting. And things have picked up recently. Something's wrong. It's been getting noticeably worse since, ooh, 2016?

Bad spirits are abroad, and right now they're particularly around Coldbay Island, which isn't even abroad, it's only 20 miles from Skegness. The Rooks' 'quick call out' to the island picks loose a thread that begins to unravel the whole place, and the world beyond.

Is this the apocalypse? This might be the apocalypse. Who knew it would kick off in an off-season seaside resort off the Lincolnshire coast? I'll tell you who knew – Linda. She's been feeling increasingly uneasy about the whole of the East Midlands since the 90s.

OUT NOW!

Also available

Darkwood
(Darkwood series, Book 1)

Magic is forbidden in Myrsina, along with various other abominations, such as girls doing maths. This is bad news for Gretel Mudd, who doesn't perform magic, but does know a lot of maths. When the sinister masked Huntsmen accuse Gretel of witchcraft, she is forced to flee into the neighbouring Darkwood, where witches and monsters dwell.

With the Huntsmen on the warpath, Gretel must act fast to save both the Darkwood and her home village, while unravelling the rhetoric and lies that have demonised magical beings for far too long.

Take a journey into the Darkwood in this modern fairy tale that will bewitch adults and younger readers alike.

OUT NOW!

About the Author

Gabby Hutchinson Crouch (*Horrible Histories*, *Newzoids*, *The News Quiz*, *The Now Show*) has a background in satire, and with the global political climate as it is, believes that now is an important time to explore themes of authoritarianism and intolerance in comedy and fiction.

Born in Pontypool in Wales, and raised in Ilkeston, Derbyshire, Gabby moved to Canterbury at 18 to study at the University of Kent and ended up staying and having a family there.

She is the author also of the acclaimed Darkwood trilogy, a modern fairy tale series for grown-up and younger readers alike and The Rooks trilogy, a supernatural horror comedy about a family of ghost hunters.

About Cursed

Cursed is a fantasy rom-com series following Fang, Lazare and Nell, three humans who are struck with the curse of immortality. As they set out to reverse the curse with the help of friends they've met along the way – Amber the urban dragon, and fae child, Tem – they realise that although they can no longer die, their newfound powers make them targets for criminals and the law alike. And surely when in grave danger, falling in love should be off the agenda, shouldn't it?

Also by Gabby Hutchinson Crouch:

The Darkwood series
Darkwood
Such Big Teeth
Glass Coffin

The Rooks series
Wish You Weren't Here
Out of Service
Home Sweet Hell

Acknowledgements

Huge thanks as usual to Nathan, Violet and Alex, as well as to Spooky the cat for her constant distractions. Thanks to my agent Dom and everyone at Duckworth and Farrago, especially Daniela, Matt and Pete. Thanks to everyone who has read and spread the word, especially Jess and Paul, and Lucy P.

Cursed Under London is heavily inspired by the absolute joys of fanfiction, which is how I started writing in earnest (I still dabble, sometimes). Thanks, fanfiction!

Note from the Publisher

To receive updates on new releases in the Cursed series – plus special offers and news of other humorous fiction series to make you smile – sign up now to the Farrago mailing list at farragobooks.com/sign-up.

RIVER FLEET
SLEEPLESS MARKET
FAE ENCLAVE
RIVER WESTBOURNE
REDTHROAT'S EMBASSY
CLIFFCAVES
DEEP LONDON